The Last Will and Testament of Lemuel Higgins is a haunting account of shattered dreams and the quest for impossible redemption. O'Connor has created a gritty and compelling portrait of a broken man, whose hopeful pursuit of atonement is set against the hardscrabble environs of small-town life in the rust belt. A gifted storyteller, O'Connor offers the reader a rare and honest glimpse inside the lightest and darkest corners of the human soul. Lemuel Higgins is a gripping debut novel possessed of exceptional and evocative narration.

–Aaron Himes, Editor, The Literate Man

THE LAST WILL AND TESTAMENT OF LEMUEL HIGGINS

by Patrick James O'Connor

BLACKBRIAR PRESS, Miami, Florida

THE LAST WILL AND TESTAMENT OF LEMUEL HIGGINS

For Bucky and for Winnie,
both men among men.

INVOCATION

It was just this morning that I watched a buck come up over the hill that sits behind the north field looking off toward East Angler. A little doe trailed along behind him, their white tails twitching in the chill of the dawn. The sun was coming up over the forest to the east, and I thought to myself that it had come on just a bit later than the day before, its rays glancing quickly off the ground and giving a hint of gold to everything they touched in the softness of mid-autumn. A line of Canada Geese appeared above the eaves of the farmhouse, honking away as they passed on out over the fields and disappeared at the horizon where the sunlight mixed with the morning fog.

I picked up Joby's binoculars with my good hand and scooted myself to the foot of the bed. I held in the coughing fit that tickled its way up my throat, and I had a good look at that buck away out over the field. He was a big animal, with a massive, broad rack standing tall and proud atop his head—a twelve-pointer for sure. He raised his snout high to a light breeze coming down off the hills to the west, scenting the air for anything untoward that might be crawling about or set high in a tree stand at the edge of the wood.

I dialed him in closer and watched his muzzle go back and forth in the air, his nostrils dilating with each inhalation to take in all the information that a gentle breeze might give, and I could tell that he was indecisive. He must have just skirted the town before the sunrise, and I guessed that he was trying to lead his little mate into the deep forest to the south, out of the reach of the instruments of man, which turn sharp and pitiless when the leaves turn to fire. I didn't doubt that he knew the country there, from the creek that runs through the south quarter and spills over Johnson's Falls to the sweet grasses that grow late beneath the canopy of pine to the conical deer lick that old Joby'd put out there early last spring. And I imagined that he was looking forward to a time of ease and plenty, where he could bed that little doe and bound through the brush for joy alone, unpursued by man nor beast, growing fat for the lean winter months that were coming along like a freight train on the wind.

He was big with the weight of the years and wise enough to know that the first chill of autumn, when the sun dips low in the sky, brings hordes of gruff, vested men out into the forest with their slim rifles that don't look any bigger or more threatening than a blackened nickel when leveled to point straight at your eyes. I was sure that he'd had more than his share of brushes over the years and he knew instinctually that he was a marked animal carrying that proud trophy back up high on his head. He also had the doe to consider. Alone, he might run or even turn and lower his antlers to fight, but that little doe wasn't any bigger than a large dog and all but defenseless against the forces that claw or bite or pierce. All this was passing through his mind, or so I imagined, as I watched his nose drift back and forth in the morning breeze.

I scanned the rim of the forest, where any hunters were most likely to be lying in wait. And I fully appreciated the irony of my concern, given that only a few years back, I might have been out there among them. Of course, nobody should have been out there, as Joby's never let anyone hunt his land except you Danners, but that doesn't mean that some punk that's a handful of years and a lifetime of experience behind me wasn't sitting behind the gnarled trunk of a big maple just waiting for that buck to make a go of it. And as I trained the binoculars on the forest, covered in a carpet of orange and yellow, I half-expected to see it crawling with two-legged predators who would surely consider those twelve points quite a prize for the walls of a country home. I stopped more than once to take a hard look at the sway of the leaves and the dance of the tall pines in the wind, thinking that I could almost pick out a man raising a rifle to his shoulder and poised to pull the trigger. But then the wind would shift and I'd see that what I thought was a vested hunter was just a pile of newly-fallen leaves and what I thought was a rifle was just the stark outline of a thick branch against the forest floor.

I turned my attention back to the buck, and I could almost see him take the measure of the season behind dark eyes and decide within himself that crossing that field wasn't worth the risk, that it was time to take that doe the long way around and find a quiet, hidden place to mate and to wait out the coming of the winter. He dipped his head and rooted at the ground for a bit, seemingly morose at having to leave the short path through the field for the longer trek that would take them from tree to tree through the forest. But his mind was made up, and he swung his big antlers back toward the brush from which he had come. The doe followed dutifully along behind him, and I saw no more than the white of their tails as they bounded off into the dense forest beyond.

I paused to back down a coughing fit that was rising slow but steady from the bottom of my failing lungs, then I set the binoculars down and raised the window sash. The metallic scent of the winter on the wind washed over me like a bucket of cold water. I craned my head out into the October morning and I listened quietly, hoping against hope that I wouldn't hear the shot ring out, but half-expecting it all the same. It never came; silence reigned, broken only by the sound of Joby tinkering in the milk house, and I spit down on the drive beneath me for luck, and quietly wished that buck well on his journey and wherever he might roam.

Autumn is well along here, Sarah, and the winter is only two steps behind. I'm predicting the first major snowfall in about two weeks. Old Joby tells me that I'm off my rocker, that the fevers and the sweats have finally cooked my brain and don't let me tell the seasons apart anymore, but I tell him to wait and see. And when it's piled up out there two feet and old Joby's griping about having to shovel the walk and pulling out the bags of salt and hasn't even put the chains on the tires, well then we'll see who had it right. There's a lot that one can see from this window that sits away up in the eaves of your family's farmhouse, and Lord knows I've been holed up here long enough to get to see a good bit of it. It's been over three years now—though in my mind it feels as if you had gone just yesterday—three years of doctors and hospitals and the care of Joby and Celia and quiet afternoons of baseball on your father's old black and white, all of it punctuated only by the discovery of the virus and the promises of a cure, and always back to this farm, this room, this half-life that barely sputters on.

The farm hasn't changed much since you left, though many of the outbuildings have been rebuilt after what the neighbors have come to call Joby's "incident." The fields across the road sit stripped of their hay and fallow as they'll remain until old Joby comes around to churn up the ground next year and sets about the planting. Old Hampton Holmwood Road still runs between the house and the

"So this is the end?" I asked him straight out, sensing that he hoped to engage me in some political side-conversation to put off the inevitable. I wouldn't let him avoid it.

But just the suggestion of it seemed to bring my own mortality down like a curtain of rain. It still doesn't seem quite fair that I won't get another shot at doing things right given my age, but I tell you, Sarah, the only thought in my mind right then was that I'd never get to see you and little Danny again.

"We're all doing our best, son," Doc said, not giving me any kind of straight answer at all, but we both knew that he might as well have said yes. "They're making new discoveries every day. You just rest easy."

Well, I looked at old Doc and laughed like I haven't laughed since my days on the field. It rose up spontaneously from somewhere in the depths of my soul and it was big and full and showed that even in my sorry state, I could appreciate the cruel joke that had been played on me after all these years. Or maybe I was finally going crazy. And then, try as I might to hold it back, my laughter turned into a wracking cough that didn't let up for a full two minutes, with Doc Tyler pounding on my back the whole time and Celia running up the stairs again from below. When I finally calmed myself back down, I was exhausted.

They both sat with me a quiet moment, and then Doc asked Celia to sit with me some more. He gathered up his tools and gave me a nod and tousled my hair just like I was some five-year old boy with the chicken pox instead of a twenty-six year old man with AIDS, and he went on down the stairs.

I really don't know how long I have, Sarah. Doc says he'll be back with the latest test results tomorrow and they'll be able to give me a better idea of the true state of my "condition," as he calls it. But

I know he means that my days are numbered. In the meantime, he left enough morphine with Joby to put down a horse, just in case the situation turns for the worse before he can make it back out here. I told Joby that he needn't hesitate. If I'm going to go, I'd rather just get there. Joby laughed and told me that he's wanted to shut me up good for nearly ten years and now he's finally got the means to do it. But I saw the film of tears on his eyes when he turned away, and I know he's taking it hard.

To tell you the truth, I'm scared, Sarah, and I wish to God that you were here to hold my hand and stroke my forehead like you did after my father passed. But then I think that it's all part of my own Calvary, all part of my penance for taking everything that was good in my world and turning it upside down and crushing it under my boot. And there isn't but one ending to the story of Calvary, as we all know. In the meantime, I have the kindness of Joby and Celia to sustain me, and I have my memories of you. As the end draws near, it's those thoughts of you that consume me, Sarah, you and my little boy that I barely know anymore. My heart fills to bursting and I want to carve out that part of me that killed us and throw it in the stove to burn as it surely deserves to burn.

But I won't let my emotions run wild here, or I'll never get to the task I've set myself. I don't know how long I'll be able to write, but I do know that time is short. Doc tells me that they might want to stick me in a room at Mercy again, maybe enroll me in some more experimental treatment, but I think I'm beyond that now. I don't think I'll go. And so, yesterday afternoon, I asked Joby to fetch that fat Horace Riley down to pay me a visit and instruct me in how I could put my affairs in order before I grow too weak to write. He's a good old boy, Horace is, even if he's as round as the day is long and a lawyer to boot, and he left me some forms that I could fill out to be sure that the state doesn't take the little that I have to my name in taxes and probate fees. He says that I only need to hit the highlights and the document will be recognized as official by the great State of New York. As long as I do so, he says, I can put down whatever comes into my head and he'll read it out to those that I leave behind.

Horace told me right out that he can't make you be there nor can he force you to send along Danny so that he can understand something of his old man, but I haven't got many options at this point, and I figure I have to put it all down before I can't anymore. Of course, I haven't sold a million books like you and, at bottom, I'm still just an ignorant ball player from the sticks, so you'll have to pardon my mistakes. Horace did promise that he'd send along a copy to you and to Danny even if you don't come home to hear it read, which makes this my last best shot to get across what I need to say to you and the boy. So here goes.

I, Lemuel Ryan Higgins, a resident of the State of New York, being sound in mind and somewhat less sound in body, having twenty-six years of age and having been lawfully married to the most beautiful Sarah Danner Higgins for the best years of my life, and leaving behind me one son, Daniel Conor Higgins, known to one and all as Irish royalty as the rightful and true High King of Tara, and not being under any duress, menace, fraud, mistake, or undue influence except that of my present condition, my own writhing demons, and an unforgiving conscience, do make, publish, and declare this to be my last Will, hereby expressly revoking all Wills and Codicils previously made by me. But I haven't had any, so that last part doesn't matter.

EXECUTOR

I hereby appoint my one true friend and former brother-in-law, Joseph Bartholomew Danner, as Executor of this my Last Will and Testament. Even if I thought you'd do it, Sarah, it doesn't seem fair to saddle you with an obligation that's bound to bring you in close contact with a lot of painful memories that I know you'd rather simply forget. No, Joby's the man for the job—I know he won't shrink from it—and so, I give old Joby all necessary powers over all my rightful goods and possessions and all authorization to carry out my wishes as expressed in this document, as well as to pay my just debts, obligations, and funeral expenses.

Now, I don't want anything special, Joby, but in a fit of undeserved generosity you once offered to bury me beneath the boughs of the sugar bush that stands up in the north field along with those that have gone before. You Danners have been the only real family that I've ever known and there couldn't be any greater honor than to lie my bones down beside them beneath the shade of that stand. But I also don't want to be a source of conflict. After all is said and done here, if Sarah doesn't want me buried in your family's plot, then so be it. After all that we've been through, I could hardly blame fields and out past the Village Pub to Collins, the town itself hidden just out of sight by the stubborn foliage of the trees and a dip in the road. Off the road and under my window here sits the circular drive that you know so well. At the moment, it's our old F-100 that sits at the bottom, after Joby finally abandoned that worthless Chevy that was falling apart on him and took me up on my offer of a real American truck. Just behind the Ford lies the same worn path that leads on down to the door of the same milk house, where the sloping concrete dips beneath the rafters of the barn to the milking floor and row upon row of stanchions where the heifers stand by morning, afternoon, and night, churning feed into the milk that's been the Danner family business for more than a century now.

There've been some changes too, especially in the lands around the farm, but also on it. Cooperative Foods bought up just about every scrap of land and family holding to the south and west of us. Your brother, Joby, figures they must own more than half of Cattaraugus County by now. The barn that you remember above the milking floor has been replaced by another after Joby turned the older building into what looked like a set of charred matchsticks. But I give him credit. He and those Dickerson boys put their hearts and souls into the new structure, which is half again as big as the old one and mostly aluminum. I watched them pull it up from the ground day after day while I was first laid up here, lying in this same bed and looking out of this same window, wondering then as now if I was ever going to hear from you again. Anyhow, Celia swears that the barn is even better than it was before, so maybe some good came out of all that nonsense at last.

The farm is still quite a sight in the rising of the morning, Sarah, as the golden light shines through the reds and browns of the maple and the beech and the oak, like someone set the world on fire. I watch that sun make its run through the autumn sky, just a little bit lower every day, as it quietly bakes fallen leaves into the soft brown soil that has done its duty to you Danners for yet another year. I know it's autumn when even the land appears tired from its exertions, and I feel more of a kinship with it now than ever before. We both await a well-deserved rest beneath the snow until the world turns and we peek out dark and loamy and refreshed next spring, moist and thick and hungry for seed.

It's in these slanting rays of the autumn sun that I think I can see the world beyond this windowpane most clearly. I see the charred remains of the old barn stacked up next to the drive, the blackened timbers stark like the mark of my pencil against the paper here, a reminder of that time of blind destruction that all started with me. I see the stand of maple that old Joby calls the sugar bush in the north field, the white crosses beneath like some misshapen albino progeny of the woods, and I can't help but think of those that have gone before. I see the defeated carcass of an old baler that sits up next to the burnt timbers, and I think of the squeeze that Cooperative Foods so heartlessly put on us all a few years back. And I look down upon this stump of an arm that hangs useless at my left side and I see it in these last days as nothing more than a mutilated reminder of my own stupidity and weakness.

Now I don't mean to get sullen or bitter, for the autumn light is a kind light too. The new barn came up straight out of the old, and it helped to almost bring the old farm into the modern age. The maples shed their leaves but remain as we all take our lumps and go on. One look at old Joby proves that a man's right-headed determination can overcome the violence of his fellows and even himself. And even though I've been holed up here as half a man (and rightfully vilified by many of those that I used to call my friends), I've managed to accomplish something right and good and lasting. And seen from that angle—the angle that I choose so long as the choice remains with me—it's a scene that is at peace with itself, a scene that is wiser for the years, a scene that has moved beyond violence and hatreds, jealousies and misunderstandings, resentment and regret. And I think it's the kind of place where we might have done well, if only we had met when we each had a bit more experience of the world about us.

I've got something to tell you, Sarah, but I'm not sure that I've got the time to write it all down. Doc Tyler was in to see me again yesterday. He's just about the same as you'd remember him—a little whiter about the temples and a little heavier about the midsection—but his eyes still smile down at you through those thick black frames that haven't changed for thirty years or more. Well, he poked and prodded me as has become his daily routine over these past several years, and he drew blood from me twice so that I thought he'd leave me pruned up and dry as a raisin in the sun.

"How've you been breathing, son?" he asked me when he was just about wrapped up.

"It ain't getting no easier, Doc," I told him in a whisper, and even that little speech had me doubled over and hacking up phlegm into the handkerchief that Celia always keeps at the ready.

"Rest easy, Lem. Don't talk," he said to me then and turned to your sister-in-law. "And the fevers?"

"Night and day, Charles," Celia answered him. She glanced at me then and I caught her eye before her gaze settled back on the floor beneath her. It was obvious that she was holding back tears.

"Whatever it is ... just go on and say it," I wheezed to the both of them.

The statement hung in the air and the room fell silent. Old Doc

Tyler set his bulk down on the edge of the bed and looked me full on in the face and gave me a smile as he always does before he gives me some devastating news. It was that same smiling face that finally told me that I had AIDS about a year back, just after the government identified the virus and announced that they were on the edge of a cure. I'd already been sick for some time at that point, and I can't really remember now whether he actually used the word or whether that was something that I attached to the memory later. Anyhow, the tension in the room grew unbearable and Celia couldn't take it anymore. She jumped up from the rocking chair at the foot of the bed and hurried out into the hall, where I heard her take great breaths of air to hold back the sobs. There was more silence and then we heard the tap of her footfalls as she headed down the stairs.

"I've always given it to you straight, Lem," he said to me. "So here it is. You're immune system is shot, and there's nothing left in you to fight off the infection. It's pneumonia and, what's more, it's the same sort of pneumonia that has been killing people in your situation."

"The queers, you mean," I spat at him. And I was surprised to hear myself say it. I'd never been a bigot before, but then again I knew that there was talk about me all over Collins and East Angler, and the more I knew that I was associated with that particular group, the more I seemed to lash out against them.

"It's not just the gays anymore, Lem," he said quickly, looking down on me with a stern condemnation. Doc never did have much of a tolerance for a small town mentality, though he'd lived in Collins all his life. "It's beyond the gays and the addicts now, and it always was. It's a virus like any other and, given the chance, it will attack us all just the same—young or old, male or female, gay or straight."

"So this is the end?" I asked him straight out, sensing that he hoped to engage me in some political side-conversation to put off the inevitable. I wouldn't let him avoid it.

But just the suggestion of it seemed to bring my own mortality down like a curtain of rain. It still doesn't seem quite fair that I won't get another shot at doing things right given my age, but I tell you, Sarah, the only thought in my mind right then was that I'd never get to see you and little Danny again.

"We're all doing our best, son," Doc said, not giving me any kind of straight answer at all, but we both knew that he might as well have said yes. "They're making new discoveries every day. You just rest easy."

Well, I looked at old Doc and laughed like I haven't laughed since my days on the field. It rose up spontaneously from somewhere in the depths of my soul and it was big and full and showed that even in my sorry state, I could appreciate the cruel joke that had been played on me after all these years. Or maybe I was finally going crazy. And then, try as I might to hold it back, my laughter turned into a wracking cough that didn't let up for a full two minutes, with Doc Tyler pounding on my back the whole time and Celia running up the stairs again from below. When I finally calmed myself back down, I was exhausted.

They both sat with me a quiet moment, and then Doc asked Celia to sit with me some more. He gathered up his tools and gave me a nod and tousled my hair just like I was some five-year old boy with the chicken pox instead of a twenty-six year old man with AIDS, and he went on down the stairs.

I really don't know how long I have, Sarah. Doc says he'll be back with the latest test results tomorrow and they'll be able to give me a better idea of the true state of my "condition," as he calls it. But

I know he means that my days are numbered. In the meantime, he left enough morphine with Joby to put down a horse, just in case the situation turns for the worse before he can make it back out here. I told Joby that he needn't hesitate. If I'm going to go, I'd rather just get there. Joby laughed and told me that he's wanted to shut me up good for nearly ten years and now he's finally got the means to do it. But I saw the film of tears on his eyes when he turned away, and I know he's taking it hard.

To tell you the truth, I'm scared, Sarah, and I wish to God that you were here to hold my hand and stroke my forehead like you did after my father passed. But then I think that it's all part of my own Calvary, all part of my penance for taking everything that was good in my world and turning it upside down and crushing it under my boot. And there isn't but one ending to the story of Calvary, as we all know. In the meantime, I have the kindness of Joby and Celia to sustain me, and I have my memories of you. As the end draws near, it's those thoughts of you that consume me, Sarah, you and my little boy that I barely know anymore. My heart fills to bursting and I want to carve out that part of me that killed us and throw it in the stove to burn as it surely deserves to burn.

But I won't let my emotions run wild here, or I'll never get to the task I've set myself. I don't know how long I'll be able to write, but I do know that time is short. Doc tells me that they might want to stick me in a room at Mercy again, maybe enroll me in some more experimental treatment, but I think I'm beyond that now. I don't think I'll go. And so, yesterday afternoon, I asked Joby to fetch that fat Horace Riley down to pay me a visit and instruct me in how I could put my affairs in order before I grow too weak to write. He's a good old boy, Horace is, even if he's as round as the day is long and a lawyer to boot, and he left me some forms that I could fill out to

be sure that the state doesn't take the little that I have to my name in taxes and probate fees. He says that I only need to hit the highlights and the document will be recognized as official by the great State of New York. As long as I do so, he says, I can put down whatever comes into my head and he'll read it out to those that I leave behind.

Horace told me right out that he can't make you be there nor can he force you to send along Danny so that he can understand something of his old man, but I haven't got many options at this point, and I figure I have to put it all down before I can't anymore. Of course, I haven't sold a million books like you and, at bottom, I'm still just an ignorant ball player from the sticks, so you'll have to pardon my mistakes. Horace did promise that he'd send along a copy to you and to Danny even if you don't come home to hear it read, which makes this my last best shot to get across what I need to say to you and the boy. So here goes.

I, Lemuel Ryan Higgins, a resident of the State of New York, being sound in mind and somewhat less sound in body, having twenty-six years of age and having been lawfully married to the most beautiful Sarah Danner Higgins for the best years of my life, and leaving behind me one son, Daniel Conor Higgins, known to one and all as Irish royalty as the rightful and true High King of Tara, and not being under any duress, menace, fraud, mistake, or undue influence except that of my present condition, my own writhing demons, and an unforgiving conscience, do make, publish, and declare this to be my last Will, hereby expressly revoking all Wills and Codicils previously made by me. But I haven't had any, so that last part doesn't matter.

EXECUTOR

I hereby appoint my one true friend and former brother-in-law, Joseph Bartholomew Danner, as Executor of this my Last Will and Testament. Even if I thought you'd do it, Sarah, it doesn't seem fair to saddle you with an obligation that's bound to bring you in close contact with a lot of painful memories that I know you'd rather simply forget. No, Joby's the man for the job—I know he won't shrink from it—and so, I give old Joby all necessary powers over all my rightful goods and possessions and all authorization to carry out my wishes as expressed in this document, as well as to pay my just debts, obligations, and funeral expenses.

Now, I don't want anything special, Joby, but in a fit of undeserved generosity you once offered to bury me beneath the boughs of the sugar bush that stands up in the north field along with those that have gone before. You Danners have been the only real family that I've ever known and there couldn't be any greater honor than to lie my bones down beside them beneath the shade of that stand. But I also don't want to be a source of conflict. After all is said and done here, if Sarah doesn't want me buried in your family's plot, then so be it. After all that we've been through, I could hardly blame

her for wanting to erase me from the Danner collective memory. If that's the case, Joby, just stick me in the ground next to my old man in the cemetery up on Vermont Hill Road and don't give it another thought.

We've had some times, old Joby and me. Some of it you know already, Sarah, and some of it happened after you left. But if he's played one part consistently, it's been the part of country psychiatrist, listening to me jabber away as I've tried to piece together the history of our relationship and figure out where it all went wrong. He never says much, except to tell me to think about those years from your perspective, but his simple listening has brought me to some interesting conclusions about myself and about our life together. I've come to understand, for example, that it all started downhill long before we met, you and I. And so that's where I'm going to start here as well. It all began with my own old man, God rest his soul. He made as many mistakes as I have and maybe more. But I've been to hell and back since you left, Sarah, and I haven't got the right or the strength to condemn him anymore.

Conor Higgins was born on the eve of the Nazi invasion of France, and by the time he was two years old, his father was drafted into the U.S. Army along with nearly the entire male population of East Angler. So for the next five years, my grandmother, along with my father and baby Aunt Katherine, had to tighten their belts and make a go of it alone. They weren't the only ones. My grandmother took a job as a secretary at Harold O. Brumsted Elementary School, and though he was just a child, my father started to take care of himself and his baby sister for long stretches after school and on weekends, while my grandmother tried to make an extra dollar or two by mending clothes or baking pies or doing laundry or just about anything else. My old man never complained about it by name—at least not to me—but I know that he resented having to become the man of that house while he was still a child. And even when my grandfather returned from the war, his mind never really made it back, and so my father used to say that he and my grandmother and my Aunt Katherine were as much casualties of the war as anyone else. I've had long conversations with old Joby about the effect that war can have on a man and how long it took him to recover from all that he saw in Vietnam. And he's admitted to me that it's not really something that you ever recover from, though most learn to go on living as if they had. I guess in some ways it's helped me to understand my father and grandfather both, and to forgive some, which is the more important.

That's not to say that the case of my father was in any way special. The old boys that sit outside the hardware store will tell you that the war seemed to take a toll on everything and everyone about East Angler at that time. All points of reference were lost to the war effort and everybody was searching for something to hold on to. Some found rebirth in the Lord and some found rock 'n' roll, some found drugs or the bottle, and some found baseball. That was my old man, as you might have guessed. He played ball, just like me, from the age of five. With my grandfather over in the Pacific, it was his mother that showed him how to throw from a crouch and how to step into the ball just before he made contact. She was quite a coach, from what I understand, and she was followed by others and by the time he was seventeen, my old man had scouts coming from as far away as Minnesota to watch him squat behind home plate and throw out runners that thought they were too fast for anybody. And he'd crack the bat too when his time came. He was a damn good ballplayer, just like his son would be, and he had his sights set on a life of it.

Then my grandfather died, or I guess you could say that his body finally joined his mind, which had never really made it back from overseas. As my old man told it, one summer day about ten years after the end of the war, his father came through the front door, kicked off his boots and told the family in a quiet voice that he had a lump in his throat. He'd dipped a tin of Copenhagen a day since he was twelve, so he knew the score, as did they all. Two weeks later, the biopsy confirmed it and my grandfather went under the knife. The doctors told them after that the cancer had spread from his trachea to his tongue and esophagus, and in trying to dig it out, they had severed an artery. He bled out right there on the operating table.

Outside, the snow had begun to fall in buckets, and my grandmother and my father and my little Aunt Katherine had to spend two days snowed in at the hospital where the body of my grandfather lay decomposing in the morgue. It was so bad that the undertaker told them that because of the facial deformities from the surgery and the two days of delay the funeral had to be closed casket. And so it was.

The way my father told it, my grandmother seemed to shrivel up into an old woman once my grandfather was gone, as if the needs of her family and the hope that her husband would someday make it back from the Pacific was all that had kept her young and energetic all those years. But the world turned and my father stepped up to take care of his aged mother. At seventeen, and just on the cusp of living his dream, he dropped out of school and took a job in the lumberyard. My grandmother would tell me that the light left his eyes with the death of my grandfather, and I know she meant that Conor loved his father in spite of the space between them. But I know better what that light was. When that light went out, my father said goodbye to the dream of playing in the big leagues that had pushed and sustained him since he was five years old. And it isn't easy for a man to live without his dreams, let me tell you.

He supported my Aunt Katherine until she graduated high school and married and moved on out to California, and he took care of my grandmother until her dying day. And I never heard a word of complaint or resentment about them. But he was broken inside, in that way that you and I know so well. He drank for a while early on, mostly without consequence. He grew a belly and a beard, and he lost some of that blaze-red hair, but his chest was broad and his arms were big, and no one dared to mess with him, at least not when he was half sober. He joined the union, and he worked hard to better the situation at the mill, mostly without success. But it occupied his time, and he made enough of a wage to support a small family as well as his mother and younger sister. He was a quietly angry man, as I remember, with a cold, blank stare that would freeze you when it lighted upon you. And I know he had packed away his dreams and settled in for a long and bitter life of putting his nose to the grindstone. Lord knows he isn't the first man to make that sacrifice, nor the last, to be certain.

I think he might have made good if he had just caught a break or two, and for a while it seemed like things were turning his way. He met my mother down at the mill, where she helped to keep the accounts. She was the third daughter of a Scotch-Irish family from way over in Aurora that was in a precarious position itself with eight mouths to feed. It didn't take much for my old man to sweep her off her feet. She had a certain softness to her and a pale beauty and long fingers that I always picture floating above the keys of a piano, though I have no idea whether she ever actually played. I do remember quite distinctly that there was a sadness about her steel-gray eyes, which I assume must have allowed the two of them to understand each other.

Within a year, they were married. They had me soon after and bought the little house that sets about two miles out of East Angler on Main Street—you'll know the one, Sarah. And there was a wistfulness that passed across my old man's face whenever he talked about those years just after my birth when they moved out of my grandmother's house in town and out on their own.

They tried for another baby just after I was three years old. They conceived a little daughter and had one of the rooms of the little house outfitted in pink and frills. And my mother settled on the name Colleen after my great-grandmother that came over from County Cork in old Eire. And for nine months, we all lived in anticipation.

I remember the walk up the drive to my grandmother's house on a cold winter's night—the snow floating down softly in the spotlights over her garage—as my parents rushed off to the hospital in the city, but I have only flashes of memory thereafter and there isn't any story to connect them, except as was told to me in my later years. There's my grandmother reading to me from some old book of fairy tales, there's a peanut butter and jelly sandwich and a simmering pot of chicken soup, there's the feel of hands lifting me out of bed in the dark, and then there's the face of my father, alone and defeated in that way that I've only recently come to recognize in myself.

He told me once that we stayed there with my grandmother for a month, given that he couldn't bear to go back to that room that they'd done up so nice and frilly. And he must have changed it soon after, because I don't have any memory of that room whatsoever other than what I've been told. By the time we did get back, he had become just about like you and I remember him—a solitary, joyless, hard man, just like my grandfather, and I can count on the fingers of my one good hand how many times I heard him laugh after we lost my mother and baby sister.

He did his best to swallow the sadness and be a good father to me. I see that clearly now. Some of the first solid memories of my life are tagging along behind him at the end of the winter as we worked our way down the path cleared to lay the gas line that stretched along behind our house, over streams swollen with the runoff of spring and through still-barren cornfields to the low country. He'd pause periodically and sweep the brush to the side of the trail with a walking stick, looking for the game traps that were lying there in wait for the fox, the rabbit, and the deer that came in search of water. He'd spring every one and pull them up and throw them into the forest if they weren't secured to the ground.

"A man that can't look his kill in the eyes doesn't deserve to eat," he'd say to me, and I still hold that as the truth.

After a mile or so, the ground would even out and we'd cross the old wooden bridge that sat atop two steel girders that were placed there before any of the neighbors could remember. We could hear the slap of beaver tail on the flat water even as we made our approach. And it was there, to the left of the old bridge, that the family of beaver would be putting the finishing touches on its dome-shaped, mud-packed hut of that season, where the female would spend the three-odd months of her confinement before giving birth to her litter of kits. We'd sit on the bank and look out over the lake that they'd created by sheer industry. My old man would crack a beer and give me a sip now and then and we'd sit quietly, just staring at the hut and watching the birds come and go and listening to the slap of beaver tail and the low gnawing of wood and not saying a word.

Later on in the summer, he'd come back with some of the other men of the neighborhood and kick down the dam to let the water run to where it wanted to be. They'd learned early on that if they let the beaver alone for more than a season or two, the whole valley would flood, right up to the gas line. They didn't take the kids along back then, what with all that pent up water rushing over and around the broken dam. But he'd often tell me that the damnedest things would rise to the surface when they broke it up—old tires and discarded clothing, street signs and rusted old appliances and, once in a great while, the bloated body of some poor animal that got just a bit too close to the kits and was swarmed upon.

Maybe all that I can say about Conor Higgins is that he was a sad and complicated man, and he stayed that way until he took his last breath. The days of his satisfaction were few and far between and he spent his life working from before sunup until long after sundown and trying hard to forget his station when he wasn't at it. But we shared two loves, he and I: the memory of my mother and the sport of baseball.

I never felt closer to him than during the summer of my seventh year, when we both discovered that I had inherited his athletic talent. I had been playing Pee Wee for two months at that time, mostly making a fool of myself like the other kids in stumbling after the ball across the infield or flailing away and missing it entirely when it was lobbed over the plate. My father spent hours showing me how to choke up on the bat and to step into the swing, and not to take my eyes off the ball as it crossed the plate. After a few weeks, I could tell that he was getting frustrated, and I imagine now that he took my first clumsy steps as the sign of yet another burden for him to bear.

Then, I connected. It was one of those picture-perfect June afternoons in East Angler, when the daisies and the buttercups cover the field and wild goldenrod and Queen Anne's lace peek through the fence that rings the ballpark behind the old middle school; when the sun sits up high above and it doesn't get dark until nine. You can smell the contentment of life on the air, and everybody gets caught up in it, even the kids. The opposing pitcher looked diminutive away up on the pitcher's mound, where he went into an exaggerated windup, and I watched that ball come in as big as a ripe melon. Time slowed as I stepped forward and stretched out my shoulders and pivoted on my little hips with my eyes firmly trained on the ball. I could feel the contact reverberate through my forearms and I watched the ball sail up and away through the clear blue sky toward left field. I stood there astonished, just relishing the feel of the hit in my hands and arms, too shocked to even run towards first base. The ball sailed high over the fence and into the field of wildflowers beyond as nine fielders and both benches stared stupidly along with me into the afternoon sky. I heard my father shout "Run!" and eventually I made my legs obey. I rounded the bases then as fast as my feet would carry me, careful to touch every one, and my teammates welcomed me at home plate as if I had just won the Little League World Series.

Something had clicked, and from that moment on my play would improve, and I'd rarely miss that or any other ball again, whether lobbed over home plate or thrown at eighty miles an hour by some poor sod from a neighboring town. And I'll never forget the face of my old man when I crossed home plate and finished high-fiving with my teammates. It was pure ecstasy, pure adulation, pure pride, and I knew I had found the way to soften my old man's heart.

Now, it's a dangerous thing for a child to know how to win a father's love. I know by long experience that it upsets some universal balance in the family system. And when that love depends upon athletic success, you can be sure that disappointment and resentment are just around the corner. But I didn't know that then, and from that day on we were inseparable. My father became assistant coach of my Pee Wee team, then head coach, and he continued to coach me right up through high school. We watched baseball together every weekend, we travelled to the city to see the Braves whenever we could, and we made the long trek along the southern shore of Lake Erie to Cleveland at least twice a year to see the great Gaylord Perry and the Indians play. It was the happiest time of my life and, I think, his too. I liked to play ball, and he liked me playing it, and I liked him being happy, and it seemed that we were both content, at least for a time.

By the time I joined the varsity team as a sophomore, I was throwing fastballs at eighty-five miles per hour, and I had a curve that'd jump from one side of the plate to the other. My swing held steady at .350—which is damn good—and I had the expectations of all of East Angler riding on my fifteen-year old shoulders. I couldn't walk down Main Street without six old timers stopping to tell me about how my old man was the pride of the town when he took the East Angler Hornets to the Class C state championship game back in 1956, just before he dropped out. That they lost that game by ten runs nobody seemed to remember; they only recalled that, for a brief moment, our little town was in the spotlight. It wasn't much of a spotlight either. I know because I've been there—Class C is about as small as you can get, there being only four classes in state high school sports. And we wouldn't have lasted two innings against one of the teams in Class A. But everything is a matter of perspective. And the town's perspective on that game was that it was the be-all and end-all of small-town sports, and it was too, that is until I led our team to that same game and we came away with the trophy in 1977.

I remember that championship game almost as well as I remember that first home run, and in some ways, better. As to how I played, I only remember the stats. I threw a two-hitter, and I hit two home runs, with five runs batted in. But I remember the very picture of the stadium crowd, and the same star-struck look on the face of my old man as I looked toward the dugout in the bottom of the ninth, when I was about to throw the final fastball (at ninety plus now) past that tall, skinny shortstop from Haverford Park to end the game. The old man's face was older now, worn with battle and the work of years, but his expression carried all the hope and wonder of a child. I had never seen my father shed a tear, not even at the death of my mother and sister, nor at the funeral of his own mother three years before. He told me afterward that I was imagining things, that it must've been the reflection of the stadium lights, but I swear that even from fifty yards away, I saw a single tear roll down that gruff cheek over the stubble that felt like heavy sandpaper to the touch, and it hung glittering in the bright lights for just a moment, before he had a chance to wipe it away.

You'll know the other reason that I'll forever remember that game, Sarah—it was the first time that I laid eyes on you. You that owned my heart even with the first glance, you that I dreamed about every night on the road for four years, you that I broke myself against with my own anger and stupidity, and you that I'll forever seek forgiveness from. Lord, Sarah, when I look back on it now, I see myself so clearly. I want to shake myself by the shoulders, slap the bottle out of my hands, and give myself a hard right to the jaw, anything to wake me up to the gift that I had in my young hands and to keep me from spiraling down into the darkness as I did. But I can't, and I've got to live with that for whatever time remains to me.

I already knew your cousin, Owen, from the years we had spent battling each other on the field. He was a hell of a second-baseman, and he made some plays against me that had me red in the face and cursing up a storm. But he wouldn't ever leave the field after throwing me out without telling me what a nice hit it had been. He's a hell of a competitor, but also just a genuine nice guy. Anyhow, I was coming off the field after the win, headed toward the dugout to await the awarding of the championship trophy and the naming of the most valuable player, when I heard Owen shout out to me in that deep, twangy voice of his that no one this side of the Niagara can mistake.

"That was a hell of a game, Lem-boy, one hell of a game!"

I looked to the stands searching for his face. I admit that I wanted to rub it in a bit. After all, we had beaten the Collins Bengals—his team and yours—in the quarterfinals by only one run two weeks before. I found him ten rows up and still standing. I smiled and gave him a thumbs-up and a wink, but my gaze was soon drawn down to a pair of the most beautiful, big brown eyes that I had ever seen on a human being. They were the pure eyes of a doe that wanders shyly, carefully into the clearing—wholly innocent and vulnerable, trusting in a world that doesn't deserve trust. The eyes were framed by the most perfect oval-shaped face, the skin pale and pink at the cheekbones, with dark eyebrows and black hair flowing out behind down past your shoulders. I was thunderstruck then, and in spite of the mess that I've made, I don't think I've ever recovered. You looked me full in the face and smiled politely, but then looked away in that shy way that you do. And even that simple, demure act made my heart jump. You might not even remember that game at all, but I tend to hope that you do.

The rest of that evening is a blur to me. I was riding high, drunk on the title we had taken and the excitement of the fans that had followed us to the game and tailed us back, horns blaring all the way. And that bottle of Southern Comfort that our short-stop, Brian Alston, brought along for the bus ride back didn't hurt either. I looked for you as we headed out, that I do remember. And I asked around to all my rowdy teammates on the bus until Billy Giles told me that you were Owen's cousin from over in Collins. The boys could tell right away that I was into you, and I didn't try to hide it. I knew even then that there was something about you that I was destined for—that life had put you in my path for a reason, and I wanted to open that door right that very minute. But it wasn't until I saw Owen more than two weeks later that I was finally able to ask him about you. It took some convincing, because nice as he was, he was also protective; but he finally agreed to ask you along to Tyler Goodwin's cabin that Friday night for the bonfire—a sort of belated celebration of our win without the parental supervision.

A month after that game, my father and I were sitting at the kitchen table with a scout from the Yankees, who wanted me to skip college and roll right into their farm league organization out in Oneonta. It was the twentieth such meeting we had had that year with pro scouts and college recruiters, and though I had already committed to Florida State, we both thought it worthwhile to at least talk to the Yankees. Now, everybody thinks a kid should go to college, and I agree—it's not a statement that you can argue with for long. But I also think that you have to take your chances when they come, and my father and I both knew that this was a chance that only comes along once. And so in June, the Yankees officially took me in the third round of the amateur draft and I signed up to play starting the following spring. I think my old man was more excited than I was, though truth be told I was just about pissing myself in those days. It seemed like the Higgins family had finally caught a break, that all those years of practice and work were about to pay off, that I was going to be able to take us up two giant steps in money and respect and put it all back on track.

And looking back, I can see how college would have tempered that spirit. It would have forced me to grow up at a normal pace, not thrown out into the world as I was, on the road all the time and leaving you to fend for yourself. And I think that, just maybe, if I had gone to Florida State, you might have followed me and taken your degree down there. I can see us living in Tallahassee, a nice little house with a great big yard, Danny's pitch-back off to one side, and a great big oak covered in Spanish moss out front. I see that as clearly now as I saw us together back the day of that championship game, and it makes my heart ache for what might have been.

Now, this is the way I get: frustrated and angry with myself if I spend too much time in the past. I feel like the future that we always dreamed of is close enough that I can reach out and touch it, and then I remember how I destroyed it, and I suffer the death of those dreams all over again. But I've changed too. I've learned to let go and to walk away from the past until I can come back to it with calm. If I had only known that back then, we might be walking along the Seine right now. But it's enough that I know it today—it has to be—and so I'll be putting my papers away for a bit. I'll come back to them tomorrow, God willing.

FIRST BEQUEST

I hereby bequeath my 1978 World Series ring to my son, Daniel Conor Higgins. It's not worth as much as you might think, but it's just about the only personal item of value that I have left to my name. And it means something to me. Not that I can say that my talent contributed in any large part to the Yankees' great comeback over the Dodgers that year, but I did throw for two wins during the regular season and apparently that was enough for management to vote me a small share of the glory in the form of that ring. I think it's important that the boy knows that side of me—the side that worked hard and believed and held a tiny flame of talent cupped between his hands as the storm wailed about him.

There are times that I fear the memories both you and Danny hold of me will overwhelm everything else about us. I wake up in a cold sweat, reliving that night that I lost you both for good, and I go about the next day thinking that my son's only thoughts of me are going to be of freezing on that cold concrete floor while I lie next to him, dead to the world in my own piss and vomit. And maybe that's what I deserve—to be remembered for my worst. But as bad as it was, no one can say that it represents the whole of me. There was an entire history before and there have been a few worthwhile acts since. And I want Danny to know the good and the bad, to see me as a man who is fallible in every respect, but loyal and hardworking from morning until dusk and on through the night. In the end, I guess I just want the boy to know that he was loved by someone that mattered, even if I don't deserve his love in return.

It's almost too much for me to relive those days that are so long gone that they feel like they belong to another man. My heart fills with the memory of joy and expectation when I start to remember us in the first days of our courting, and I think of all the little attentions that you paid to me then and I to you. And there was so much feeling to it that I wonder where it all went. I've heard it said that no moment in time ever dies, that it just goes on being somewhere in a parallel universe. And I take comfort from knowing that somewhere out there tonight and for all time, there's a pure and unbroken Lem Higgins that's come upon the most tender and beautiful creature in all of his life. But then sure as night follows day, I know that there's a Lem Higgins drunk out of his mind and dragging his little boy through the ice and snow of a December night, with hatred on his broken mind. I want to grab him by the throat and pin him to the ground and shout full into his face that he's throwing away all that will ever matter to him in this world. But I can't, and I've got to be okay with the fact that those two Lems are out there working against each other for my soul day after day.

Now where were we? That's right, back at Tyler Goodwin's cabin that soft night in June of 1977. It was only a few days before I announced that I was joining the Yankees and my life seemed like it was rolling along some soft, clean red carpet that led straight on to true love and fortune and fame. Do you remember it, Sarah? Do you remember the cool breeze and the smell of the pines and the crackle of the fire and the muted conversation as I walked you away and into the night?

"I saw your game. Congratulations," you said to me.

Now, I don't have much of a memory for detail, but I remember you that night as if I had the very picture of you right here in my hands. The firelight played softly over your face and your black hair cast a shadow on your cheek. You brushed it back with one hand and smiled up at me. You wore that blue flowered sundress that you kept as long as I knew you and I always liked so much. It flowed easily over you in the night breeze, hugging your slender hips and your breasts, which you always thought were too small but I thought were just perfect. You wore sandals, and your face and your nails were unpainted, as if you recognized that no color could do you justice. It's one of the traits that I've always loved about you and love about you still—that you don't make any apologies for who you are and you don't try to hide behind any wall or paint or foundation. And I felt then that I was seeing you as you truly were, naked in every sense of the word but the literal. The fire was blazing, and a crowd had grown as it always does around the libations up on the porch. The entire East Angler high school was there, or at least three-quarters of it, and there was a smattering of friends from the surrounding area, including you and Owen, who said hello and proceeded to look sideways at me now and then from across the other side of the bonfire.

The night was starlit, and I was glad of that, because it gave me an excuse to walk you away from the crowd.

"I saw you there," I mumbled, "but I had to go a good ways to get Owen to tell me about you."

"He's always been that way," you said. "I think it's my brother, Joby, that puts him up to it. They won't be happy until I'm locked up in a convent like Suzanne Simonin."

"Who?" I said, thinking you were talking about some friend of yours from Collins.

"From Diderot," you said, shyly. "She was a nun … in a book. Never mind."

I didn't know Diderot then and I don't know Diderot now, except as some old French author that once tickled your fancy. It would be years before I learned to take your literary references in stride. You sighed heavily then as you did a thousand times in the years to follow and it felt like someone let the air out of my lungs. I realized even then that I would always be the brute to you and that you would always be exasperated by my ignorance. Yet somehow, even that felt right.

"Well, I guess I can understand that," I said, turning on the charm, and I saw you blush in the golden firelight. "But it doesn't make getting to know you any easier."

You nodded and looked across the smoke and flames at Owen, who was chatting it up with Billy Giles and throwing looks over our way every few seconds. I stuck my hands in my pockets and looked at the ground, feeling as though I'd failed already without ever having really begun. But I wouldn't give up that easily.

"Maybe," I said and swallowed hard, "maybe we should head away from the fire. Find somewhere to talk … away from all the prying eyes?"

You nodded and I took your hand and my heart jumped inside as we walked off into the dark, our eyes adjusting to the dim moonlight after the glare of the bonfire. I felt tongue-tied and about as agile as a bull moose on a frozen lake, but I can still remember the smell of pine needles and the crack of fallen branches as we made our way into the woods to the left of the cabin. The pond just beyond gave onto a clearing from which the stars were lit bright as could be. I lay my jacket down for you on the bank of the pond and sat next to you on the grass. The fall of night had caused dew to form and I could feel my seat getting wet almost as soon as I sat down, but the night was beautiful and perfect, as were you, and I wasn't going to let a little damp ass bring down the mood.

"Where do you want to go from here?" I asked after we had covered the small talk and moved on to graduation, which was still a year away for you then. Knowing that you had a love of the books, I expected you to say that you wanted to go to college somewhere nearby. Your answer said everything about you that I didn't yet know—that you were large and intense and fearless—and it nearly blew my small-town mind.

"Everywhere," you said, and I could see from the steady gaze in your eyes that you were telling it to me straight. "I want to see every corner of the world, eat every dish, learn every language, read every book, write a thousand more, and really stuff myself with it. And if it can't be done in my lifetime, then I want to come back again and finish it until it is."

If before my heart had jumped on a whim, I knew then without a doubt that you were the end of me and the beginning of someone new. You were truly the first person that I had ever met that saw the world as it was—large and grand and just waiting to be explored. That night was the first time that you talked to me about the Beats—about Ginsberg and Kerouac and Kesey and a dozen other names that I had never heard before, about hitting the open road and living in the moment and expanding the mind beyond its narrow human confines. It was like meeting you had opened a door in the recesses of my mind and I could see the cloudless blue sky of the great wide world beyond. I stepped through and I was flying. I hardly knew what to say, ignorant as I was and mostly still am, but you didn't make me feel bad about it. You just lost yourself in the telling.

"It's getting cold," I said after we'd been talking for a good hour. I had a genuine concern for your comfort, though I wanted to prolong the moment as long as possible. "You want to wander back?"

"No," you said, moving yourself closer to me, "let's just lie here for a while."

And we did. I asked you where you'd start and you said Paris. And how I wanted to take you right then, to jump into it and let the current of life half a world away carry us along. We'd never get the chance for a thousand reasons that were still unknown to us as we lay there, but it didn't affect our dreaming. Back in the dark and limitless woods of East Angler, Paris was just a formless idea in our heads, a poster of some beret-wearing painter pedaling back to his studio over cobblestoned streets with baguettes in the front basket.

Now I still haven't ever been there, but I feel like I carry a part of it with me, like the two of us might have been something different there, and that our shared idea of Paris still exists somehow outside of our time together and always will. At least that's the way that I like to remember it.

I could feel that bull moose slipping and sliding across the ice, just trying to hold on for dear life and not make a mistake that would show you just how ignorant I really was and send you laughing back to your cousin, Owen. I was nervous as a boy could possibly be—and I had to fold my hands in front of my legs to stop them from shaking. But I screwed up what courage I had and leaned over then and kissed you. Your lips were cool against my own and I felt you press back towards me. You tasted of peppermint, and I was suddenly embarrassed once more because I knew that I tasted like cheap beer. But I kept on, probing, testing you with my tongue. You lay back flat on my jacket and I went with you, not willing to tear my lips from yours for even a second. I felt the dew against my cheek and I knew it was getting your hair wet too, but you didn't pull away. How I wanted you and I knew then that you wanted me too.

And as I lie here, eight years later and a broken man, I can still taste the peppermint on your lips. I can still feel the breeze blowing over the pond and the musty scent that it carried over us. I can still smell the burning wood and taste the stale beer. And I can still feel that knot of adrenaline in my stomach—the same one that I got from that moment on whenever you walked into a room. For me, that night still lives brightly in my memory. Truth be told, it's one of my most precious possessions—much more valuable than any World Series ring. It's a sanctuary from all that I've caused and endured in the years since, and I visit it as often as I can.

"Uh um … I think it's time we get going, Sarah," said Owen from the shadow of a nearby pine.

I bounded off of you, tripping over my own feet, and ended up with one leg in the pond up to my knee. You laughed from where you sat in the grass, and I stuttered some sort of apology to Owen, who just looked at me sideways. You stood up calm and straight in the starlight and smiled at my clumsiness. Then you led me out of the rushes at the edge of the pond, and stood on your tiptoes to kiss me lightly once again.

"Call me," you said and you squeezed my hand. "I'll be waiting."

I told you I would, but I was suddenly seized with a panic that I would never see you again. And I was desperate not to lose the night to propriety and good manners. I told Owen that I could drive you home. I knew from his look that he thought I wanted to take advantage of you—and I did. I mean, I did eventually want to be with you. But that night all I wanted was another minute or all the minutes that the world would give, to lie next to you and to talk about your favorite books and faraway places and to kiss your lips until the sun came up and then to do it all again.

"All the way to Collins?" Owen asked doubtfully. "And you've already been drinking? That's alright, Lem. I promised my cousin Joby that I'd watch over her. I ain't done such a good job thus far, but I mean to get her home safe. You take it easy now."

And he was right. I was drunk as could be, but the beer didn't have anything to do with it. I was drunk on you. I had tasted you only for a moment, but I was irrevocably and forever addicted to you. I watched you disappear into the trees and then I watched your shadow as Owen led you past the bonfire to his old truck. I lay back on the grass when you drove away, and I closed my eyes and replayed every second of our being together. My heart was flooded with the feel of you, and in a rush of the adrenaline of young love, I took off toward the pond and plunged into the cool, dark water head first, my face tickled by the grasses and lily pads that lay just below the surface. I turned over on my back and floated out to the middle. I was already dreaming of you, and the sliver of moon winked its approval as the stars shone down upon me.

It was more than a week before I was able to see you again, though I called you every night and we talked until the wee hours of the morning. Even my old man took notice, which he did about few things other than baseball, and he asked me about it. When I finally told him about you—that I had never felt for anyone what I felt for you after only a couple of weeks—he just grunted and told me to be careful.

"Now, boy, don't you go doing anything stupid. It ain't no time to screw up now," he said, and I knew exactly what he meant, though pretty much all I could think about was laying my hands on your beautiful naked body.

We had only just announced that I was planning to join the Yankees in Oneonta the following year, and the congratulations were flooding in from all over. It seemed like every old timer in East Angler was thrilled that a hometown boy had finally made good. Daryl Kozinski, the Town Supervisor, even told me that he'd call for a Lem Higgins Day the minute that I made it up to pitch with the Yankees in New York. And he was true to his word too, though it was only celebrated the one time. I told everyone that I was thrilled, that I'd make them all proud of me, that the pros never had to deal with a rough and tumble farm boy from East Angler before, that I'd be up there in New York in a matter of months and show them how to play. But inside all I could think about was you, how I couldn't wait to kiss you and to touch your soft skin again, about how I couldn't think to leave you even if I was only going to be a couple of hours away. But there didn't seem to be any limits in those days, and I assumed that you'd come with me wherever I went, that we'd do all those things we dreamed of doing, and together.

After just a week, I was desperate to see you again. We had talked that Friday night through on the phone, and I asked you when we were going to get together.

"I hear Celia rattling the pans downstairs now," you said. "Why don't you come over for breakfast?"

That wasn't exactly what I meant. My dreams of you and I together were generally of the private type and I could feel the quiver in my lips that so longed to touch yours again, even if only for a moment. But I wouldn't give up any chance to pass the time with you, heavily chaperoned or not. And so I said that I'd be right over and I screwed up my courage and took off early that morning on my old dirt bike across the hills to your father's farm. It took me damn near an hour to get there, not knowing exactly where it was and trying to stay off the roads to avoid the state troopers, but I pulled into that drive—that drive that I look down on from the window before me now—for the very first time on a beautiful Saturday morning in late June just as the sun had risen over the hills to burn off the fog of the musty night that preceded it.

It wasn't your father that came up out of the milk house to see who was making such a racket so early in the morning, but your brother, Joby, with his son, Devon, hard on his heels. Joby stopped about five paces from where I sat after cutting the engine on the bike, looked me up and down, and spit a stream of tobacco juice on the ground at his feet.

"Well, I expect I should have seen this coming. Yes, sir. Well … I suppose you want to see her …"

Now I'm a big boy—tall that is with a good amount of meat on me—but that Joby's about as broad as a bull and twice as strong, with forearms that make him look like he's Popeye when he's throwing hay bales around like they're empty cardboard boxes. But it isn't just that stout build that put me on my guard, it's that Joby's got the most penetrating blue-marbled eyes that go flat as seawater in the sunlight. They make him look like an errant black bear that's deciding whether to pounce on you and take a chunk of your hide. He intimidated me right off, and I could see from the look in those blue eyes that he wouldn't think twice about stepping between you and me if he thought I was acting with dishonor. And it made me love and want you the more, because that sort of snorting and pawing and blustering only occurs when the herd circles around something precious to it.

I think he might have read me right there on the spot—old Joby always was good at reading folks right off—because then he softened a bit, his eyes gained some depth, and he walked toward me wiping his hand on the back of his jeans and then sticking it out to me. I took it gratefully.

"I'm Joe Bart ... Joby if you like. And I'll be playing the part of the overprotective older brother," he said deadpan, then his face broke into a half-smirk. "Now I know of you, Mr. Professional Baseball Player, but I don't know you as of yet, and so I feel duty bound to tell you that that little girl that's peeking through the curtains above is about the most precious thing this family's ever had. You go messing with her in the wrong way, and you'll have me all over you like stink on shit, big ball player or no, and that's a fact."

He spat another stream of tobacco juice at his feet to punctuate his last statement and Devon aped him with all the threat that his skinny twelve-year old body could muster, though I could tell the kid was more interested in that dirt bike than anything else.

"Now go on in the house and see her before she pees herself. Lord knows she ain't talked about nothing but you for more than a week now."

We sat down to breakfast that Saturday morning with the farm coming to life about us. Joby and Devon came in after they were done milking the heifers and your father made his way downstairs to sit at the old kitchen table that we still eat at today. He was older than I expected—much older—but still in full control of his mental capacities even so. Celia whipped up some pancakes with sliced banana and tiny bits of apple like she does and we all smothered our stack with Joby's homemade maple syrup. I remember saying that I couldn't believe something so pure and sweet could ever come out of such a nondescript mason jar, but Joby just looked at me and squinted his eyes like he knew exactly what I was up to.

We talked about baseball, of course, and what it would be like in the majors. And I continued undaunted to ask Joby all about making the syrup that really did slide down my throat like liquid silk. Your father picked up the conversation and told me about the sugar bush and boiling sap in the old days before they had log splitters and such to make the work easy enough for a woman to do. And he invited me back that spring to join him and Joby when they tapped the maples that lined the fields behind the barn. I accepted, of course. I was so into you that I would have gladly come back to clean out the heifer stalls if they had asked me. Lord knows I've done it enough times since then anyhow.

The table grew quiet and reverent as your father told the stories of your mother, and I could see the tremendous loss in his eyes as he described losing her overnight to an aneurysm only ten years before. I saw you watching him then, and I knew that you didn't have but a child's memories of her yourself. And I recognized then that we were both children left out in the cold rain of life with only a flat, hard board to stand beneath. Our fathers did their best in that, I know, but it doesn't change the fact that we never again were able to draw comfort in the storm.

I stayed at the farm a couple of hours, never getting time alone with you, which is what I was dreaming about on a nearly constant basis then. But I knew that I was putting your family's mind at ease, and I was glad to have met Joby—just how glad I wouldn't know for years. They gave me a tour of the farm, this same farm that seems to have become the totality of my universe. Devon even took me up one of the towering grain silos to look down at the feed contained within, and from the top he told me how Jorge Martinez had fallen in last year and went unconscious in less than a minute from the fumes. If Joby hadn't grabbed a rope and gone in after him, he would have died for sure. As it was, despite all his gratitude to Joby for saving his life, Jorge decided that life was too short and precious to be working someone else's fields and risking death and injury, so he headed on back to Mexico.

Joby never said it, but I could tell that he needed a hand around that farm. I started coming every Saturday, then every Sunday too, just to help them milk the heifers and spend a couple hours with you and your family that soon enough became like my own. Though I started training with the Oneonta Yankees that summer, I wouldn't officially join them until the following spring. And it turned out that the training wasn't quite the full-time job that I had expected, so I was able to spend most of my time hanging about the farm and running away to Oneonta for team meetings and practices three to four days a week.

It was late that first summer that me and Devon discovered the woodchuck den that set against the north side of the old barn. It was a good-sized hole, maybe two feet in diameter, which is plenty of space for a small man to get through. We spent two days listening to the squealing that came out of that hole, Devon poking about with a stick to see if he could drive that woodchuck out and into the light. He always did love animals, and he'd have adopted a lion cub if he had happened upon one out in the fields. Lord knows he had enough frogs, snakes, mice, and damaged birds for three boys his age. Well, we were all sitting down to a late afternoon dinner of pork chops and corn on the cob on the picnic table out in the yard on one of those summer days when the temperature was on the rise and the mosquitoes and flies were down, when Devon walked up covered in mud from head to toe and showed us that he had a little life squirming about in his twelve-year-old hands.

He had finally decided that afternoon that those squeals weren't the sound of a woodchuck at all and so he'd screwed up his courage and wriggled down that hole head first. Feeling along in the cramped, dark space underground, he came upon a bundle of wet fur that squeaked like a chew toy and latched onto his nose when it got close, sucking away for all its little body was worth. Even Devon couldn't be sure that it wasn't a little woodchuck or a little bear cub for that matter until he wriggled backwards out of that hole and held the thing up to the light. And that's the story of how your family got this fine specimen of canine that lays here at my feet, scratching away at some bite that she picked up out in the fields with Joby.

We learned later that the Hamil bitch had chosen the abandoned woodchuck hole as her birthing place, but left the runt behind when she took her pups on back to her own house, trotting them up to the front door proudly one by one. I wanted to name her Runt, which would have been appropriate, but Devon named her Woodchuck, which wasn't half-bad either. He nursed her right along, just like he'd done a dozen baby calves, until she didn't need the bottle any more. From that day on, she was his constant companion right up until the end.

It was that same beautiful, innocent summer that we started dating in earnest, heading out to the old movie house in Colbyville at least once a week, where we'd steal out in the middle of the show and spend the rest of the night kissing and touching each other in that old '68 Chevy Impala that I bought with my small signing bonus from the Yankees. The rest of my life that summer is a blur, though I know I went to practice and team meetings and hit the gym as often as ever. And we must have spent the Fourth of July together and my birthday. But all my memories of that time are of the barn, the breakfast table, and holding your beautiful, slender body in my hands by the light of the dashboard, though you never let me go too far.

By August, the leaves were beginning to turn and the wind had picked up and the air held that spark of electricity that seems to rise right out of the ground as the big storm clouds roll in, when it seems anything in the world is possible. School hadn't started back yet, and I was spending every waking moment at the farm or elsewhere with you. The truth is that I could have spent the rest of my life in just that way. Most days I wish I had.

Devon's pigs had grown to a ripe old size and he was sure to take a prize at the Cattaraugus County Fair over in Shelburne. Old Joby did the polite thing and asked me to come along that Saturday morning, seeing as I'd spent just as much time feeding those pigs as Devon for the three months prior. I told him that I had to take a physical for the Yankees organization that morning—just a formality, but a requirement of my signing package—but that I'd be right on over that afternoon before the prizes were given. You looked at me then, and I saw the mischief in your eyes. I had a good idea what you were thinking when you said that you'd wait for me and we could ride over together. But it wasn't until later that you asked.

"Lem? ... I was thinking ... do you think you could see the doctor some other time?" You said it so shyly that I couldn't miss what you were after, and I felt my stomach tighten into a double half-hitch knot right there on the spot. "It's been three months and we haven't spent hardly any time alone together, except in that old car of yours, which isn't all that comfortable to tell you the truth."

I raced through the chores of that afternoon with an energy that made Devon look at me sideways. I kissed you goodbye and sped home over the hills, where I rescheduled my appointment with the team doctor and set about counting the seconds until Saturday morning. I didn't feel quite right about keeping the truth from Joby, but one thought of you and me alone in that big old house wiped away any guilt in an instant. My thoughts ran wild over untouched country, and I could barely stand still for more than a few seconds at a time. Even my father noticed my agitation, and he thought I was getting nervous about playing for the Yankees.

"You'll be just fine, Lem," he told me kindly, and I nodded. "You're the best this town's ever produced and I ought to know. I'd have had my cup in the majors if it weren't for the old man's cancer, and you're a sight better than I ever was. You'll make it … you'll make it just fine."

The days of milking the heifers had gotten me used to rising early in the morning, or maybe it was the anxiety of knowing that we would first be together, but that Saturday I was up to watch the sun dance up over the pines from the wooden deck that I'd built with my father five years back. I would have run right over as soon as I got up, but I didn't want to show up with your family still around and ruin our chances. So I waited an hour, and I can honestly say that it was the longest hour of my life. There was a nice, warm breeze, the last of its kind for that summer, and it rustled the newly-dried leaves and pine needles as it swept over the undulating hills behind our house. I watched a family of red squirrels busy gathering acorns at the foot of the grand oak, carting each nut off to a knotted old apple tree to bury it within.

Finally, after an eternity, when the shadows had grown smaller by a touch and the sun had burned off the first clouds of morning, I thought it was safe enough to make my way to you. I scrubbed myself down and even stole some of my old man's cologne, though the overpowering smell of it made me queasy on the ride over and I tried to take it off with water and a napkin. I wore my lucky rugby shirt and a pair of jeans, not wanting to appear over eager, but also to be dressed for the fair later that day.

Nervous as I was, a strange calm came over me as I pulled into the drive and parked the Impala behind the house and up close to the barn so it wasn't visible from the street. It was like I knew that I was crossing some invisible plane, moving from childhood to adulthood in the space of a single, bright August morning. And nothing in the world meant more to me at that moment, and every moment since, than you and the love of you and the having of you then and forever.

You met me at the door and nodded with a smile when I asked if they had gone on to the fair. You had let your hair down and you had on a soft, ruffled brown skirt that fell to your knees and a white peasant blouse of the kind that they wear down in Mexico. I caught a glimpse of a lacy, black bra beneath and it lit a fire in me. I picked you right up off the floor and carried you up the stairs to your bedroom, where you already had candles burning and where the radio was playing the soft tones of Paul Simon.

Those moments are some of the very clearest memories I have, and I remember second by second what happened next. I think about it often—especially now and at night when I can't get back to sleep—and I relive every touch of your soft skin on my own, every sound that escaped your lips, every caress of my hands and fingers, and the feel of your moist lips on me again and again. I once had a first-base coach that believed that you make your own heaven or hell out of your memories of the life you've left behind. If he's at all right about that, I know that I'll get to live forever in your sweet caress of that morning in August, when we made love three times before noon and pledged ourselves to each other forever.

If I could only go back and be more careful or more restrained, I think sometimes that it all might have worked out differently.

But regret is a useless emotion, and we were following our passion then as God had intended for us. And I know that it's blasphemy to most to even suggest it, but I say that God was fully present in that room—this room where I now sit and write—where one nervous eighteen-year old boy entered body and soul into the deepest reaches of one calm and passionate seventeen-year old girl and they became one. I whispered words of commitment against your ear and my hands ranged over every inch of your body. We pressed each other until we were spent and then lay holding each other and talking close and laughing until the urge was more than we could bear and we came together again. And again.

And I remember your gasp as I pulled out of you that last time and we both looked down to see that the thin rubber sheath that was meant to contain and protect our youth from the creation of another had torn while I was inside you. At the time, we did all that we could do to push back the frightening reality and cling to the paradise we had temporarily created together, which was to ignore the danger. We spent the rest of that morning in each other's arms until we couldn't put off the trip to Shelburne for another instant. And I told you that I loved you and would love you forever, to which you smiled and said that you knew I was telling the truth. But a fog had settled over our clean, crisp young lovemaking, and it would grow progressively thicker until six weeks later you said those words that we both were afraid to hear.

"Lem, I'm pregnant."

SECOND BEQUEST

It may seem an odd article to include in a will, given that it isn't tangible goods, but I feel strongly that it should be put down on paper and made known. And so, I hereby bequeath forgiveness to my father, Conor Liam Higgins, for all that he did to me and all that he left undone for me. It's been eight years since our falling out, but I feel like I've grown at least a hundred in the interval, and I know now how hard it can be for a man to try to hold together a family, especially while the forces of chaos are trying to break them apart. I see clearly now that it wasn't just the loss of his dream that set my father on the path of his own destruction, but the loss of my mother and sister and both at the same time. It's a wonder that he still had the love to raise me as he did, and I understand now why he focused all his hopes and dreams on me until they were so heavy that I folded under them—or at least I think that's how it looked in his eyes. I wasn't in any position to judge him back then, though I did, and I feel that we might have made amends if I hadn't been so goddamn stubborn and determined to prove him wrong about me.

So there you have it old man, a long-awaited response to that "I'm sorry," which were about the last words that we ever exchanged.

You're forgiven, God rest your tired soul.

It's hard for me to relive all that I'm putting down on paper here, Sarah. But I want you to know everything that I was feeling at that time of our beginning, and I want Danny to know it too. Between the pain and fever that are creeping along my insides, and the sorrow that's rattling about my brain for all that I've lost, it's quite a chore. But I'll keep on as long as I can. As for that, Doc Tyler came back this morning with the results of my latest blood tests. Joby came up with him, though he looked like someone had sucked all the color right out of him. I could tell right off that what they carried wasn't good news.

"Advanced pneumocystis carinii pneumonia," Doc said to me, and it was as strange to hear it as it is to write it now. Truth be told, I didn't understand the Latin and still don't, but I made Doc write it all down for me on a scrap of paper.

"Now, what the hell does that mean?" I asked him, the words hissing out of my mouth like the air from of a punctured tire.

"It's what we talked about yesterday, Lem," he said. "The pneumonia develops because the virus in your blood has torn down your immune system. And because the body has nothing to fight it with, it builds quickly beyond the point even where antibiotics will help. They've been seeing more and more of it lately in cases like yours."

"So, then … how much time?" I asked him straight out.

"Without treatment, not much, I'm afraid. Weeks maybe … days probably. But there's always hope, son," he said with a forced smile, and I felt a shudder go down my spine, as if the Grim Reaper himself had just tapped me on the shoulder with his scythe.

I told him he didn't have to go tiptoeing about me, that I knew the score, that every breath was harder to take and rattled about in my lungs as if I were pulling chain, and that I knew that the end was coming fast. Doc looked over to Joby as if giving him his cue.

"Doc thinks you should head on back to Mercy, Lem," Joby said. "It might buy you some time, which might be enough for them to find a cure, which is something we all can hold on to. Celia and I think it's worth thinking about, but I told him it's up to you."

"I ain't going back," I said, and hacked away into the handkerchief that he pulled from his back pocket. The two of them exchanged a glance as if it was what they'd expected me to say.

"Lem," Doc said slowly, looking me in the eyes, "I can't treat you properly way out here. You need specialists and treatment and analysis on a constant basis now."

"Well, you do what you're gonna do, Doc, but I ain't going back. I've spent enough time there already and it don't seem to have done me an awful lot of good."

And so we left it at that. Doc's still got me on antibiotics in any case on the theory that maybe they'll slow the infection at least enough to give me some additional time. And now there's that Pentamine, which I'm taking five times a day, and that's in addition to the shots of God knows what that he's giving me in my ass twice a week. They all twist my stomach up something awful, but I keep on thinking that it's worth it if they let me get out all that I need to say here. And so I'd better get back to it while I still have the ability.

I was one hundred percent completely unprepared for all that happened next. Not that that's news to you. But I've got to make something clear because I know—I hope—that someday Danny will be reading these lines. While it may have been that we would've waited to have a child, we would have had him eventually. I have no doubt about that. Back then, our love was pure as the December snow over the north field and anything that came out of it had to be good. Truth be told, that little life that grew inside you for the next nine months turned out to be the best thing that could ever have happened to us. And, at the very same time, it was the worst. It brought us together as never before, but it put more pressure on us than two kids are meant to bear. I admit that I didn't handle it as well as I might have. Now isn't that an understatement? The truth is that I took something beautiful and delicate and trampled it under my boots because I was stupid and childish and afraid.

Just as we discovered that you were pregnant, school started back. I kept on showing up early to the farm and driving you to class in the morning before making the long trip back over the hills to East Angler, where I'd work out with my old high school team in preparation for the minor league season that spring. But I would count the moments until I could find my way back to you again. There were rumors flying in both our circles, and my old teammates asked plenty of questions about you and all the time that we were spending together. I mostly put them off at first, but later—when the word got around that we were having a baby—it seemed that all their questions had been answered.

After you told me that you were pregnant and we both agreed that we wanted to keep the baby, we did the only thing we could have done. We sat your family down and we broke the news, hand in hand. It was during Indian summer when the air was warm and dry, just before Joby and Devon and I headed out to bring in the last cutting of hay for that year, the barn being almost full to the rafters with the bailing that we'd already done. I thought that it was Joby that I'd have to answer to, but he took it as well as one can take news of that sort about a baby sister, meaning that he didn't accidentally run me over with the tractor that afternoon or stick me in the brains with a hay hook. And your nephew, Devon, fairly beamed at the thought of having a little cousin to chase about all over the farm. He always did love the little ones.

It didn't endear me to your father at all, but he was getting on in years, and I could tell from the beginning that he was just a little bit glad to have another grandchild on the way, even if it was unplanned and his baby girl had to become an adult overnight. I knew then that he looked forward to holding that baby in his arms and spoiling him as grandparents are wont to do. And so, it was your family that was most affected that took it the best and let us know that they were there for us in whatever we might need.

My father was a different story.

I told him that same afternoon after I got home from the farm. I knew that he'd be disappointed and angry and probably yell and stomp about and, if so, I didn't want you there. If there was a price to pay, I wanted to take it on myself. And so I did.

He had come home from working an extra shift at the lumberyard that Saturday, and he was sitting at the kitchen table, unlacing his work boots, while a couple of cans of soup simmered away on the stove. He just stared at me at first, his head cocked to one side like he'd suddenly lost the ability to understand English. And time stood still as I waited for his judgment of me to rain down.

"You stupid son of a bitch," he finally said.

The veins stood out starkly against the sweat-stained skin of his neck, and I could see his fists clench. He had never hit me before, but we'd come close a couple of times over the years, and I knew he looked at me as a man, not a boy, and capable of putting up a fight or taking a good beating.

"All the years that I put into this job so that you could have your shot and you've gone and pissed all over it like it was nothing. NOTHING!" he yelled suddenly, "GODDAMN NOTHING!"

I told him that he was wrong, that I could still do it, that I was still going to Oneonta, that you wouldn't let me give up my dreams, that your family was behind us both, and that there were plenty of hands over on the farm to pitch in, but he didn't hear me. I could see through him to the flames that were consuming his dream and mine too, like a pile of kindling in the dry heat of August. I tried to get to his heart, telling him that he should be proud that he'd have a grandson or a granddaughter to show off around town, someone to spoil as children deserve to be spoiled, but he didn't hear that either. And so then I told him that I loved you, that I had no doubts that we were supposed to spend our lives together, and that you would be the daughter that he'd always wanted. But I think the memory of his dead baby girl only poured more gas on the flames.

"Don't you mention the name of that whore in this house again. Do you hear me? She ain't no daughter of mine. I don't want to see her or any godforsaken spawn that comes of her. And you tell that bitch that I said so!"

It was like he had ripped into my heart with his dirty bare hands, Sarah, and I became something else entirely—not his son, not even an acquaintance—but something animal and determined to protect what was mine. I flew at him. He didn't have time to stand up from the chair before I knocked him over and we tumbled against the bricks of the wall on the far side of the table. He still outweighed me by about fifty pounds and he was still a powerful old bastard, but I was quicker and I got a few good shots in to his face and ribs before he flipped me over and started to go to work on me. I struggled at first to try to regain the advantage, but after he broke my nose, I didn't have the strength. Still, every time that he asked me if I'd had enough, I found the mettle to spit my own blood—our blood—into his face. After he'd swollen my eye shut and cracked two of my ribs, he stood up, shook his head like he was waking from a dream, and stomped out the door. I think I passed out then, because the next thing I remember is looking up into the face of Kylie Jakes, that nosy old hen from down the street, through eyes that were still tearing on account of the pain in my side. Kylie was shaking me and then telling me to lie still. Behind her, I could see the mailman and other faces crowded at the door.

"Now you just lie there, Lem, honey. Buster's gone to call the ambulance. You'll be alright. Now you just lie still ..."

I crawled to my knees at the thought of being hauled off in an ambulance, and I could just see the police hunting down my old man for the damage he had done to me. I fell once and let out a whimper from the pain. But I managed to steady myself on the second try. I told them all to get lost, that it wasn't none of their business, and that I didn't need any goddamn ambulance. When I closed the door behind them, I went to the phone myself and dialed 911 to call them off. They told me that they had to come out anyway because a call had been placed and that was the law, but I told them that they'd find an empty house if and when they did.

When I hung up, I hobbled on to the bathroom to clean the blood off my face. I was staring into my own battered reflection and I suddenly saw the ugly mug of the old man staring back at me. The same eyes set too close together, the same heavy eyebrows that were slowly growing into one, the same crooked mouth that always looked like it was enjoying its own private joke. And I got to thinking about how our lives were running on the same track. It was his old man's passing that finally turned him off of baseball, and here I was taking on a new baby just when I needed to be focused on playing. And I realized even then that it wasn't me that he was mad at, but himself. It didn't make me like him any better. I snarled at the image in the mirror and told it that I was my own man, that nobody's destiny was written in stone, and that with the right attitude, any burden can be carried over the mountain. I could do it all, and I would, and I'd be goddamned if I'd end up like him. I was young then and foolish.

Then I went to my room and packed a duffel bag full of clothes. I threw in the ball from my first varsity no-hitter, and I headed for the door. I pulled it open to find my father on the other side, and I was gratified to see that he had a shiner on his right eye that'd last for the next week or so. He looked unsteady on his feet, like I'd either got to him more than I thought or he'd had a couple rounds down at the hotel before he calmed himself enough to come back.

"Lem, boy, I'm sorry," he began, but I cut him off. I think we both knew that it was done between us.

"This ain't your goddamn life to lead, old man. You had your chance and if you don't like the result, well that's too damn bad. You leave me to make my own mistakes," I said coldly.

I was gritting my teeth against the pain that almost forced me to sit down there on the step in front of him. But I sucked it up and pushed past him into the yard beyond. I'd be damned if I'd let him see me suffer. I settled into the old Impala and threw her in reverse, and the wheels kicked up a storm of gravel and dust. I caught a last glimpse of him sitting on the steps, his head hanging down almost between his knees, as I pulled out of the driveway. He was as big as ever, but he looked defeated, and it brings a tear to my eye now to think that I had anything to do with that and all that happened afterwards. But he had crossed the line—I knew that as surely as I knew that I loved you—and he couldn't take it back once it was out there.

I drove slowly over the twisting roads to the farm. My ribs were hurting so bad that I couldn't sit up straight and my left eye was pretty near swollen shut. Joby was sitting on the front porch when I pulled into the drive. The sun was just setting behind the eaves of the barn and the sunlight bounced easily off the red and brown of the autumn leaves that were scattered about and it cast a mellow light over the new-cut hayfield across the road. Devon had just turned the herd out into the field and I thought to myself that it would soon be too cold to let them wander out there on their own.

I could see from the expression on Joby's face that he knew what had brought me out to the farm for the second time that day. And if he hadn't guessed right off, I'm sure the blood and bruising on my eyes, nose, and forehead gave it away. He didn't say anything at first, just reached into the cooler at his feet and pulled out a beer and set it on the arm of the rocking chair next to him. I thanked him and settled down beside him, content to drink in the waning of the day and try to put my troubles aside. I brought the cold metal of the can to my swollen eye and winced when it made contact.

"It looks to me like your old man didn't take it so well, Lem," he said slowly and spit a stream of tobacco juice over the side of the porch.

"That's a fact."

He nodded, looking me up and down.

"You know, I been thinking," he continued slowly, measuring his words. "It's been a hell of a season and we got more machinery broke up and on the sidelines than any year that I can remember. The old man's too old to be much help and Devon's a bit young yet. What say you stick around for a bit and help us out? I know Sarah'd love to have you around to help get things ready for that baby."

I nodded, but I didn't say anything as I felt the tears start to come—and I wasn't going to cry in front of your brother. I took a pull from the cold aluminum can in my hand. Then I put it to the bridge of my nose, where I could feel the throb of the break that Doc Tyler wouldn't set until the following morning, and I looked out into the last of the day graying into night. Behind us, Celia had turned on the porch light and the moths began to gather. The crickets came up and a strong hum of the night soon enveloped us. Hardly another word passed between Joby and me, though we sat there for the better part of an hour or so, working our way through another couple rounds. At the end of it, Joby put a hand on my knee and smiled his crooked, tobacco-stained smile.

"Well now, I expect we better get you cleaned up before Sarah finds you in this shape and calls the whole thing off on account of you're ugly. Come on now."

I didn't realize it then, what with the anxiety caused by the baby coming and me on the outs with my old man, but for the first time in my young life, I was part of a real family. I guess I still am a part of that family, though the most precious part of it has gone from me. That's my own damn fault, I know. But I don't mind telling you that those years that we spent on the farm and in our little house in Collins are some of the most precious memories in my head. It hasn't been easy to know that I'll lose them before too long.

THIRD BEQUEST

I hereby bequeath my F-100 to old Joby. It probably doesn't have but five good years left, but you can't ever have too much equipment on a farm, and I hope that he gets some use out of it before it graces the scrap yard down on East Holland Road. I'm not as attached to it as I was that old Impala, where so many of our memories were made in that big backseat, but I thought the F-100 was about the biggest, baddest truck on the market when I traded in that old car, and the truck seemed an appropriate prize for the success that I was coming to have in the minors. It's just about the only thing I have left from that time other then the ring and a few old clippings that aren't worth the paper they're printed on.

I can see the truck down in the drive from where I lie here. It's parked tight up against the barn and covered with a fine dusting of snow. It's only October, but it's turned cold about here, Sarah. I look out the window and I can see this morning's flakes swirling in eddies along the gravel and right out into the road. And as I lean in toward the windowpane, I feel the cold fingers of Jack Frost reaching out to my cheek and digging beneath my skin, pulling me in closer until I'm flat against it and it begins almost to burn. And I think to myself that it's too early, that the winter has come too soon, that the boys are still playing ball, and we all still have the Indian summer to enjoy. But I have my doubts that it's going to come at all this year. It won't be long before the snow starts coming down in earnest. I'm glad that you and Danny are safe down in Virginia, where the weather is more moderate. I hope you've got him bundled up there just the same, for it doesn't take but a minute even in the mid-Atlantic to catch your death of a cold.

I feel the weather right down to my bones, Sarah. I noticed a draft in this room a few days back, though Joby and Celia have both searched high and low looking for cracks in the siding and drywall and they can't find a thing. They look at me like I'm crazy, and then like I'm feverish again and about to die any minute, but I tell them that it isn't so, there's just a draft, and I think we'll find it sooner or later. It doesn't help the temperature of the room that they keep coming in and out like I was back at Mercy Hospital, bringing Doc Tyler in every other day. I told that old man that he must need to do some advertising in the Penny Saver, given that it's obvious he hasn't got any other patients but little old me. He just nodded his head and smiled like he was proud of me for making a joke, then he proceeded to prick and prod me as usual.

It's a sorry state that I'm in today, but it isn't half as bad as I was after that fight with my father. I had a hell of a time explaining the ruinous state of my body, first to my coach and then to the doctor sent out by the Yankees just a week after it happened. I had been making the trip out to Oneonta to train with the team a couple of times a week. I met Coach Lidel on my first trip out. He was a short, round man with a kind face that seemed to sag about the eyes and in the jowls as if his skin was just tired of sitting upright on the bones of his skull. He told me straight out that first meeting that they all knew that I was talented and of the high expectations that the organization had riding on me. I promised to do my best to measure up and he said that he knew that I would.

The truth is that, before the fight, I had been making good progress. My fastball was coming up and even the pitching staff was pleased with my curve, which had only grown more pronounced over the summer and early fall of 1977. But I know they had their doubts when I showed up just a short time later all busted up like a boxer on the back side of his career. I told Coach Lidel and the doctor that I had fallen face-first from a hay wagon back on the farm. Coach didn't push me further, but the doctor was a sly one—I expect that he'd heard just about every lame excuse in the book—and he told me that he could see how that'd account for my nose and maybe even my ribs, but there wasn't any way on God's green earth that three rocks jumped up and hit me on both my eyes and my nose at the same time. I stayed silent after that and so did he. Later, he showed me that he put down that I'd had a farming accident in his report, but that otherwise I was healthy as could be and passed the exam with flying colors.

The cracked ribs had me sitting out team practice for another six weeks, and I resented the fact that I had to wait to live the dream. There had been talk all up and down the Yankees farm organization about my arrival and progress in training with the boys in Oneonta—and everyone had high hopes that I'd make the jump up the ladder to Syracuse that season, which was just below New York itself in terms of the organization hierarchy. But it all had to wait. My teammates began looking sideways at me and thinking that I might not have what it takes to make it in the bigs—and they were right, but not for the reasons that they thought back then. There wasn't anything I could do with busted ribs except let them rest and try to get my head back in the game. I went to the team meetings and I promised my coaches that I'd show up better than ever and ready to play when the season commenced the following May. In the meantime, I headed back to the farm, to you, and to little Danny growing fast in your belly.

The October winds were moving in by then and the storms built cold and grey on the horizon all morning until they made their charge over the fields about midday, whipping up every dead leaf, fallen branch, and wisp of dry grass in sight. The air was charged with electricity, and it sometimes seemed as if the whole scene might explode about us in one giant thunderclap. The sun rose slowly during those days, more often than not behind the clouds, which bathed the farm in an ominous half-light. But once in a great while, the risen sun would sneak in an appearance beneath the cloudbank on the horizon and a soft glow would float over the land, giving a sort of golden aura to everyone and everything that it first touched alive in the newborn day. It was on those days that I felt a calm deep down inside, like we were all being swept by a gentle current toward our common destiny, like all I had to do was hold your hand tight and put my head on your belly and let go. Looking back now, I think that something or someone was trying hard to tell me that I had already found my end—that life on the farm was so soft and beautiful that I should never want to leave it. And I should've listened, but I was still just a boy and I had to go and knock myself against the world before I learned to be content.

You'll remember that I spent a week in the guest room, sneaking around at night just so that I could kiss your sweet young lips and run my hands over your belly, though you wouldn't begin to show for a month or more yet. But then your father decided he could turn a blind eye to our living in sin—it wasn't like we were fooling anyone anyhow—and I started spending the nights in your soft, tiny bed, my arms and legs entwined with yours, kissing your lips, your belly, your temples and your forehead from sundown until your nephew Devon would give three soft knocks on the door and I'd get up for another morning in the barn.

I took over the milking chores with Devon so as to let old Joby sleep in for a change with Celia. And I got to know your nephew well in those days. For a twelve-year old at the edge of adolescence, I decided that he was alright. He loved sports and, despite his original promise, he'd started to test my baseball knowledge from the time we walked in the door until the last heifer was milked. When the wind wasn't up, we'd head out behind the barn and I'd show him how to throw a good curve or a knuckleball, and we'd spend some time just denting the aluminum siding to show how tough we were. He wasn't any kind of prodigy, but he learned fast, and I thought he'd make a nice addition to the varsity team over at Collins in a couple of years. And so he did for a time.

When you were squirreled away in your room writing or gone off to see Doc Tyler or shopping for new clothes when the old didn't fit you anymore, Devon and I would spend the afternoon about the farm and the fields, with old Woodchuck jumping about and nipping at our heels. The cold weather held off in that year and, on the warmer days, we'd head off to Johnson's Falls and let the cold waters that came down off that rock shelf pour over us in the pool beneath. That dog loved to swim and was normally paddling about the water even before we got within sight of the falls. Other days, we'd head a bit further downstream, where the beaver set up shop every spring. The walks sometimes reminded me of the good times with my old man, and I'd either grow morose with the memory or angry at what he'd done that was so fresh in my mind. I talked with Devon about it a bit, cursing my father up and down. But we mostly had ourselves a good time that autumn, and we grew into friends even though there was more than five years between us.

Most days Joby didn't sleep in at all, but got up anyways, and we'd find him tinkering with some piece of machinery or other in the shed when we were done throwing the ball around. We'd help him finish up whatever it was he was working on and then all three of us would come in out of the chill of the early morning to find you and Celia putting food on the table. And it was always an event—piles of pancakes with sweet maple syrup, dozens of eggs with big round slabs of Canadian bacon, fresh-baked bread and pastries, and all washed down with the sweetest buttermilk that my throat had ever tasted. I've always said and still do that milk straight from the cow quenches a man's thirst better than any glass of water or sports drink or even beer that I've ever had, not that I was drinking much in those days. We'd sit down the seven of us to a traditional breakfast nearly every morning, which wasn't something that I'd ever done before, and we'd talk over the price of milk and feed and the weather and the million little things that still needed to be done before the farm ran just right.

Later on, once your family had truly taken me into their confidence, that talk turned to how Cooperative Foods was buying up the land, one family farm at a time, and how they had their sights set on old Joby, who cursed them even before they caused him any real trouble. In those early days, your old man would tell stories of years gone by and we'd all sink into a sort of post-breakfast meditation until one of us would realize the time and you'd jump up to get ready for class.

October rolled along, the brittle leaves mostly blew down from the branches and grew soft and moist underfoot where they were pummeled by the showers, which turned to freezing rain and hail long about Halloween. The morning air turned downright cold and Devon and I could see our breath hang in the air as we made the tired journey from house to barn. The grass woke brittle with the frost, which began to burn off later every day until it didn't anymore.

The first real snow floated down in early November and it was getting harder to leave the soft touch of your embrace to stomp around in the cold barn with those heifers. But I did it, and Joby told me that I was a welcome addition, milk prices having fallen so low that he couldn't afford to hire out help anymore. I told him then what I still believe today—that I got more from the Danner family than I could ever hope to repay. And it seemed to be proven to me once again that Thanksgiving, when your relatives came from all over to fill the farmhouse to the rafters. They took me in just like I was one of their own. Every cousin and aunt hugged me until I was worn through, and even your cousin Owen seemed genuinely happy to have me as part of the family, drinking with me and sharing old baseball stories well into Thanksgiving night.

My ribs had finally healed and I got back to training with the team out in Oneonta, where it felt like everyone had their eyes set straight on me to see whether I would actually make it back. When I first started throwing again, my curve was as strong as ever, but my fastball had lost a good portion of its spunk. It was a month before I got it back up to the heat that I was throwing before the old man and me had it out. But the break seemed to have done me a bit of good too, as my fastball ticked up over ninety-five miles per hour. And the coaching staff at Oneonta started to talk openly about moving me up the chain to Syracuse that first season. I bit my lip to keep from shouting when they told me, and you and me celebrated the way that we always did. It never did matter to me that you were pregnant. I wanted you every moment of every day, and your beauty grew as did your belly the closer you came to having little Danny.

I saw my old man hanging around the gym at East Angler High late that autumn when I was putting in some extra time in the weight room. He quit coaching that year after I graduated, partly because of all that passed between us, but he still put in an appearance at the school every now and again. Well, he turned his back to me as soon as I caught his eye, and I watched him walk straight out the double doors of the gymnasium, which closed behind him with a loud snap. I went back to the bench press, where I upped the weight by a solid fifty pounds, and I pumped out the repetitions until I couldn't anymore and one of the football players had to help me pull the bar off my chest. I damned the old man to hell in my mind, and I swore to myself once again that I wouldn't end up like him, some two-bit has-been that hangs around the edges of someone else's dream.

It wasn't until the first heavy snow of December dumped two feet of pure white flakes on the ground that your father started coughing. It was such a hacking cough that almost immediately started bringing up blood that none of us had any doubt that it was serious and forced him to go to see Doc Tyler right off. Now I know you loved your father as much as anyone could, and I'm willing to bet that his passing still brings tears to your eyes, so I'm not going to belabor what happened next except to say that it was cancer and the doctor said that it was too late to do much of anything except make him comfortable for the last months of his life, which you did along with Celia.

We weren't operating under any illusions in those dark weeks, and the cancer settled a question that we'd been going over for some time. Everyone knew that we had a baby coming, that we were living as man and wife in your family's house, and that we loved each other as much as two people can, and so we were asked time and time again, even before your father got sick, when we were going to get married. By that time I had asked you about a dozen times to give me your hand and about wore myself out trying to explain how it'd be better for you, me, and the baby to be together in fact and in law before he was born.

But you were unsure and rightly so, knowing that I might be headed to Syracuse in the spring and out on the road after that, and neither of us knew how much time I'd be able to spend back on the farm. We had talked about you coming with me, the two of us setting up house in a little apartment upstate, but we decided that I'd be on the road a good piece, that the road wasn't any place for a young mother and her baby, and that you'd have more help and support if you stayed on the farm with your father and Joby and Celia and Devon. Besides, you had your own dreams of becoming a writer, and the peace and tranquility of the farm lent itself to your intellectual pursuits much better than the life of a minor-league baseball groupie. And so we decided that you'd stay on the farm, and we were right for deciding it that way. But the news of your father's illness put one question squarely before us and so we made the decision: your father would see his daughter married before he closed his eyes for good.

And so, it was the last Sunday in January of 1978 that I stood next to Father Murphy at the altar of St. Mary's and watched you walk down the dark red velvet carpet past Celia, who was crying even before the ceremony started. You held your father's hand coming down the aisle. He was thinner by then but sitting up tall and straight and proud in his wheelchair with Joby pushing him along from behind. He'd cough every now and then, and Joby would lean on down and wipe the bloody spittle from his lips. I know that both father and son suffered a thousand miseries in those final days, but I never heard a word of complaint out of either of them.

Most of the rest of the town was out, including hundreds of our friends and classmates from East Angler and Collins both. St. Mary's was near to capacity and you were beautiful in the flowing white bridal dress you'd chosen. Although you'd begun to show by then, the folds of the dress hid any hint of the pregnancy, and I heard fifty people if I heard one say that you were the most beautiful bride that town had ever seen. And I know it was true because I don't remember anything about the ceremony except that dress and staring into your beautiful brown eyes and knowing that I wanted to stay there forever. But I must've said something because Father Murphy suddenly pronounced us and the crowd jumped up clapping and we were off to the reception down at the American Legion post.

The hall was fairly packed to bursting with friends and family and acquaintances that came running at the words "open bar." We drank—well, I drank for both of us while you sipped your apple juice from a champagne glass—and we made the rounds and danced to "Unchained Melody" as the first real act of our union. And we were making our way back to the table when Joby, who was dressed to the nines as my best man, tapped me on the shoulder and let me know that your father wanted a word or two.

As I mentioned, he was thin by then, barely half of the man that I had met only five months before, and he was on oxygen, with those tubes snaking over his upper lip and behind his ears, where they disappeared under the suit jacket he had on. But the strength was in his brown eyes—your eyes—and they didn't waver as he took my face in his hands and brought me down to hear his whisper. And the room fell silent—or maybe that's just how I remember it.

"You're my son now," he said to me quietly, though his mouth worked in an exaggerated manner as if he were fairly shouting. "You're part of the family. And we all stick together …."

I nodded and put my hand on his shoulder and started to pull away, but there was strength yet in those hands that had worked the land for better than sixty years and he pulled me back in close.

"Some people call 'em stubborn," he said looking at Joby, and I couldn't tell whether he meant Joby individually or as a member of the family, "but that ain't it. We stick because we love, Lemuel. We love the land and we love each other."

He paused to take a breath and continued.

"Now you try to measure up."

"I will," I said, and I meant it, and I hugged his bones to me.

Two weeks later, your father passed. And was missed. And still is.

We buried him just as he wanted, beneath the first of the great maples in the sugar bush at the head of the north field, where he said he could keep a watch over the making of his precious syrup for every spring thereafter. It was Devon and I that dug the hole through the frozen earth with that little Bobcat that your father had bought for putting in fence posts. Father Murphy did the service at St. Mary's again and then half the town of Collins followed him out to that frozen field where we sat shivering and teeth chattering in the depths of February while we committed his body to the Lord and he was lowered in the ground.

It wasn't until we lay down to bed that evening that you finally broke down and wept on my shoulder for the loss of a great man, and I promised to do my best to be a piece of flint and look after you and the baby forever. I thought then that I was strong like him inside and out—I was wrong. But I haven't ever given up on trying to make things right between us, or at least as right as they can be, and I'm still not giving up, though time feels short about me now.

Given all that we'd been through, we didn't even consider a honeymoon, though I told you that we'd fly off to Paris once the baby came and we were settled. But other events soon got in the way of that promise as well. Later that month, I got the call from Coach Lidel over in Oneonta, telling me that the last lefty in the bullpen in Syracuse had just been called up to Spring Training with the Yankees down in Florida, which meant that there was a spot on the Chiefs' roster that needed to be filled. And even though I hadn't thrown a single pitch in a single game with the Oneonta Yankees, I was the only southpaw that fit the bill. And so, Coach Lidel told me, I should report to Coach Anderson of the Syracuse Chiefs the second week of March.

Now I was turning cartwheels that I had fallen ass-backwards into the Chiefs, but it had been nearly two years since I had thrown a pitch in a real game, and that was before the broken ribs and all the atrophy that followed. I know you'll remember that I told you more than once that I was nervous and afraid that I'd lost the edge. I also didn't like it one bit that I'd have to leave you alone and pregnant little more than a month after your old man had passed, but I promised to return whenever I had a day off, even if it was only enough time to make the drive west and kiss your beautiful lips before I had to turn around and head on back.

I kept that promise for a good long while. I wish I had kept it for the rest of my life and maybe, just maybe, you'd be lying here next to me where we could keep each other warm from the cold gale that's blowing along outside. But it isn't so, and I should stop wishing that it were.

FOURTH BEQUEST

I hereby bequeath all my baseball equipment, clothing, tro-phies, and memorabilia, including the old Hank Aaron card which should be worth a pretty penny by now, to my son, Daniel Conor Higgins. Take good care of them, Danny, or at least make sure that you get a fair price for them. I'm fairly certain that there is a card or two of George Brett buried in those boxes as well, so be on the lookout for those. Old George's stock is up again after he helped the Kansas City Royals take the World Series in seven games against the St. Louis Cardinals this year. I never did get to throw against him, though I dreamed about it from the time that I was twelve years old. That chance is lost to me now, but it wasn't so back then, when it looked like my star might go on rising forever.

It was the first week of March, when you were in your seventh month and getting round as a prize pumpkin, and I was a week from reporting to pre-season training at Syracuse when I first got the impression that something wasn't quite right with Devon. It's true that we all worried about him after his grandfather's passing, as he seemed to take it even harder than you and Joby. Woodchuck followed him about with a concern that sometimes came out as a whimper when the boy failed to pay him the attention that he was used to. And to us, Devon was dead silent for a couple of weeks, so that Joby and Celia even talked about taking him on to that psychologist over in Aurora. But before any decisions could be made, he seemed to bounce back, taking an interest in all that a thirteen-year old boy should take an interest in, which is to say, sports and girls. He brought two or three pretty young things around the farm over the course of that winter and more than once I walked in on him only half-dressed in some dark corner of the house or barn while he sputtered excuses and I just about rolled on the floor laughing.

As the spring rolled in, I tried to help Joby get as much done as we could before I had to head out to Syracuse. It was that week before I left that Devon and I were out plowing the west field across the road in preparation for planting the following week. The land was still sopping wet with the run-off of that winter and the rains that were coming through about every other day. We'd had to pull each other out of various ditches and sinkholes all the early part of that season, and we'd even had to use the winch on a couple of occasions. Anyhow, I was driving that old John Deere that your father had bought when you were just a baby, while Devon was in that blue New Holland with the heated cab that Joby had bought just off the assembly line only two years before. We'd been plowing opposite ends toward the middle when we found ourselves on a collision course at the north edge of the field along the ditch dividing your family's land from that of old Crazy Earl on the other side.

Well, that little devil gunned the engine as he came toward me, and I could see the smokestack sputter with the effort of the machine as he down-shifted to pick up speed. The plow went bouncing along behind him and I cursed him because I knew that we'd have to redo that row before we went on back to the farmhouse. Then

I saw him lean into the windscreen of the cab as he came bearing down on me and he spit a stream of tobacco out the open window. He'd taken up chewing tobacco in the weeks since his grandfather had passed and old Joby couldn't find it in himself to be a hypocrite and scold him for it. The sun was out for the first time in months, and Devon had on a cheap pair of dark glasses so as I couldn't see his eyes, but I felt them on me, giving me the challenge from behind those dark lenses. Well, I'd be damned if some little young punk was going to get my goat, so I gunned the engine of the old John Deere and headed on toward him determined to teach that little bastard a lesson in who had the balls around that farm.

As I downshifted and the big machines came closer together, I expected to see his face still pressed up against the glass of that cab, coming at me with all the determination of a young buck making a run at the leader of the herd. Instead, I saw him sit back and lean his head on the rest behind him. Then he stuck his left hand out the side of the window and made it do barrel rolls in the air current that was flowing past. He was large before me now, and I could see that he was staring up into the blue sky through the sunroof above, while managing to keep that tractor heading straight for me with barely two fingers on the wheel. I suddenly came to the realization that his tractor was somewhat bigger than mine and he was protected by the cab in the case of a rollover. But then I steeled myself again—I wasn't going to let some punk drive me off my game. I was headed to the pros goddamn it, and I'd be facing down big, nasty, aggressive animals at home plate day in and day out. And so I hunkered down, my knuckles turning white on the wheel and the throttle pushed all the way forward.

"Turn, you bastard," I breathed to myself. "Don't be stupid now. You turn now, you young punk."

But he continued to ride that mound of steel as if nothing in the world could have broken his serenity, and as I leaned over the steering wheel of that old John Deere, I swear that I could see the lips of that boy puckered like he was whistling. Truth be told, it had me a little spooked. My resolve began to crack, and I started thinking how fuming mad your brother Joby'd be if we wrecked one or both of his machines screwing around out there the first days of spring, not to mention the fact that we might get hurt. But still I held on.

We came to within five meters of each other when I finally saw him laugh and feint like he was turning to his left into the field. In fact, he didn't turn one inch, but kept on straight for me. I took the bait and did the natural thing and swung the wheel to my left and before I knew it, I was waist deep in the freezing water of that ditch, the old John Deere sputtering and sinking under my very bones. I jumped off it, soaked straight through to the middle, and while I was wading back to the high ground, I saw Devon unhook the plow and back the New Holland up on me, then he jumped down and called to me to see if I was alright. I waved at him, then gave him the finger, and he started unrolling that heavy chain from the back winch and working his way down toward me. Now we hooked it up and pulled the old tractor out of there in about fifteen minutes. That it would still turn over and catch was a surprise to both of us considering that it had been almost entirely underwater. Once we had got it checked out to our satisfaction, I turned to Devon and asked him just what in the goddamn hell he thought he was doing.

"Ain't found nobody can beat me yet, Lem," he said to me half with pride and half with a creeping sadness that gave me the shivers. "Not with a tractor or with no dirt bike neither. The boys say I got nerves of steel, but I'll tell you the secret. You want to hear it? Well, listen good. The secret to playing chicken ain't to steel your nerves, but to let it all go—to crank the music to its highest, feel the wind on your cheek, watch the earth slide by beneath your feet, and embrace the very last seconds of your life. Before you know it, it's over."

We never told old Joby about that day, and he never asked, though I'm sure he wondered how we managed to get cattails under the seat of that old John Deere. But the truth is that it wasn't at all unusual for one or the other of us to get stuck once in a while. And so we all let the thing pass without comment or discussion.

The following week passed like a blur before my eyes, though I do remember more than one bout of you crying on my shoulder. You were sad, and rightly so, but the hormones of the pregnancy were making their presence felt too and some of those sobs turned downright emphatic. I told you that I'd be back as often as the team would let me, and I said that I'd be right by your side when the baby came, but nothing seemed to help you to feel better in those days. And now I think maybe it was a premonition, like maybe you knew deep down that you, me, and Danny weren't supposed to put two hundred miles between us when our love was just a seedling struggling to reach the light.

Joby and Devon were so busy tapping the maples in the forest behind the barn that they barely said two non-syrup related words to me those last couple of days. The sap was already running thick and heavy, and old Joby still tells me that the sweetest syrup he ever produced came from that season when we were still young and in love and had everything before us. I helped them out when I had a free moment, but those weren't many as I wanted to spend every last second by your side before I had to leave.

You might remember it and you might not, but old Joby had a meeting with the bank managers the Thursday before I left. He came back from that meeting about as white as a sheet, which made him look even funnier considering that he was wearing a shirt and tie for about the fifth time in his life. But the worry on his face shut me up before I had any chance to make fun of him. I asked him how it had gone, but he just shook his head and bit his lip and headed up the stairs to change.

I chased him down atop the sugar shanty later on that afternoon, where he was replacing some shingles that had come off in the heavy snows of that winter. I asked him again what was wrong and he ignored me until I fairly shouted it at him a third time. He came down then and told me to hold my tongue, goddamn it, that old Horace Wiggin down at the Bank of East Angler had given him the full measure of the situation that morning, and that we were working borrowed land just like some Georgia sharecropper after the Civil War. I didn't understand what he meant until he explained it to me in plain terms.

It seems that the farm had been turning losses for a number of years and, while your old man owned the fields that he turned over in the years after you were born, the price of milk had hit rock bottom in the decade that followed and it never recovered. Joby had known that times were tight and that the price of milk was putting a squeeze on the profits of the farm for all those years. It wasn't like your father was hiding it from anybody. What he was hiding was that he had borrowed nearly every last cent against that land, including a hefty chunk just to pull off our wedding, and it was pretty near impossible for old Joby to make payment on the mortgage month after month. Your father had been two months behind when he passed as it was, and it took some clever maneuvering—and the sale of that old John Deere, the cattails still stuck underneath the seat— for old Joby to catch back up.

"Fat Horace told me flat out to sell the whole shebang to one of those suits from Cooperative Foods that's always calling," Joby said to me then. "And I told him just as flat out that he could stick that idea right back up his ass where it come from. There's five generations of this family that's grown up on this herd and plowed these fields, and I don't aim to be the last."

But I could tell that Joby was shaken. I watched him age ten years in two days, the lines growing deep across his forehead and the gray peeking out at his temples. I told him that I could stay on, that maybe it was best that I stay near you and the farm with the baby coming on and all—and I half-wanted him to ask me to do it, even though it would mean giving up my dreams. But you know old Joby—he told me that he'd personally kick my ass out of principle for being just plain stupid if I ever mentioned such a harebrained idea to him again. And I believe that he would have. He told me that Devon was just about a man now and that they'd get her done come what may, then he spat a stream of tobacco juice on the ground and the shadow seemed to pass.

Before we knew it, I was packing that old Impala with my necessaries for the trip to Syracuse. I said goodbye to Celia and Devon, then old Joby give me a clap on the shoulder and told me that they were my family now and to make them proud. I said I would. Of my father, not a word did we hear. I had seen him now and again while tooling around East Angler, but I think he got the message that I didn't want anything to do with him after I failed to invite him to our wedding. Later, I heard some of the boys say that he had been spending a good bit of time down at the bar of the East Angler Hotel and old Teddy Bailey had to toss him out just about every other night. But my life lay before me then, and I didn't have time to coddle an old man that was nursing regrets.

When I last hugged you to me and felt your swollen belly

against my own, I nearly started unpacking that old car. And then you kissed me with your sweet, soft lips and you held my head in your hands, standing on tiptoes to look into my eyes.

"Now you do well by me and by this baby of yours I'm carrying, Lem Higgins," you said to me. "You knock them dead on the field and when the game is done, you call me. And you come back here whenever you get the chance. Because here I'll be."

I nodded, the tears beginning to well up in my eyes. I moved forward to kiss you again, but you held my head steady and said those words that echo still in the caverns of my mind.

"We're your family now, Lem Higgins. And don't you forget it."

After some further kissing and waving goodbye, I was out on the open road, and I wouldn't stop for three hours until I turned off the New York State Thruway, just outside of Syracuse. The ground was still spotted with snow cover across the Finger Lakes, the wet warmth of spring not having made it up that far north quite yet. And it gave me nothing to look at, nothing to think about, but you. It hurt me something deep to leave you, Sarah. But I did it because I thought it was the best for me and for us. I don't think either of us could've seen what was coming, and for the moment at least, it seemed we both had faith in our love such that we were sure that it would see us through. But it's a fool's game to be young and in love, and the world is unforgiving, especially to the foolish.

FIFTH BEQUEST

It's a promise that was made so long ago that you may not even remember it, but it weighs on my heart as I sit here and relive the first days of our young love. I picture you, lying on your side on the wet grass in the starlight, telling me about all your dreams and expectations, and I can feel your warm breath on my cheek. Of course, it should've been me to take you—that was the promise, after all—but that doesn't seem likely or even possible after all that's passed and all that's about to pass. I've got no choice but to do the best I can with the time I've got left. And so, I hereby bequeath the two first-class tickets to Paris that set atop the dresser here to Sarah Danner Higgins. Now, it took some doing and they didn't come cheap, that's for sure, but they don't have to be used by any particular date, and you can decide who you want to take with you, though I hope you take little Danny. I gave Joby all the contact information for the agent at Air France—you just give them a call whenever you want to make the arrangements. And when you get there, and you're crossing over the Seine on your way to Saint-Chappelle, and you look down at the water that runs along beneath, I want you to remember that I loved you and that I said I was sorry for all that passed between us.

I showed up in Syracuse in the second week of March and reported to Coach Anderson straight away. I was excited and I was nervous and I knew that I had to keep myself busy if I didn't want to go crazy thinking about you and little unborn Danny. Coach set me up with the pitching staff on the day that I arrived and they set me to work to see what I could do. I was back completely from the fight with my old man, and I was still throwing heat at better than ninety miles per hour. The coaches mumbled together as I threw out the first few heaters and then they asked me to switch it up a bit. I threw a couple of change-ups and then worked up to my curve. They watched that ball arc across the plate like a slice of the moon and their eyes lit up like young boys coming down the banister on Christmas morning. And that was that. It wasn't but a week before they worked me into the rotation for our first series against the Toledo Mud Hens in early April.

There were seven of us that were a part of the rotation in those first days, although one or two were almost always on injured reserve, and I was the only lefty, which means that I was pretty much called up in every game, except when I pitched more than three innings at once and my arm needed a rest. I ended up bunking with our shortstop, a quick-footed Mexican named Bucky Lopez, and I'm pretty sure he got tired of hearing your name within the first two days that we were roommates. I could tell that he hadn't ever been in love himself, and I told him so, but he just muttered a string of words in Spanish that I couldn't understand anyway. I introduced him to the Jameson early in that first season, telling him that it was the preferred poison of my old man, and Bucky took to it so much that I told him that he must be the darkest Mick that ever came out of old Eire. He didn't know what that meant, but neither of us much cared about the details of our conversations, being generally content in our mellow when we were throwing it back.

Having been a reliever in our first series, the coaches scheduled me to start on the second game of our road trip against the Richmond Braves toward the end of April. I threw a two-hitter my first time out and we came away with a five to one victory. The coaches were duly impressed, and told me so. And back in the dressing room, Coach Anderson told me not to get too comfortable with the team or make any long-term plans in Syracuse, as the Yankees were hunting for lefties and I was coming along better than anybody had expected. My mouth hung open for about ten good seconds until Bucky walked up and closed it for me as he clapped me on the shoulder and said congratulations.

If ever there was an excuse for a celebration, I figured that was it, and so old Bucky and me headed out for a night on the town in Richmond. I was still getting used to the life of a professional ballplayer and all the temptations that accompany it. Each new city seemed like a metropolis to me, small though they generally were in the scheme of things, and full of people that dressed and spoke and lived different than what I was used to back in podunk East Angler. In short, a small part of the world seemed to open up before me. And like you, Sarah, I wanted to get out and meet and experience it all as we were passing through, though I recognize now that it was partly just the love of the vice that was drawing me on. But there wasn't anyone there to hold me back and so our road trips eventually became somewhat of a constant, rolling drunk, though I was always sober and ready to play by practice or game time.

Anyhow, we must have hit ten joints that night in Richmond after we left the stadium and headed down Broad Street toward Shockoe Slip. The two of us threw back an ungodly amount of whiskey and even some tequila at old Bucky's insistence, though

I remember him saying after that it wasn't the real stuff like they have in Mexico. And we nearly got ourselves killed by a pack of equally drunk rednecks who were mouthing off about how much they hated Mexicans and why didn't they all just go back where they came from. I hit the first bastard that had made his opinion so loudly known and tumbled with him to the floor. Bucky went at his friends, but the bartenders pulled us off them before we could do much damage and told us to get lost because they were calling the police. Well, we stumbled out of that place and on to the next bar and maybe one more—it's damn hard for me to remember anything about that night clearly—before we crawled into bed just as the sun was coming up over the James River.

The coaches were none too pleased with us at practice the following day and we both got a good talking-to by Coach Anderson, who told me on the side that I had a chance of making it and that I'd be a fool to throw it away by being a drunkard. I took it to heart and swore off the bottle, as I've done a hundred times since, and it was a good two weeks before Bucky and I were out drinking again. But I managed to keep myself more or less under control for the next several months and to put in some good performances besides. I got a call along about the beginning of May from Coach Rojas, the pitching coach for the Yankees. He told me straight off that the team had their eye on me and that if I kept up the improvement, I'd be moved up to the bigs before the season was over. I about fell over and peed myself with excitement at those words, but for once I remembered the words of Coach Anderson and I hit the gym for an extra session instead of running out to the bars.

Despite all the good news, I was missing you terribly, and I think that made the drinking worse, and I think Coach Anderson understood that when I told him about you. So, when I asked him if the team would put you up in a hotel room for our series at home against the Charleston Charlies, he agreed right off. With the hotel room taken care of, old Joby put up the money for Devon to come along with you, which we all thought was a good idea, given that you were eight months pregnant. It worked out for Devon as well as he was just starting with the junior varsity in Collins and wanted to learn everything there was to know about pitching. And so I started counting the days until I could wrap my arms around you and nuzzle your belly where little Danny was growing big.

I remember that week that we spent together as among the happiest in my young life. I was in love and headed to the majors, and I felt like nothing in this world could stop me from going right to the top. But I had my moments of clarity too, moments when I knew that it was all too good and that someone somewhere was just waiting to pull the rug out from under me with all my dreams piled high like some tottering, triple-dipped ice cream cone in the hands of an unsteady child. What Coach Anderson saw back then was that I was the one that already had that carpet by the frayed edge in my hands and I was just bracing my shoulders to give it a good yank. He tried to stop me from doing it to myself—I see that now—but he failed like so many more would over the ensuing years. Only your brother Joby ever managed to reach me and pull me up out of my destruction—this time for good—but I'm getting ahead of myself in the story again.

I took you and Devon to the ball field straight away and introduced you both around to my teammates who were just finishing up practice. Knowing me better than I knew myself, old Coach Anderson thought it'd be a good idea to give me some time with you, so he let me off that day and a couple more between games later that week. You were big and beautiful and radiant and I felt like the proudest man that ever walked the face of the earth showing you around to all the guys, most of whom were still single and had never been struck by the thunderbolt like me. And Devon was in his glory, staring open-mouthed at the pros that were scattered around the field. Many of them went on to play for the Yankees or other teams around the country and old Diego Barra even went on to become an All-Star second baseman two years later with the L.A. Dodgers. Devon was still talking about meeting him right up until the end.

After I showed you around, we went back to the apartment. I had old Bucky clear out and bunk with Manny Ortega, a Dominican that had just been called up from Oneonta and one hell of an outfielder, on account of I planned on spending every moment I had with you alone. We made love for the first time then in months, although it wasn't easy, given how big you had gotten. But I needed you then and you needed me just as much and we spent hours wrapped in each other's arms, me listening to the heartbeat just below the skin of your belly.

You inspired me and the rest of the team that week and we swept the Charlies in four games. I earned saves in two, which means that I came in and saved the game when the Charlies looked like they might come back, and I threw a one-hitter in my only start of that series, which we won six to nothing. And it was while we were packing the car to send you and Devon on your way back to Collins that I got the call from Coach Rojas who gave me the news that I was being moved up to the Yankees the following week.

And that was it—my dream was suddenly a reality.

We hugged and kissed, and I begged you to stay just one more night to celebrate it all with me, but Devon had to be back in class the very next day, and you couldn't drive back on your own even if we were to send him ahead by bus. And so the two of you headed out into the bright morning sun of that glorious day on which I had finally made it all the way from tiny East Angler to major league baseball. And I had to chase down old Bucky to join me in a right proper celebration of my achievement. He called up a handful of the guys from the team and we made a night of it. But even in my inebriated state, I realized that it all meant nothing if I didn't have you by my side to share in it. And for the first time ever, I wanted to go home more than I wanted to play baseball.

But I didn't go home. Instead, I reported to the Yankees the following week, the bright May sun shining down on that city of a thousand bitter failures to every one success, and I took the plane up to Boston with the team for a three-game series only two days later. There wasn't any doubt in my mind that I was on to a higher caliber of play, but I was still holding my own in practice and Coach Rojas told me that I was still just a young buck and that I should keep doing what I was doing and not worry about measuring up just yet. It was good advice, and I knew that even at the time, but there wasn't anything that could have held me back from giving it my all in those days. I knew there were thousands of pairs of eyes on me back home and I wanted to make them proud—one particular pair more than any of the others. And I'd be damned if I was going to head back there with my tail between my legs. That's all to say that I was throwing my goddamn heart out morning, afternoon, and evening, and my shoulder was sore by the time that I hit the field for the first time during that trip to Boston.

It was the bottom of the sixth inning of our second game against the Sox. We were down five to two with one out and there were two men on, which is to say that things looked bad and nobody expected that we would pull out a victory. I had thrown up in the bullpen when I got the call from Coach Rojas to take the field and my legs were as wobbly as cooked spaghetti, but I sprinted out there just the same and gritted my teeth and willed my body to produce the adrenaline that would fortify that shoulder and those legs for what I had trained all my life to do.

Coach Rojas stood over on the benches while I warmed up, and he gave me a wink as if to say that he knew that I could do it. When I was done getting my arm in the groove, Don Gables, one of the best catchers to ever play the game, gave me the signal for a fastball, high and tight, and so I tried to settle myself the best I could and put my foot against that pitcher's rubber and went into my wind up. I knew it was wrong as soon as it left my hand. It sailed up and to the right and the batter had to duck to get out of its way as it sped toward the back wall, hitting the matting with a dull thump. The batter looked at me with menace in his eyes because he thought I was going after him, there was a chorus of boos from the crowd, and I thought for a split-second that maybe I was in over my head. But I carried on. I didn't hit him, but I walked him on four straight pitches, which loaded the bases and caused old Don to come jogging out to the mound, shaking his head the whole time.

"Look, rookie," Don said to me, "I know you're shitting bricks out here, but get it together. You ain't gonna get but one chance to prove yourself here and if you fail and get sent back down, it's a long climb back up. So suck it up and start throwing right, you hear me?"

I nodded my head, and I guess I had heard him, because I started throwing heat like I had never thrown in all my life. I struck out the next batter on five pitches and got the following guy to send up a foul ball that Don chased down to the right of home plate. And the inning was over and my stomach wasn't full of butterflies anymore, and I was determined to give my teammates every chance to win the game. Don slapped me on the ass on the way to the bench, gave me a wink, and told me that was more like it. And right then I knew that I had the stuff.

My teammates knocked in two runs in the seventh, and I held the Sox to one hit in the bottom of that inning, a looping shot into near right field. But the following batter grounded out to end the inning anyway. We knocked in two more in the eighth on a series of grounders and an error by the Red Sox's second baseman, and we took the lead never to look back. Old Don Gables sent one into the right-field stands in the bottom of the ninth and I struck out three in a row to end the game.

We won the game seven to five, and I got my first win of the majors. The papers around East Angler went more than a little over the top with a front page story the following day.

LOCAL BOY MAKES GOOD:
LEM HIGGINS LEADS YANKEES OVER SOX, 7-5

Boston, Massachusetts. In the first Major League appearance of his budding professional career, East Angler's own Lem Higgins led the New York Yankees past the Boston Red Sox last night, 7–5, at Fenway Park. Warming up in the bullpen, Lem got the call from Yankees Coach Francisco Rojas in the bottom of the sixth inning, with the Yankees down 5–2. In a shaky first series, Lem walked Red Sox outfielder, Jason Sebring, on four straight pitches to load the bases. A brief conference with Yankees catcher, Don Gables, ensued and Lem was back to the form that East Angler knows so well. He struck out Red Sox All-Star Jorge Arriaga on five pitches and caused the following batter to fly out to the infield.

Over the next three innings, Lem held the Red Sox to two hits, while the Yankees climbed back into the game, finally taking the lead in the eighth inning 6–5. Yankees catcher, Don Gables, added an insurance run in the top of the ninth, and the Yankees won 7–5 with Lem striking out the last three batters to end the game.

In the locker room, Coach Rojas was quoted as saying, "Lem played well tonight. I'll admit that the first pitch had my heart in my throat, but once he settled himself down a bit, he started throwing like we knew he could. He's one hell of a southpaw, and he has a long future in this league." With the season headed toward the mid-point, the Yankees are bunched in the middle of the pack in the American League pennant race. But with the addition of Lem Higgins, the future looks very bright indeed.

East Angler Town Supervisor Daryl Kozinski has declared next Friday, June 2, the first day of the East Angler Wild-flower Festival, to be Lem Higgins Day in celebration of the ongoing achievements of our native son.

And so it was. Two lefties came off of injured reserve for the Yankees the next week, and the short season was already over for Syracuse. Coach Rojas knew that you were expecting, and he thought that it might be a while before I made it back into the rotation, so he sent me home with instructions to stay in shape in case the Yankees needed to pull me up later in the season. With a single win under my belt, I went back to East Angler and to you.

Having been on the road for almost ten weeks, I was never so glad to be back in that little podunk town in my whole life. You were already overdue and we knew the time was short and I wasn't going to miss it for the world. Meanwhile, the whole town turned out to greet me that first Friday of the Wildflower Festival. The kids were following me around the amusement park rides and games during the day, a dozen or more already with Yankees jerseys with my number 88 and "Higgins" stitched across the back shoulders. And the adults packed the barroom of the East Angler Hotel that night, everyone wanting to know how it felt to throw against the big boys. I must have repeated the story at least a hundred times. It was a hell of a high, and my face was beet red from embarrassment from the time that I stepped down from the car to the time that I threw back that first tumbler of Jameson.

You were understandably tired after the day of walking around the parade grounds, and old Joby did me the favor of taking you back home so I could bask in my glory a little bit longer. You kissed me sweet and told me to be good. And I tried to stay away from the whiskey, I tell you, but it was damn near impossible what with every swinging jack wanting to buy me a drink up there and old Teddy the bartender telling me I could have anything I wanted on the house. By the time that midnight rolled around, I was two sheets to the wind and singing "Take Me Out to the Ballgame" at the top of my lungs along with the entire male population of my hometown.

I was feeling pretty good, when I caught sight of my old man sitting behind the old pool table and watching the goings on at the bar. Now, my eyes were just about crossed at that point, but I swear that I saw a smile on that man's face, like he was enjoying the festivities that hung around me as much as I was. The flames of anger shot up in me as they sometimes do when I'm on the whiskey and that voice in my head shouted that the old son of a bitch didn't have any right to enjoy my success after what he'd done, and I jumped off the barstool to go chase him down and give him a piece of my mind. But just as quickly as my rage had risen, my heart softened as I made my way through the crowd, a chorus of hands slapping me on the back as I passed, and by the time I got over to the pool table, I had nothing in my mind but to give my old man a giant hug, pour my heart out to him, and make amends. When I got there, though, he was gone. I just caught sight of him walking out the door and into the warm summer night. I ran over there to catch him before he disappeared down the street, I flung open the door, and I shouted his name into the soft light of the street lamps. But he was nowhere in sight, and I began to wonder if I had imagined the whole thing.

Your cousin Owen found me outside, sitting on the concrete steps of the hotel and looking off into the night.

"You doin' alright, Lem?" he asked, coming to sit at my side.

"Goddamn perfect, I should say. I got everything I ever wanted. But I thought—" I stopped as the whiskey-driven tears welled up in my eyes and my throat got tight.

"You thought … " he urged.

"I just thought that I seen my old man wandering around out here, and I thought I'd say hello. I miss the old bastard, in spite of all the fighting that we've done. Never mind, Owen … I'm just drunk … don't pay no attention to me."

"I ain't seen him, Lem," I remember Owen said to me, "but they say he spends a good bit of time here at the hotel as of late, drinking his sorrows away and wandering home when they throw him out. I hear tell that old Donut at the Red & White found him propped in the doorway at six o'clock in the morning not too long ago, muttering to himself about how he was the best that ever played the game."

I nodded my head in recognition, as Owen wasn't the first to tell me how my old man was spending his days lately, but my throat had tightened again and I couldn't speak.

"Now I know that you're just back in town and on top of the world and all that, but you best watch yourself so you don't end up the same," Owen said with genuine concern. "Now what do you say we get you home before you go and do something stupid?"

I agreed, and we climbed into Owen's old pickup and he drove me back to the farm. I stopped in to kiss you goodnight, but decided to spend the night in the guest room next to Devon when I found you dead asleep on your side and cradling your big belly in both arms. At five-thirty the next morning, Devon came in and shook me awake and we went down to milk the heifers like always and it was like the whole thing hadn't really happened—like I had just stayed here on the farm with you for the summer and dreamed of pitching in the majors. Only the pounding of my head and the sorrow in my belly let me know that it hadn't been a dream at all.

SIXTH BEQUEST

I hereby bequeath all my personal effects to Father Murphy over at St. Mary's. There isn't much, and most of it still sits in my father's house and needs a good going through and cleaning up, but I send it along just the same. I'd ask Father Murphy to put it to the best use that he can, though I know I don't have to. I haven't been to a Mass that wasn't a wedding or funeral since I had it out with the old man, and I guess my relationship with God has been strained right along with my relationships with all of his children here on earth, and that too is my fault. I hope this gesture is the first in a series of steps back toward him, for like it or not, I'm headed toward his house in short order.

I had old Joby start me on the morphine this morning. He didn't say a word, but just asked me whether I wanted a beer, a whiskey, or an Irish Car Bomb. I told him that he was a smartass and there wasn't any call for disparaging my Irish heritage by allusions to terrorism. But he just laughed and eventually I laughed along with him—though it caused me to launch into another coughing fit that nearly did me in right there—and told him that I'd start with a beer, thank you very much. I couldn't stand the pain, but I didn't want to be unconscious for the start of the World Series tomorrow night either. Well, he gave it to me just like Doc Tyler had instructed and the pain that was spreading from my back over into my chest and down to my hips seemed to wind up and disappear. I lay stupefied for a bit, but I eventually came to and asked for the paper again so I could continue our story here. I know that there'll come a time when the morphine will overcome any ability I have to write, and so I want to hurry to get it all down without having to leave nothing out.

I knew that old Joby'd go along and call Doc Tyler as soon as he left the room and he did. Doc showed up not more than an hour later and asked me how was I doing. I told him honestly that I could feel it getting worse but that I still had a bit of kick left in me.

"Lem, son, as your doctor and your friend, I have to tell you that you need more treatment more often from here on out. I truly believe that you would be more comfortable in the hospital."

I had no doubt that Doc meant well, but I had already made up my mind about it. I'm going to spend the rest of my time here in this room and in this house and on this farm where I've spent the best goddamn days of my life. And when that time's past, then so be it. I have amends to make here on earth and in heaven too, and I'm not going to let the last image that runs through my conscious brain be that of some sterile, white hospital room while strangers run about pulling at the tubes that sustain me. But I didn't say all that to old Doc—I didn't have the strength.

"I ain't going back," was all I could muster.

Doc nodded, but he didn't bother to hide his concern and disappointment. He told me quietly then not to be afraid to ask for the morphine when the pain kicked up. And then I asked him about the birth of little Danny. He must have spoke for a good hour or more, telling me that he was just about the happiest little boy that Doc'd ever had the pleasure to first hold in his hands. He said it wasn't the easiest birthing that he could remember, but that he never saw a woman take the birth of her first child with more calm, though you were only eighteen.

Well that just about set me to bawling right there, knowing that you were forced to be the strong one after all those promises that I'd made. The truth is that I was gone more often than I would have liked and I left you with the responsibility of raising our family. And as I see it now, that was another big step down in our relationship. There were many, and for each one I want to go on back and shake myself by the shoulders to force a different outcome.

It was the second day of the Wildflower Festival, and you told me that you had slept well the previous night, although you were feeling heavy, and we talked about whether it was a good idea to just stay home. But you wouldn't hear of it, knowing that the town was counting on me to ride in Horace Wiggin's Corvette at the head of the parade. And so, we packed up the old Impala and headed on into town long about noon. Truth be told, I felt just plain stupid waving at all those people for an hour as the parade wound its way through the center of town, past the hotel, and back to the parking lot of the elementary school. I wondered whether my old man was in that crowd. Try as I might, I just couldn't get the image of him from the previous night out of my head. But I didn't see hide nor hair of him that whole parade route.

I waved extra hard at you and Joby and Celia and Devon when we made our way past the drug store, and I could hear you all whooping and hollering my name as we went past. You looked huge, and that isn't a slight, because you were more beautiful in your bigness than I think I had ever seen you before. The sun shone down through your long dark hair, and I could see plainly what every-one calls that glow of pregnancy as your skin was the color of ivory but infused with a light that came up from within. And I wanted to jump right down out of that car and take you in my arms and scream to everyone about that I was the luckiest son of a bitch in all the world. And I guess I should've done so while I had the chance, but I couldn't know that I'd throw it all away right then.

Anyhow, Devon ran right out into the street to jog on beside the car with me for a piece, and he handed me a bottle of water, which I was truly grateful for, being dry as a bone from my libations the night before. And we continued on. My wrist was damn tired by the end of it. But I did my duty, I guess you could say, and I found you and Joby and Celia and Devon still standing on the steps just outside of the drug store. I could tell that you had had just about enough for one day, and so I turned down the multiple invitations to head down to the hotel that seemed to come from all sides and above and below too, and we set off through the crowd toward the car in the lot next to the liquor store. We were headed back to Collins, where life seemed always constant, and I knew that there were gutters to be cleaned and heifers to be milked and a hay wagon that needed mending that afternoon, while you and Celia set about the preparations for dinner.

I was adjusting the seat in that old car, which seemed to stick more with every passing day. I wanted you to be as comfortable as possible for the long drive back, as I could tell from your face that you were hurting. I was struggling with the under seat lever when you yelled out to me.

"Lem ... oh my God, Lem ... my water broke."

And we all jumped into action. I yelled over to Joby that it was time, and then I forced that seat back with all my might. I helped you into the car and gently closed the door and we were off to the hospital. Old Joby being what he is, he didn't let a single car get between us the entire drive to Mercy Hospital, and that's saying something, being that the drive is at least an hour, though I think we did it in less. The traffic was light, and it seemed that the Lord had cleared the way for us, and we pulled up into the emergency drive, where I helped you out and we hurried up to the nurses' station.

Old Joby was already there, telling them to get a room ready for you and to call Doc Tyler because little Danny was coming then and there. I handed the keys off to Devon to find a parking space and helped you into the wheelchair that the orderlies brought out. It wasn't like it is today, where everybody and their brother gets to sit in the birthing room. Back then, you'll remember, they didn't let nobody in. It was just as well. Joby and I didn't consider ourselves particularly clean after all the slop we worked through day in and day out. And so, they took you off through the swinging doors and the nurse led me and Joby and Celia into the waiting room, where Devon joined us not two minutes later. I was pacing the floor and wearing a hole in the carpet waiting for Doc Tyler, but he made it in after about forty minutes and told us that you were fine and that we should buckle in for a long night, this being your first birth and all.

"Doc," I said, taking his hand and looking him full on in the eyes with my best and most insistent stare, "this is my wife and child we're talking about here."

He gave me a pat and chuckled a bit and told me not to get worried over nothing, that giving birth was the most natural thing in the world, that he hadn't lost a mother or baby yet, and that he didn't plan to start with anyone as beautiful as you.

"Please, Doc," I said, thinking back to my own mother and dead baby sister.

But he kept on chuckling as he walked through the swinging doors, muttering something about how he had never seen anyone so big and strong afraid of something so perfectly natural. I swallowed hard and sat down and stood up and sat down again. Eventually, I took to pacing the floor again in front of Joby and Celia, who were glued to the game shows on the black and white that was setting on an end table in the corner of the room. I didn't know how they could be so goddamn calm about it. Celia tried her best to talk me down and let me know what was going on in that room down the hall, but it didn't do any good. All that talk of needles and blood just made me think about the fragility of life and I got to worrying all over again. The time seemed to slide by in slow motion, like pouring cold syrup out of a jar that's been setting in the refrigerator all night long. And every so often, I'd hear a groan from down the hall, and I'd bounce up to the round little window in the swinging doors to try to gauge if you were alright until Joby or Celia would get up and guide me back to the seat with soothing words.

At last, I wore myself out and I must have dozed off, because I woke to Doc Tyler shaking me awake, still chuckling as he had when he come in, though you could tell that the long night of work had taken something out of him. He led me back to the birthing room and there I found you, a true-to-life Madonna with our little Danny cradled there in your thin arms. Well, I lost it right there and then, my knees went weak with worry for you and the baby and I collapsed to the floor.

Old Joby still gives me shit about it, saying that you were the one getting poked and giving birth and bleeding all over and I was the one that ended up on the floor. And I guess he's right. But I was overcome. When I came to, Doc Tyler gave me an orange juice and made me sit in a chair in the corner for a good half an hour before he'd let me take hold of little Danny.

And when I finally held him in my arms, he wasn't any bigger than a catcher's mitt, and he kind of looked like one too, all purple and wrinkly as he was. I tried my best to steady those big, clumsy man hands that I thought would crush or fumble something so tiny and fragile. But I didn't. And he squirmed in my arms and gave little snorting noises just like he was a tiny newborn calf. I saw his eyes squinted almost shut and trying to make sense out of the explosion of light and color that was all about him then. And that was it. I worked my way back over to you to tell you how much I loved you and how I was always going to take care of you and our little High King of Tara. You told me that you knew that I would and we both melted into the sight of our little boy there cradled in my arms between us.

And so began the quiet days of our life together, the days infused by the light that only a new life can bring into the relations between a man and a woman. We were both tired for months on end, staying up late, getting up in the middle, and rising early to pick up little Danny and cradle him and sing to him softly and give him to suckle or just to calm him and put him back down. Celia and Joby and Devon helped us out on occasion, though they knew enough to leave the hard work of parenting to the parents and they didn't get in the way at all. And though they were days of sleeplessness and irritability for us, they were also days of wonder and happiness and we knew that we had accomplished something that had long been planned for us both and that made us feel whole and complete.

About four months later, just as the steady winds of Danny's first winter were tapping the branches of the oak on the glass of the window, we had pretty much gotten the hang of parenting and settled into our own version of family life. And just about the same time, Danny seemed to get the hang of being a child too, as he left off crying and carrying on and waking us in the middle of the night. He became a child of calm and quiet observation and that too made us as happy as could be. I started to work him into my daily routine where I could, taking him out to the milking floor when the weather was mild. He'd lie awake and stare wide-eyed at the broad backs of the two hundred heifers that were all lined up in a row. And he'd giggle and turn away whenever old Joby or Devon would upturn a teat in our direction and let fly a long string of milk that petered out on the floor before us.

And you gradually came back to your own life too, putting pen to paper in a serious way for the very first time, though it seemed you'd been talking about it forever. I could feel the words within you and I never had any doubt from the beginning that they were going to make you famous. That they would make me infamous wasn't within my comprehension at that time. But you used those late-autumn afternoons that father and son spent ranging about the fields or in the recesses of the barn to set your life on the course that it had always meant to take, and I'm damn proud of you for it. It would be another six months and hundreds of rejection letters before you were first accepted for publication, but I never had any doubt. And when that first story came out, and I saw the spark in your eyes, I knew that you were in for a life of it.

And stupid me, I thought that I was just the man to support you in it—that we'd be the professional ballplayer and the professional writer, living a privileged life over and above the concerns of the everyday because things were going just that right for us that they didn't seem like they could go wrong. And I know what you writers call that too—hubris—the fatal flaw that brings down the protagonist who runs about blind in his confidence and his pride, sure to his soul that he's above the petty problems of this world. But I didn't know that then and, besides, I was focused on you and little Danny. And for a time, there weren't any problems, and these were the happiest days of our lives together.

And now I've gone and got myself all upset again. I was a different man back then, Sarah, closer to the man that I am right now, but somehow I got lost in the middle. Like something took over my body for those years in between like in that alien movie. Or maybe that's just me ducking the blame. Anyhow, I've been writing for quite a long time. It's three o'clock in the morning here, and I know that I'll be hearing Joby and Celia making their way downstairs in a couple of hours. They've had burdens aplenty of their own to carry, and I'm ashamed to say that it makes me glad to know that you and Danny are safe down there in Virginia. For I still love you both.

SEVENTH BEQUEST

I hereby bequeath my father's house to you, Sarah. I know you haven't been there more than a handful of times, but it's a sturdy structure and should be used for something other than the home for raccoons and red squirrels that I found after the old man had passed. I haven't got any advice as to what you should do with it. It's more like a hunter's lodge than a home at this point, but there is a good bit of land behind it—almost six acres, with that little old stream running down to the beaver dam beyond. It's a beautiful place if you forget all the fighting that we did on it and over it all these years. Anyhow, I got the silly idea that you might tear it down and convert the land into a writers' colony, but I'm not going to press it on you. If you want to put it on the market and use the money for something else, you go right ahead and do so. Given all that's happened there, maybe it's better to just get rid of the thing and move on.

Well, after I'd left that house for good, and before I returned to inhabit it again, two years passed like the blink of an eye. I spent most of my time in Syracuse and on the road, and each time I came on back it was like getting to know you all over again. That isn't easy for any relationship, much less one that was as young and fragile as was ours. I can tell you that it wasn't the ideal situation for me either. I missed you and little Danny, and when I got down, I got to drinking again, which caused me to fall behind in my training. I'd end up hung over and hating myself for sabotaging the very thing that we were sacrificing our time together for. I know you think it wasn't enough, but I promise that I brought you and Danny over to Syracuse to watch me play every chance I could get. And I held on to those moments like they were my very last days on God's green earth. I remember them in every sunshine-filled detail, so much so that I sometimes think that I continue to live then and not now.

In spite of the lapses in judgment, Coach Anderson still had high hopes for me, and the pitching staff of the Chiefs was pretty near dedicated wholly to me over those next two seasons. I jumped up to the Yankees every so often when they needed an additional lefty on the roster, and I got to pitch two more games over that stretch, winning one and losing the other by a single run. And even though I was settled in good in the minors, the organization recognized that I was a valuable commodity, so they held on to me for the moment and paid me a nice salary besides.

In the off-season, I did a few local appearances around Syracuse, but I tried to keep them to a minimum. I stayed about on the farm as much as I could, going through the routine of years that had developed with Joby and Devon. I knew Joby preferred to have me there full time, given that the price of milk had fallen yet further and he couldn't afford to hire out any more help. It was obvious by then that he was being squeezed tighter with each passing season. We all noticed that the herd was getting thin and by the end of that second year, we were down fifty head.

We weren't the only family that was set upon by hard times. There were more than a handful that lost their farms to foreclosure, and it was a right sad day for all of us when the news came that old Tommy Reese had put a shotgun in his mouth and pulled the trigger when Sheriff Haney had come to do his duty and clear Tommy off the farm that had been in his family for five generations. It became known that Cooperative Foods was buying up the mortgages to every family farm about and putting the squeeze on those that wouldn't sell on the cheap. And I imagined that they were especially interested in your family's farm, given that you Danners always did own some of the best land about those parts. But you know your brother, he'd never say a word to bother nobody, even if they were choking the life out of him, so I never knew just how serious matters had become until later.

You and I were doing alright financially in spite of the time we spent apart, and it was into that second year that we decided that the farm just wasn't big enough for both families anymore. Joby and Celia and Devon were a full house anyway, and they all treated you like you were their little girl, even though you were then a mother yourself. And it was damn uncomfortable sleeping in your double bed night in and night out, and there wasn't any extra room to put the baby in, so it was either convince Joby to let us add on to the old farmhouse or go on out and buy a house of our own. Joby was focused on keeping the farm up and running, and your preference was clear, and so that's the way it was.

Little Danny had grown big over that stretch, and it seemed to my eyes that he'd gained six inches and twenty pounds every time I came on back through the door to kiss you both after my time out on the road. And I'm never going to forget the feeling of joy and anguish at walking through the front door to hear him yell out "Daddy!" and realizing that he'd been talking a blue streak for a month while I'd been finishing up the season in Syracuse. Once he found his voice, there wasn't any way to stop him from asking a million questions about anything and everything there is in this world. At a year and a half, he declared himself a big boy and wouldn't stand for a car seat on the road nor a booster seat at the table and we didn't press him, though we knew that there was a certain risk to it. He came with me nearly every morning to meet Joby and Devon for the milking of the heifers, and I could see him gradually becoming the little farm boy that he was by the time everything went south on us. That's not to say that he lent us much of a hand quite yet—he was still too tiny to do any of the hard work about the farm—but the will was there and we knew that he'd be a right good little helper when the time came.

Anyhow, we started looking for houses closer to town and about five minutes from the farm. Danny was a handful in those days, talking a mean streak and running from one place to another so fast that we had to tend to a hundred tears and dozens of scraped knees every week, so we didn't waste any time, seeing all ten houses for sale in Collins in two weekends. We finally bought that little white house on Marie Road off of Main from the old Polish couple that was so nice and so excited to be moving down to Florida with the purchase money. We moved in right away. And for a bit longer, our life was just about perfect. Then the walls came tumbling down on me, and what was left standing I pulled down on myself and on you and little Danny.

I hadn't seen much of my father for those couple of years and though my anger at him had cooled, I was focused on my own home and family and had no time for the drama I knew it would be to reach out to him as a good son probably would have. But he knew that he had a new grandson that he hadn't even met, and he knew where to find me too if he wanted to patch things up. But he was a stubborn old goat, and I wasn't about to give in to him after all that had happened, and that's just how it was. I generally avoided him while I was at the farm or running about in Collins, but East Angler isn't really a town that it's possible to hide from somebody in, and I'd catch a glimpse of him every so often coming out of the drugstore or hanging out in the bar of the hotel. He even caught my eye late one Saturday evening as he sat at the hotel bar with a tumbler of the Jameson while some of my old teammates invited me to the same along with a quick game of pool. I was more than a little surprised to find him there looking down on me, and I turned away. When I looked back, he was gone and old Teddy was wiping up the ring that his glass had left on the oak of the bar. And that was the last I seen or heard of him until Joby came down to the barn at four-thirty on a cold February morning to tell me that he'd just got off the phone with Teddy over at the hotel in East Angler.

Turns out Teddy had become my father's only friend and family in those years, and my old man spent more time on that hotel barstool than he did in his own home. It shouldn't have surprised me any, as I've seen the same demons in my own soul, but I didn't recognize them then. I was blind and so self-centered that I thought just maybe the old bastard had done it to spite me. Anyhow, you know what happened. Joby told me that Teddy had found him frozen stiff as a board, leaning against the doorjamb of the hotel where he had passed out the night before after Teddy had thrown him out for the third time that week. I've got to believe that he was just waiting for the morning sun to rise so that he could take up his seat once again. They say that Jameson, like vodka, doesn't freeze, but it dipped below zero that night and a vicious wind had kicked up like the last gasp of winter itself. And I can still see the steam pouring out of Joby's mouth as he told me that my father was dead.

I didn't cry then and I haven't cried since over that stubborn old man who did himself in with no help from me or anyone else. We buried him next to my mother and little Colleen in the cemetery up on Vermont Hill Road, which was frozen solid as his own heart in that late February snowstorm that covered the ground about us and made us feel we were at the very edge of life itself. There wasn't anybody in attendance except your family and old Teddy, who felt responsible for what had happened, being that he was the last one to see the old man alive and threw him out into the cold of night. I told him not to worry, that the old man would have hung himself or smashed his car or fallen off his roof or some other nonsense, but that he surely would have killed himself one fine day, old Teddy or no. The drink just made it easier. And believing that to be the case, I pulled a flask of Jameson from my jacket pocket, splashed a bit on the ground where it left a honey-colored hole in the snow beneath, and took a good long pull down on it in memory of my father, the sorry old bastard who lay dead beneath my feet.

Time moved on and I thought I had it beat, but the thing crept up on me. One day, we were pulling hay down for the heifers from the last recesses of the old barn about a month after the funeral, when I first came to the realization that I'd never get the chance to make it up with him. The finality of it left an empty space in my gut, and I got just as scared as I had when, at five years old, I spent half a day lost in the forest behind our house. I had chased a rabbit out of the hedges in the front yard and followed him into the brush while my father dozed through the later innings of a Jays game that was broadcast on the radio that sat on the floor of the porch just outside our front door. The chase only lasted a few minutes, but it was enough so that, when I looked up, I was out of sight of the house and each tree looked like every other. Desperate and frightened and eventually exhausted, I wandered in circles for hours until I finally collapsed and cried tears of loneliness and abandonment as only a child can know. And that's how he found me two hours after sundown, wailing at my misfortune and full of the knowledge that I was going to die out there in the wild that night. Back in the barn, I came to the double realization that not only was he gone, but that I was on my own and near to getting lost and no one was coming to find me this time.

Devon hit me square in the chest with a heavy bail as I stood stock still and contemplated all those lost chances and my new solitude. I fell backward on the dry planks of the barn ceiling, shaking my head to try to get back to where I had been fine with his passing. But I didn't ever get back there, not then and not now.

I know that you did all you could to help me through those times. And it's not exactly as if I was crying out for help. There were times that, with your arms about me and little Danny cuddled into the bed next to us, I could see through the loss and the pain. I knew that I had some blame in all that had happened, but with you and Danny there, I knew that whatever bad I had done was made up for by the good that we had created between us.

But his passing had shaken me inside. I was drinking too much, following straight along in his footsteps, and I just couldn't bring myself to do the training that the coaches had assigned to me over the offseason. By the time that I reported to Tampa for Spring Training in March of 1981, I was twenty pounds overweight and I'd lost five miles per hour on my heater. Coach Rojas was understanding, but he was a practical man with a job to do. And so he took me out of the rotation until I was back to form and ready to throw again in the bigs. Coach Anderson gave me a call and told me that he understood that I was having some trouble and to take my time in reporting back to Syracuse. I knew that he meant well, but time on my own was the last thing that I needed. I was in the worst shape of my life when I finally did make it back to the Chiefs three weeks later.

And that's where it started to go really bad. Though he'd talked about my situation with Coach Rojas, Coach Anderson was clearly surprised at my sorry state and put me on the disabled list with my injury listed as "unspecified" until I could pull myself together. But I didn't do so even then. Travelling with the Chiefs for weeks on end and missing your soft touches and the smile of my little boy and thinking about all those years that I might have made it up with my old man, coupled with no prospect of playing for the Chiefs for the immediate future, and I continued to look to the bottle for solace. My teammates were understanding at first, and mostly accompanied me on my nights out, especially after a hard-fought victory on their part. And when I'd drink too much and start spouting off about what a bastard my old man was and end up throwing up all over myself, well they'd mostly clean me up and take me back to the hotel and put me to bed. It was a long stretch, and there were a number of fights, some of which I picked with the members of my own team. And over the course of that season, I was kicked out of bars in Pawtucket, Charleston, Rochester, Columbus, Toledo, and several more that I don't even remember now.

But there came a point that the team's patience was worn thin. The coaches saw that I was becoming more of a liability than anything else, and they told me to shape up or I was out. And even my teammates started to distance themselves from me. Timmy Holloway, a veteran of twelve years, told me straight up that I was a danger to everyone around me, and that I was going to throw away a perfectly good career if I didn't straighten up. And the messed up thing is that I knew that he was right. It was like I was watching myself run a red light in slow motion. I knew that the crash was coming, but there didn't seem to be anything that I could do about it.

After a disastrous five-month stretch, the organization finally sent me down to the Fort Lauderdale Yankees in Class A, which is barely professional baseball at all. Before I left, Coach Anderson told me that it was the last chance I was going to get from the organization, which had had such high hopes for me three years prior but was now looking at me as a considerable liability to any team at any level. He was still a good old boy, and I know that he meant well. I got the feeling that he was watching the same crash that I was watching, but he didn't realize that I had no control over it. He set me up with a shrink in Miami to talk about what had happened with my old man. He also told me that I should spend the off season quiet with you and Danny and get my head back on straight and I could come back to talk to him the beginning of the following season.

By the time I reported to Fort Lauderdale that August, the season was basically at an end, though management had scheduled a two-week swing through the Midwest League for some inter-league play that didn't mean anything to the standings. I went along, still hoping that I might be able to salvage something good out of that season, though I should have recognized that I was in no shape to do so.

We had just lost a game against the Quad Cities Cubs away out in Davenport, Iowa, and the team was pissed with me. I had lost four straight heading into that game. And I threw a deplorable four innings, giving up a full dozen hits and nine runs, and I committed two unforced errors before they hauled me off the mound and sat me on the bench where I belonged. It was humiliating. There I was, throwing against teenagers and old men that had no business calling themselves professionals and they were consistently taking me over the fence. And with the extra twenty-five pounds of fermented barley hanging off my belly, I could barely move myself off the mound to pick up a rolling grounder. I hated being on the bad side of my teammates, but I was more worried about the coaches scheming a way to get rid of me before next season. And so I spent the balance of that game huddled into one corner of the dugout, licking my wounds and waiting to head out on the town to forget my troubles.

I skipped the showers and changed into my street clothes and headed out into the night before any of the coaches could pull me aside to tell me how downright awful my performance had been. I found a bar right along the river, with a nice view of the barges and gambling boats that make their way up and down the Mississippi. I started with a double of Jameson and a beer, and I tipped back three more doubles before I ordered a second beer, with the bartender leering at me the whole time. As the night wore on, the place began to fill to bursting, with men coming in from the barges and crowding about the old mahogany bar, sometimes pushing right up against me from behind. It wasn't any different than any other night in any other bar. Lord knows that I frequented enough crowded bars to know that being pushed and jostled is just a part of the deal and to be accepted with either stoicism or geniality. But I was in a constant funk in those days, and I couldn't see any way out. More importantly, I couldn't see that it was my daily habits that were creating that funk, even though it was right in front of my eyes.

The crowd was getting louder as it grew and the dusk turned to night. It was a Friday, and it seemed that some of the bargemen had been out for a week or more on the river and had just come on back to town. The group right behind me was laughing up a storm and pushing each other around. When one of them dropped his beer, it hit the floor and spattered along my leg. I turned around, but before

I could object, they were calling the bartender over and asking him to set me up with another of whatever I was drinking. I stared them down for a few seconds, then nodded my head in thanks all serious-like and turned back to contemplate my damnation in the gnarled wood beneath my glass.

It wasn't five minutes later that the same sloppy drunk stumbled against me and caused me to spill my new drink half over the bar and half into my lap. And that was it. I turned to that boy over my right shoulder, dragging my left hand from way down near my hip and clocked him in the jaw and heard the bone shatter beneath. He went down like a pile of rags, but it wasn't two seconds before three of his boys had jumped on top of me and were pummeling me something fierce in the gut and the shoulders and the face.

I managed to break free and stand up and the crowd formed a circle despite the protestations of the bartender, who was rapping his billy club against the bar and telling us he was calling the cops. Well, you don't get to play ball for two decades without knowing how to throw down when the time comes, so I took up my stance and took on the first two as they came at me. I ducked a slow roundhouse from the first and punched him in the belly and he went down like a sack of potatoes, gasping for breath on the beer-covered floor. The second latched on to me from behind and had me in a sort of a headlock until I sent an elbow into his ribs and spun him around and kicked out his knee, which buckled beneath him like a match-stick. His scream was louder than any other noise in that small bar-room, and a crowd gathered about him as he clutched at his leg and yelled for an ambulance.

I bent down too to see how much damage I had done—I never wanted to maim nobody, just to teach those boys a lesson—and as I did, the third came at me from behind, screaming at me that I was a son of a bitch. I turned just in time to see the chair that he was holding above his head and I put up my arm to fend off the blow. I took it full on the arm, and I heard the splintering of the wood at the same time that I felt the shattering of my own bone beneath it. The splinters rained down about me and I opened my eyes to see my forearm hanging at a right angle where no joint had ever been placed on a human being before. Then the pain hit me and I was out.

I have no idea how long those boys continued to pummel me while I was unconscious on the floor, but the police report says it was a good bit. In addition to the shattered forearm, I came away with three broken ribs and a fractured pelvis. When I woke, I was staring at the white ceiling of the Davenport Medical Center and half of my body was set in a plaster cast, so that I couldn't hardly move to scratch my nose. The doc came in and told me that the police were coming around to see me that afternoon to get a statement and see about who wanted to press charges. Then he asked me if there was anyone that they should notify that I was there and would be for some time yet. I was pretty drugged at that time, but I must have told him to contact Coach Anderson from Syracuse, because there were three messages from him the next time I woke up. Then the doc asked me what I did for a living, and I told him that I was a ballplayer.

"I sure hope you ain't a lefty," he said.

I just stared at him blankly in response and he sat down next to me and told me that I'd shattered my left forearm into a hundred bone fragments and that there wasn't any chance of putting it back together without major surgery and a whole lot of metal. He also told me that I'd left more than a liter of blood on that barroom floor and they had to give me multiple transfusions.

"It wasn't easy, either," he said. "You're O-negative as you probably already know, and you can't take any blood but the same. We were even lower than usual when you came in, and we had to send the Medivac over to Chicago just to pick some up. All things considered, you're lucky just to be alive."

They sent me to a specialist in Chicago about a week later, and he put in a titanium rod that ran nearly from my wrist to my elbow, with just the nub ends of the bone attached with screws. The surgery left a long zipper of a scar along the inside of my forearm that looks like I got drunk and fell asleep on a miniature train set. A lifetime of training and year after year of sacrifice—not just mine but my old man's and yours and everybody that was near to me—and it ended in a split second on that barroom floor in Davenport, Iowa. I used to shake my head and damn something or other for the fate that had befallen me, but I know that I damned myself and there isn't anybody else that had a hand in it. It was all me, and so I had to pay the price for my own foolishness.

I wish that I had just put my tail between my legs and limped on back to your loving arms, licked my wounds, and confessed that I was dreaming about my father near on every night. They were strange, tortured dreams, where I was running about a deserted East Angler in the dead of winter. I would wake up in a sweat, not knowing if he was alive or dead. I know that you could have healed me, and more even than my stupidity in losing my shit and drinking myself into a bar brawl in that godforsaken town, I curse myself for not having the balls to stop when I could have, should have, needed to in order to save the life that I had been blessed with. But I didn't, which you know all too well.

EIGHTH BEQUEST

I hereby bequeath the mug that hangs from the ceiling at the Village Pub and all the tokens that have been dropped into it by the good old boys of Collins to the very best friend that I have in this world, Joseph Bartholemew Danner. By way of explanation to you, Danny, there was a time when they used to turn out to the Village Pub to cheer on your old man, and every one of them wanted to buy me a drink, which was symbolized by a red plastic token that they placed in that mug that hung from the ceiling there. By the time I got back from playing ball in the autumn of 1981, I was a wreck of a man, but I had enough tokens in my mug to drink just about forever. For obvious reasons, it wasn't the best of situations. But despite what might be said on the streets and sidewalks of Collins, it wasn't those tokens nor the liberal consumption policy of the Village Pub that caused all that came to pass. The simple truth of the matter was that I was on a path of destruction that no man nor god could have dissuaded me from.

Anyhow, old Joby never had the problems with the drink that I had, and I'd hate to see all those tokens go to waste. Lord knows that the Pub's owner, old Frank Taylor, has got enough money as it is—it isn't like he needs the rest of the town to go donating their hard-earned cash to him by leaving those paid-for drinks hanging from his Pub's rafters.

As I said, after the bar fight, they flew me on to Chicago for the surgery, and I was there in recovery for about two weeks. You came to me then, Sarah, leaving little Danny in the care of Joby and Celia. And when I saw you come on through those hospital doors, I broke down in tears. You were sweet to me as always, and you stroked my head and told me that everything was going to be all right.

"I feel almost that I'm the one that caused this to happen," you said to me as I lay in that narrow bed and you squeezed my good hand. "I've asked God to send you home to us so many times, Lem. I think I willed it."

"It ain't your fault, Sarah," I said to you then, and I was right. "It wasn't anything more than my own stupidity."

"But now we all get what we want," you went on. "Danny gets a full-time father, and Joby gets some help around the farm, and I have needs of my own that went unfulfilled all those nights that you were gone. We all get something, Lem, except you."

Well, I was about as discouraged and low as a man can get, but your words and the love in your tone and the twinkle in your eye made it all fade away. I was a man and a father and I was loved by a good woman—what else in the world could possibly matter? And for that one moment, I truly felt and believed that everything would be all right and I meant to make sure of that.

"I can promise you one thing," I said. "I'm done with baseball and I'm done with the drink. Seems to me that my life to this point has been the life of a child and an adolescent. I tell you now, Sarah, that I'm putting all that behind me. It's time now to be a man."

And at the time, I meant every word of it.

The rod in my forearm took some getting used to. They managed to save near on all of the muscle, but it was bruised and atrophied and I had no great range of motion with my hand for a good many months. But the physical therapists worked with me well for those couple of weeks and I started making good progress even before we left that hospital in Chicago.

Coach Anderson drove on over from Syracuse to see me and shook his head at me and called all that happened a damn shame. And I told him that he was right and that I should have listened, but I was a headstrong fool and a child. He agreed. Then he gave me the news that he had come to give me and which I had been expecting.

"The Yankees are going to cover all the medical bills, though the lawyers keep telling us that we don't have to given that it was your own actions that put you in the hospital and no fault could be laid at the door of the organization."

I nodded, knowing full well that this was small recompense for what was coming.

"And," he told me, "the Yankees want to do right by you and will pay out ten thousand dollars in severance, which should give you and Sarah enough to get back on your feet while you look for work."

And then he said it.

"But, Lem, the doctors and all the boys in the front office agree that playing ball ain't in the cards for you anymore. Your arm is just too torn up to give you the kind of strength that you used to have. It ain't anyone's fault, son, and I wish things were different, but it is what it is."

He was right about playing ball and I accepted it—hell, I even welcomed it after my promises to you. But he was wrong about assigning fault, and I knew it even then. It was my fault, plain and simple. And I remember thinking that the last part of my father had died on that barroom floor in Davenport, Iowa—the last vestige of his dreams for himself and his only son.

It was at the hospital in Chicago that they started me on Percocet, and it did a credible job of distracting me from the dark thoughts that began to crowd about my mind at that time. I didn't know much how to be a father, much less a husband like all the others—taking my Thermos and my lunch pail off to work with me in the morning and coming back to a beer and three hours of television before I hit the sack and did it all over again. In spite of all my love for you and the farm, baseball was just about the only home that I'd ever known, and I wasn't sure that I could live a normal life without it. I thought maybe that if I could just hide for a while, just long enough that everyone, including myself, could get used to the idea of me not playing ball anymore, that I'd wake up one day and it would all be okay. But it doesn't work that way, as anyone with half a brain can tell you. The desire to escape sinks you deeper in the hole and you find yourself buried at the end with less hope of escape than you started with.

The reception that we received upon my return didn't help either. Just about everyone knew what had happened, and they all stopped us to express their condolences, just like they had done after my father passed on. I wanted to tell them that no one had died, that I was still a man and capable of doing my part in the world, but I knew that they were just being friendly and supportive in their own way and so I didn't. But inside it seemed to me that, like everything else in my life, I went and squeezed any true respect for me out of that little town with my own stubbornness and all I was left with was the pity of all those that had cheered me on so in years past. I started taking double my prescription almost as soon as I set foot back home just to put myself into the gelatin state of half-consciousness where baseball seemed like a silly game for children and the loss of it didn't bother me so much.

The money from the Yankees came through in a little while, just like Coach Anderson had promised, and you were starting to pull in a little bit of money from your stories, so I knew that we were fine with the house bills for a while. It doesn't take much to live in a little town like Collins, and you were always judicious with your spending in any case. I knew I didn't have to worry about you or Danny quite yet. So, after a few weeks, and as soon as I could make my way about without assistance, I headed on straight to the Village Pub, where I rediscovered that gold mine of tokens that awaited me and I stared straight down into the abyss.

Now, I hadn't forgotten my promises to you and I knew that you hadn't forgotten them either. But I think we both cut me too much slack during that time that I was in transition. And since I knew that nobody was going to force me to keep my word—at least not right away—I figured that I could let it slide for a little bit and make good on all those promises at some undefined point in the future.

The effect of the Percocet was enhanced by the tumblers of the Jameson that I threw down after it, so that I walked in and out of reality and seemed to shuffle about like a zombie most of the time, or so Joby tells me now. And I woke up more than once that late summer in the ditch on my way back home from the Village Pub. In truth, it's a wonder I didn't kill myself right then by some stupid mistake or other, and it might have been a mercy given all that followed.

But I tried to help where I could too—I tried to make a go of it. You were just hitting your stride then, what with your stories being published in *Granta* and then later on in the *New Yorker*. And I don't think I'd ever seen you more proud than when you held that check from the *New Yorker* in your hands and told me that you were starting to think that you could really make something of all that writing. As dark as was the hole about me then, I was happy for you, though I admit that I could have done a better job of showing it. Still, when you told me that you needed my help to write a novel, I agreed—for God's sake, you had made every sacrifice so that I could have my dream, and it was only right that I do the same. And so, every morning I took my turn with little Danny, while you squirreled yourself away in the attic room that you'd converted into a study to write that book that you said wasn't really about us but might as well have been a diary of our lives together just the same.

Anyhow, little Danny and I would set off on down the road, hoping to catch Joby and Devon at the last of the milking for that morning or at least to help them put together an old hay wagon before we'd all head on up into the house to join Celia for a breakfast of pancakes and syrup. And you have to admit that no matter how hungover I was, I never, ever missed a morning with my boy. I never let him down, at least not that way, and the truth is that I came to love him as a person in his own right in those weeks before the cold winds set in and my life which was only sideways then got turned upside down.

When I wasn't at the Village Pub in the afternoons of that late autumn, I was usually in the barn with old Joby. I knew that the price of milk was hovering near an all-time low, and Joby didn't make any secret of the fact that he was just barely hanging on. Those boys from Cooperative Foods had continued to buy up all the small family farms about Collins. Joby explained to me that it all came about because of some change in the corporate tax laws that I really didn't understand then and even now have only the vaguest idea of. But they were coming at old Joby every other week or so, trying to get him to sell his family's land and take off down to Florida or some such warm place. But old Joby's a farmer through and through and he wouldn't know what to do with himself down in Florida with so much time and sunshine. He put them off time and time again. But he surely didn't have the money to hire out help and so, when I was sober, I tried to help where I could. But even when I was right in the head, my hands weren't as strong as they needed to be so that every dropped bail or milker reminded me that I was a half-cripple and that I had become so at my own hand, so to speak. And then the dark thoughts would come crowding in and I'd pull that bottle from my pocket and pop a couple of Percocet and count the minutes until I could escape the barn and get on to my real occupation in those days, which was drinking myself numb.

They offered to let me coach the varsity team over in East Angler, but I was still too close to the game and my exile was too recent for me to be able to do so. It wouldn't have lasted in any case, and maybe I knew that already and wanted to save myself the embarrassment of being fired from a job that didn't even pay minimum wage.

It wasn't too long after my return and just about the time that the first snows were rolling through and covering the fields in back of the barn in a sheet of white that you started to push me to decide to do something besides drink my life away. You had all the right, Sarah, and I can't ever deny that. You were just a young mother yourself, with your own dreams and trying to pick your way in the world, looking for the support that I had promised you since we had lain together at the edge of Tyler Goodwin's pond all those years before. But I was too messed up to give it, as much as I wanted to right then. Thinking back on it now, it wasn't so much the loss of baseball that had me tied up in knots as the loss of my old man and with it any chance that I had to forgive him.

Right as you were, I didn't take your demands well and we had some of the loudest, most hateful altercations that I can remember in those months when fall turned to winter and it looked like we were headed for disaster. I started spending less time at home, which was just fine with you, busy as you were with your writing. But even Joby and Celia could see that I was just sinking deeper and deeper into a depression and they started yelling louder and louder at me to get myself out of it. I could tell you that I tried—that I took that job bussing tables and washing dishes at the Village Pub just to show you that I was giving the renewing of my life the best shot that I was able—but that isn't true either. If it had been true, I wouldn't have been drunk most of the time that I was there, sneaking shots whenever young Tommy's back was turned. It lasted exactly two weeks, as you know, until old Frank Taylor told me that my money would always be welcome at the bar, but that he couldn't keep me on as an employee.

And I thought then that that was maybe the bottom of the fall, that I'd bounce right back on up and get my act together. I know that everybody about me thought the same, especially you, Sarah. But I wasn't done yet. I continued to help old Joby on the farm, though I was less than sober most of the time that I was there too. It gave me and Danny a place to go and put food on the table for the two of us at breakfast and lunch, which is all old Joby could afford. And, while he won't ever admit it, I know that the money that was being dangled before his eyes by Cooperative Foods had to start looking like his only way out.

We all had troubles to spare. Aside from the near on constant fighting, there wasn't any money coming in then. The severance was quickly disappearing into the coffers of that bar and we were falling behind on our bills. You were following your own dreams, which wouldn't truly pay off for a good couple of years yet. And anyhow, I was the man of the house and the one that everybody looked to to make ends meet. We finally gave up altogether on the house and the bank put us into foreclosure. Fat Horace told us that we had a good six months before we had to leave the premises—maybe a bit more if we wanted to pay him to delay the process—and so we put the matter out of our minds for the winter, knowing full well that Sheriff Haney would eventually show up at our door and order us to move ourselves and our belongings off somewhere else.

We were covered with three feet of snow over the course of two days early that December and the wind picked up to drive it into piles against the west side of our little house almost to the eaves. With no cars on the road and most people too afraid to leave the warmth of their houses, the view from our front window looked just like a picture postcard. It was a scene that we should have enjoyed together with little Danny, but we were at each other from sunup to sundown and there wasn't a moment of joy in our lives then. I made the trek to the farm in the middle of the storm, and I was willing to slog through the three feet of snow down to the Village Pub, but I called ahead and discovered that old Frank Taylor had closed it down until the plows came on through to open up the roads. Everything came to a standstill and, other than the milking, Joby and I spent our time drinking the last of his beer next to the wood burning stove. He told me for the twentieth time that week that you were crying to Celia about what a letch I had become since returning home.

"Now, I ain't one to judge a man, Lem, especially one that's been through as much as you over the last year and more, but I tell you Sarah don't see things that way. She thinks you're a different person now, not at all the man that she married. And she's desperate, Lem. You've got to pull yourself together, and I mean now, or you're gonna lose her."

It's a strange feeling to know that you're staring dark eternity in the face and not be able to stop yourself from running headlong into the void. But I was literally paralyzed then—paralyzed in my feelings and in my dealings with them. It was like someone had set my feet into blocks of concrete and set me out on the westbound lane of the New York State Thruway in the middle of the night, when the trucks that are bound for Cleveland and Detroit rumble over the joists with a rhythm that digs at your mind and sets you in a trance. I could see them coming, but I wasn't even close to being able to avoid the fate that was bearing down on me.

It got so that by the time Christmas was rolling around, we didn't talk at all, except for you to rightly tell me what a disappointment I was, which I couldn't take for what it was, and we'd end up in another knock-down, drag-out fight. I spent more nights than I can count at the old farmhouse until you told Joby that you didn't like that none, and I was relegated to the milk house. It was cold and less than comfortable, that's for certain, but I barely noticed, liquored up as I was on a near constant basis at the time. I'd stumble back to my cot at some small hour of the night and sleep a couple of hours until Devon would shake me awake for the milking of the cows the next morning.

You didn't trust me with little Danny anymore, which hurt me more than anything else, but I admit now that you were right to do it. Still, I'd spend the odd sober night at home and I'd see him now and again up at the house with Celia on my way between the barn and the Village Pub. On those occasions, he'd generally run on down the steps and grab me about the legs and I'd pick him up to hug him and tell him how much I loved him and that I was coming home right soon. Just the feel of his little bones against me made me realize all that I had lost and I'd get either incredibly sad or angry, either of which would send me on to the Village Pub to start the cycle all over again.

But through it all, Sarah, I want you to know that I loved you as much as those first days of our courting, and of course I loved little Danny right along. It was like I was in a car without brakes and careening about the roads with rock on one side and a sheer cliff on the other. It was only a matter of time before I broke through the flimsy guardrail and plunged headlong into the dark of night. And I did, as you well know. And painful as it is to me, I'm going to tell it.

NINTH BEQUEST

There's only one item that I've kept to remember my mother by over all these years and that's her family Bible, inscribed to the memory of my great-grandfather, who passed along in 1958. I hereby bequeath that Bible to you, Sarah, and I'd ask that you give it to Danny when he's old enough. I haven't got but the slightest memory of being held in the soft hands of a pretty and peaceful-looking woman who smiles down at me with tenderness, though I don't know if I've simply taken the face from the photos that my father used to have about the house when I was young. But I do remember the voice as she read to me from the leather-bound book in her lap by lamplight, and the walls of the room in which we sat were painted a strange color that I've never seen again.

"Be glad … for this your brother was dead, and he is alive again. He was lost, but now is found."

At the time her velvety voice just washed over me like so much water pouring off the lip of Johnson's Falls. But later, after she was gone, I thought that brother a fool for ever leaving the love and safety of his family to go off into the unforgiving world. And while the message of forgiveness wasn't lost on me, a part of me always wanted the father to tell him to get lost, that he didn't deserve forgiveness and acceptance and certainly not a celebration after he had turned his back on all that loved him. But isn't that what it's all about, Sarah? It takes the worries and temptations and failures and frustrations and bad decisions of an adult life to show us that none of us escape turning our backs on someone that we love now and again. Now I'm not making excuses, and I know that what I did was much worse than a boy who simply wanders off into the great unknown, but I hear those soft words of my mother now and it gives me a hole in my belly and sets my hands to shaking. I have no right to ask it, and you certainly have no obligation to grant it, and it's all too late anyway given that I'll be dead and gone in a few days if not sooner. But if there's one thing I know, it's that nothing's granted to the one that doesn't ask. So I'm going to lay it out.

The winter had rolled around again, and after that three-day storm in early December it turned colder than anyone about Collins could remember. The wind whipped across the fields and continued to pile snow up wherever it found an obstacle with a western wall that was even man-high, though the roads generally remained clear thanks to the constant stream of plows. I spent a good many hours digging out the drives and sidewalks both at home and over at the old farmhouse. Three and a half years old that winter, Danny was growing into a right little man, with a shock of brown hair over deep almond-colored eyes and the dimples that came from his beautiful mother. When I wasn't out drinking the morning away or laid up in bed with a hangover, you'd bundle him up and he'd tag along with me as we shoveled the walk out front or the path between the barn and the farmhouse for the milking. He wasn't big enough to be of much help as of yet, but he was smart as a whip and watched and commented on all that went on about him.

"The big brown one kicked her milker off," he'd say to me with a child's urgency, and I'd rush on over and hook her back up and tell him what a good boy and helper that he was and he'd strut about there like a proud little peacock.

You were settled into motherhood, and though we spent more time arguing then than we did at peace, I had to admit that it suited you just fine—like a duck in water as they say. Of course, you wouldn't let me near him when I was drinking, and I spent more nights passed out on the cot in that milk house than I care to count. But when I was sober, you let me slide.

"Just be careful with him, Lem. It's bad enough that you're driving him over to the farm while it's coming down so fast that you can't see ten feet in front of the truck, but I have nightmares about him crawling over all that machinery with you and Joby and Devon. It's no place for a little boy."

"I've got him, Sarah," I'd say as he was tugging on my shirt bottom to pull me out to the truck. "Don't you worry none. I keep him close and safe as a bug in a rug."

And I did, until I didn't.

My arm was pretty near back to normal, though I had lost the flexibility that you need to put a good spin on the ball. There wasn't any question of my returning to professional baseball, and the Yankees sent me notice that I was officially released from my contract. We thought we might get some insurance money out of the deal for a bit, but the police report left no doubt that I had been the instigator in that fight and that meant exclusion of coverage, and I had to finally admit that I had killed my baseball career and the best job that I'd ever have in one stupid, drunken, foolish act. Not that it stopped me from continuing to act like a horse's ass—I kept right on chasing the Percocet with tumbler after tumbler of Jameson. It wasn't easy to quit when there were always one or two good old boys about that still wanted to buy me a drink and hear me talk about those few games I pitched up with the Yankees back when the future was bright. Where the town fathers had determined to let me fade from the public scene, there were enough die-hard old ball players and fanatics to keep my whistle wet for two lifetimes, not to mention all those chits that hung from the roof of the Village Pub.

It was more than ten months after my father's death that I got a letter in the mail telling me that his house had finally made it through probate and was officially mine and, by the way, that I had to pay taxes on it that amounted to more than a third of its value at the time. Ain't that a kick in the head? A man works his whole life to leave something meaningful to his children and, when the time comes, the government comes and takes back a full third of that work just because he did the most natural thing in the world and died. Well, there wasn't any question about keeping it. Since the Yankees had let me go, the only income that we had was from your writing and the periodic generosity of old Joby, who told me he'd help us out as long as it took for us to get back on our feet. At the time, I know he thought he was talking about months rather than years, but he never once complained and paid me when he could, which was more than I could have expected given that I was rarely sober for more than two days in a row.

Anyhow, we couldn't pay the taxes and needed whatever additional money the sale would bring, and so we put my childhood home on the market. The real estate agent asked us to head on over and clean the place up a bit before she began to show it to interested buyers. I put it off as long as I could, but I finally begged off the farm early one afternoon late that December and drove the truck on over to East Angler, stopping off at the liquor store to pick up a fifth of the Jameson to steel my nerves. Then I turned the key in that lock for the first time in more than four years. I shined a flashlight inside, and I heard the scurrying of mice and God knows what else as I pushed the door open, and I prepared myself for the wreck of a place I knew I'd find, given that my old man had drunk himself to death and wasn't ever much of a housekeeper to begin with. But it wasn't half as bad as I expected. There were empty bottles lining the kitchen counter and table, and piles of straw and dust and old clothes in every corner, but otherwise the place seemed fairly in order. I stepped through the kitchen and into the living room, where the old wood burning stove sat broad as a bulldog over in one corner on a stand of brick. The picture window looked out onto the front yard, which was snow-covered and white as I remembered it from the snow days of my youth, and all the glass was still in good shape.

I turned and walked down the hall toward the bedrooms at the back of the place. When I came to my old man's room, I found it locked, and I chuckled to myself that the old man was paranoid even when he didn't have nothing worth stealing. I held the flashlight in the crook of my bad arm, took a pull on the bottle in my other hand and set it aside, then I went to work with my driver's license. The door wasn't meant to keep out anyone who was serious about getting inside, and I had it open in a matter of minutes. More scurrying came from under the bed and the dark corners of the room, which was nearly black even though the white snow made it bright as could be outside. I threw back the heavy curtains on the window, and light filled up the room. Like the front rooms, it was disordered, but my old man didn't have enough at the end to really make a mess of anything. I saw papers scattered on the bed and over the dresser, more bottles of whiskey on the floor next to the bed, and a few pieces of clothing. I walked over and picked up a yellowed piece of newsprint and brought it up to my eyes.

"HIGGINS THROWS NO-HITTER IN WIN AGAINST TIDEWATER," the headline read.

I stepped back like somebody hit me in the chest and dropped the flashlight, which rolled under the bed. It wasn't that the old man had articles about me that had shaken me, it was that the article came from the *Syracuse Post-Standard*, a small paper that wasn't easy to get your hands on in Western New York. I reached under the bed to retrieve the flashlight, and then I picked up the next scrap of paper and held it to the light.

"MUD HENS LOSE 3-1 TO CHIEFS; HIGGINS EARNS SAVE," it read and the copyright notice on the bottom showed that it was printed by the *Toledo Blade*.

And so I went from scrap to scrap of paper, finding that each was an article about my starts with the Syracuse Chiefs over the three years that I was there and each came from either the Syracuse paper or another local paper of one of our opponents. When I moved over to the dresser, instead of the ratty old clothes that I expected to find, I found the drawers piled high with old copies of those same papers, some of them carved up to remove the articles about me in the sports section, and I found one entire drawer full of the *Sports Illustrated* issue from June of 1978 that mentioned in brief my rise to the majors and the two wins that I had pulled off for the Yankees at the tender age of nineteen.

I went to the closet and drew back the doors slowly, not at all certain that there wasn't a family of raccoon that had made it their home. But it was empty except for the clothes that hung from a pole at about eye level. Behind my father's windbreaker that carried the union insignia from down at the lumber mill, I found a half-dozen jerseys from both the Yankees and the Chiefs with my name and number stitched on the back. I pulled one out, shook the dust off of it, and sat down hard on the worn carpet of the bedroom. I held it to my nose and took in the scent of my old man, a mixture of coffee and tobacco and whiskey, that I hadn't smelled in nearly five years. And I saw him in my mind's eye, wearing the jersey about the house as he tuned in the Jays from up in Toronto and set himself down to drink his troubles away. I crawled along the floor then, looking through teary eyes for my own bottle and set down in the corner and proceeded to drink my own pain into a dull memory.

I never did get around to cleaning out that old house, at least not until many months later and with my life in shambles. I was good and soused as I stumbled out the door, swearing out loud to myself that my old man was a stubborn old bastard and that things didn't have to end the way that they did. And as I weaved on up the road, crossing those hills between East Angler and the farm, I swore that things would be different with my own boy, and that he'd never have to look for my love after I was cold and in the ground.

You saw me coming from a mile away, and though I know that you felt for me in all that I had to go through since I came back and selling off my childhood home, I had already given you enough worry so that you wouldn't let me near the boy when I'd been drinking. There's no question that you were right to do so. And I'm damn proud of you for acting like the mother lion in protecting him, even if the predator at that time was me. I only wish that I had listened to you when I had the chance. But my head was full of whiskey and boiling over right at that moment, and of course we argued as had become our habit. You told me to get lost, or to head on back to the farm, and to come back when I sobered up. I yelled a stream of horrible things at you, then I slammed the door of the truck and spun the wheels on my way out of the driveway. I remember it all clearly enough, as I usually do unless I'm all but passed out, and I know that I damn near took out the mailbox and ended in the ditch, which would have been a mercy.

I meant to head on back to the farm, to complain to your brother—who didn't ever give any answer to my complaints, but just nodded his head and listened—but I never made it that far. I ended up on a stool at the Village Pub, where I continued what I had begun that morning, or maybe what I had started on the day that my old man passed, or maybe even earlier, I'm not sure any more. In any case, I threw back another handful of doubles of the Jameson and got so that I could barely sit up straight and curse you out to young Tommy as I'd been doing for more than an hour. Young Tommy told me later that I was slurring when I showed up and spitting gibberish by the end, but I remember that I wanted to make sure that Tommy knew that I loved my boy and I wasn't going to let nothing stand between me and him, not even you.

Now, Tommy has no fault in what happened next. He was handling a room full of local boys all by himself, the waitress having called in sick that afternoon. And he told me that whole time that I was sitting up on that barstool that I had had more than enough for one day, and it was Tommy who called old Joby to come on out and pick me up after I had had four or five and looked like I would melt right into the floor if someone didn't find me a bed. But when he refused to give me another, I cursed him up and down, though I doubt he understood a word, and headed back out to the truck. Tommy followed me out there and told me that he was going to have to call the cops if I insisted on driving. I told him to go right on ahead, knowing that it would take a good hour for them to get all the way out there. And he went on back inside.

For the first time, I noticed that night had settled in, and you could tell that it was going to be a cold one. My breath showed before me and the frost on the windshield took more than ten minutes to clear with the heater up full blast. When I had a nice hole in the ice, such that I could see the parking lot standing full before me, I gunned the engine and pulled out of there, slipping on the ice and clipping Horace Jeeter's 4x4 on my way out. They told me later that he never did know who had done it, though I'm sure he suspected me, falling-down drunk as I was.

I was going to write that it was a minor miracle that I got back to the house without ending in a ditch, but that isn't right. The miracle would have been if I had gotten stuck in a ditch and got to sleep off all the booze and pent-up emotion that led me to do what I did next, or even if I had frozen myself to death passed out in the cab and you and Danny could then at least have remembered me fondly for the good times that we had. But that isn't what happened, as you well know. I pulled into the drive of our little house and jumped down from the cab and was screaming my head off before I even got through the door, which you had locked and rightfully so.

I kicked the door loose from its hinges and then charged it with a shoulder, and I remember tumbling inside and falling flat on my face in the little entryway before the stairs. And then I was standing over you and slapping the phone out of your hand, though I knew that the police were already on their way. I can still feel your nails on my back as I lifted little Danny out of his bed and held him to me. He was half-asleep, but our shouts and our struggle brought him wide awake and screaming for fear of what was going on between us. In my drunken state, I had decided then and there that you weren't fit to be his mother if you wanted to keep a son from his father, and I started off down the stairs to take him away, thinking that we could stay together in my old man's abandoned house over in East Angler.

It was on the stairs that you really jumped me in earnest and I almost lost my balance and dropped him.

Now, I'm more ashamed of what happened next than anything I've done in my twenty-six years, and if there's a hell that I'm going to, I know that it's because of what I did in those next moments. I reacted as a coward on anger and instinct and turned around and backhanded you across the face, sending you flying against the banister. I remember you looking at me with disbelief in your eyes and I knew that I had broken us, though I wouldn't admit it to myself for some time yet. The blood began to trickle from the corner of your mouth as I stood there swaying on my legs and dumbfounded at my own violence. In the distance, the sirens began to howl and I knew that they were coming for me.

With Danny still crying in my arms, I stumbled down the stairs and through the door. I could hear your shouts at my back grow desperate with the concern of a mother for her child. I jerked open the door of the cab and climbed into the seat and set Danny down next to me. He rolled to the window and pawed at the glass and screamed, "Maaamaaa" into the black of the night. I was surprised by his desperation to get back to you, and I only came to when I saw the lights flashing in the distance. Then I threw the engine into drive and peeled out of our driveway, heading God only knows where. I could barely see through the frost that had come back to settle on the windshield, but I didn't let that stop me and I finally ground our mailbox under the wheels as I bounded through the ditch and out onto the road.

Not knowing where to turn, I headed over toward the south field, which had a long track that led into the woods behind old Joby's farm. We'd just plowed that track the week before in order to inspect the outlying maples for tapping, and I thought that I had a good chance of making it into the woods without getting stuck. From there, I didn't know where I'd go, but at least I figured that I could hide out for a few hours in the woods and head on up to the barn when the heat had passed. I thought somehow that if I could just hide out until morning, it would all make some sense and I would know what to do next. I had this vague idea that, if I could just explain it all to old Joby, then he'd find a way to make it okay with you and with the cops as well.

I pulled into the south field and bounced along the frozen ground until the truck was hidden completely by the forest. I killed the headlights and turned the panel lights down real low. But I kept the heater going to keep me and Danny warm, and I pulled him to me and tried to stem his crying. But it wasn't any use. He bawled right along for the next hour or more, asking for his mama, until he cried himself to sleep in my arms. I had watched the flashing lights come and go out on Hampton Holmwood Road through the shadows of the forest, but I hadn't seen anything for a good half hour or more. And I was worried about the gas that I had in that truck, which was down to no more than a quarter tank. And so I woke Danny and told him that we were going for a walk through the woods. He could barely keep his eyes open and I realized that I'd be carrying him the whole way up to the barn, which was more than a mile off. And I did, or at least I carried him halfway, until he woke up cold in my arms and squirmed until I put him down on his feet and held him by the hand. It was slow going for more than an hour, what with the snow from the storm still piled up to three feet and more in the untrammeled forest. Luckily, it was cold enough that a layer of ice had formed atop the snow. We walked along on top for long stretches until the ice grew thin and we punched through at intervals. When Danny started crying again, I picked him up and carried him the last ten minutes and on into the dark of the milk house.

I want you to know, Sarah, that I didn't ever intentionally hurt our boy, nor would I no matter how drunk I was. I know that after what happened back at our house, you thought that I was capable of just about anything, and I don't blame you. I was out of my head. But I never hurt little Danny, at least not in anger.

I was still drunk and dead tired by the time we got inside. I saw the lights on in the farmhouse, but I knew that I wasn't in any state to explain my actions of that night to anyone, and I was focused on just making it through until morning. I found half a bottle of whiskey that I had hidden in old Joby's rafters the week before, and I kept on pulling at it to stave off the hangover that I knew was coming at me like a freight train. I set up that old army cot in the corner and lay down and pulled Danny to me and zipped us both inside my coat and tried my best to drift off to sleep. But the night moved coldly through those rooms, and even the cows out in their stanchions were snorting and squirming because they couldn't get warm to sleep. Eventually, I got up, unzipped myself from the boy and started rummaging about for some sort of a blanket. I came back with an old burlap sack and I threw it over us, but it didn't keep out the cold much and we both started itching on account of the mites that crawled out of the sack and into our clothes. Danny was beyond tired by that point and so cold that his little nose was turning blue, and I started to think about heading up into the farmhouse. But I was still out of my head and I knew that old Joby would kick me out and just maybe kick my ass when he found out what I'd done to his sister and his nephew, if he didn't know already. The ruckus in the barn had died down and I knew that the fifty head that Joby was milking at the time kept the barn a sight warmer than the milk house, so I moved us both out and into one of the open stalls between two of the larger cows. I spread some hay beneath us, and we settled down for the night just like a pair of four-legged animals. It was well after midnight and both Danny and I had had enough, so we shivered together the rest of that long night, drifting in and out of sleep until someone flicked on the lights at the far end of the barn and I could hear old Joby's shit kickers coming down the aisle.

Now, I had meant to get us out of that barn and back to the truck and on to Canada before Joby woke and came on down to milk the cows, but the whiskey was still sloshing about in my head, and the part that was clearing faced a hangover of major proportions. I must have gotten sick at some point in the night, because I was covered in frozen pieces of bile and beer nuts and even though it was frozen the stuff stank to high heaven. My head felt the size of a bowling ball and the blood pounded in my ears so hard and painful that I could barely hear myself think, but I felt a shot of fear run down my spine as soon as I realized that your brother was coming down the line. If he already knew what had happened, I figured that I was done for. I saw him in my mind's eye lugging that old shotgun next to his leg, seething with anger over the wrong that I had done his sister. And with a bit of distance now, I can see that that would have been a just end. I surely deserved to be shot dead in my own vomit on the floor of that milk house.

Sarah, I relive that morning as a man lives a nightmare—all foggy and turned around in flashes and disembodied sensations—not at all like life, but something much darker and eternal. I remember Danny's small hand that shook me at the shoulder. I pushed it away and curled deeper into myself. Then it was his two hands pushing at my back. I noticed that he was crying again and between his sobs, I could hear the chatter of his teeth. I heard a grunt issue from my own throat—I wanted so badly to crawl back into the void of my

132

drunken sleep, but he was persistent and I eventually opened one eye, the pain shooting into my brain as the fluorescent light broke into me with violent force.

"Daddy," Danny said to me through tears that had frozen to his cheek, "you have to get up. Uncle Joby's coming …"

Our little boy's breath was coming in great gasps after each sob and every exhalation sprung from his lips as a torrent of condensation. It hung in the air for a moment before it disappeared, and I knew that it was still very cold. I opened both eyes then and tried to come to a sitting position. But I only succeeded in pushing the wet hay around the stall with my feet. I heard the tinkle of glass as yet another empty bottle fell into the gutter, and all the while the rhythmic clomp of steel-toed boots as they came down the ramp from the milk house toward me.

"All right," I said to calm little Danny, and I gave him my arm, though I knew he couldn't pull me upright.

And then I was flooded with images that I found hard to put in order. My head ached, and the muscles in my back screamed from being twisted into the stall all night. Could it have been all night? My mouth tasted bitter, where the whiskey-soaked mucous had dried to my lips and tongue. I saw you falling, Sarah, your hand to her face. Then I saw the boy crying in my arms as I took him through the door and out into the cold of the December night. I closed my eyes then to make it all go away, and I've been doing the same every morning since.

"Boy," Joby said, "let's go on up to the house now. Your Aunt Celia just got started on some pancakes. Come on now … let's go."

Danny looked at me with doubt in his eyes, and I nodded my head. Then he dropped my arm and jumped the gutter to take Joby's hand. Joby didn't say a word to me then, but led our little boy up the floor between the stalls and out into the still dark of the morning.

I might have run then, but the truth is that I felt so ill and broken that I wasn't sure that my legs would carry me. I would have taken death as a release if it had been offered. And so I sat in my own piss and vomit, knowing that Joby would return for me as soon as Danny was safe in the farmhouse. He didn't disappoint, and I listened to those steel-toed boots come down the aisle once more as I sat holding my throbbing head in my hands. He stopped in front of me and waited for me to look up into his eyes before he spoke.

"Now I've always considered you my brother, Lem," he said, "and I ain't never killed a man before, so you got two points in your favor right now. But I'll be honest with you as I've always been, it ain't for lack of desire or ability. I tell you this straight, Lem, if you ever touch Sarah or that boy again in any way, I will tear you apart piece by piece and make you wish you had never been born while I'm doing it."

I put up my hands and tried to explain.

"Now, hold on, Joby—"

"I ain't holding on for nothing, Lem. I don't care how drunk you was or why you done it. If you touch either one of them again, I will kill you."

Then he hauled me up by my shirtfront—he was strong as a bull then and still is—and he yelled the next words straight in my face.

"DO … YOU … UNDERSTAND … GODDAMMIT?"

I nodded that I did, knowing that it wouldn't do any good to resist, nor did I have anything truly to say in my defense. The enormity of my sins was coming home to me, and I knew that whatever fate befell me then, I deserved it. Then Joby dragged me behind him up the walk, me stumbling to get my legs the whole way, and he threw me on the floor of the milk house. It was cold as ice and I wondered that me and Danny hadn't frozen solid in the dead of that December night. He turned to the far wall and uncoiled the hose that we used for washing down the floor and he gave the handle a good crank. The water started coming fast and he turned the nozzle on me, washing me down right there on the floor of the barn. It was like a hundred knives cutting into me at every touch of the water on my skin and I screamed in protest until old Joby started spraying me full in the face to shut me up. By the time he was done, I was balled in a heap on the floor, begging him to stop.

When he was done hosing me down, Joby threw me a pile of oil-stained rags to dry myself.

"Sheriff Haney's on his way," he said, and even though I was already shivering, the coldness in his voice sent a shock right up my spine. "You can change into something at the county lockup, if you don't freeze yourself to death first."

"Joby, I—" I started and stopped as he leveled a big calloused finger at me.

"It's done now, Lem," he spit at me from across the room, "all that was is done."

And with that, he turned on his heel and walked out of the milk house, and I could hear the big bolt slam shut from the outside, locking me in so I couldn't escape what was coming for me. It was twenty minutes later that Sheriff Haney found me half-frozen on the floor of the milk house and threw me in the back of the squad car, where I finally got warm.

TENTH BEQUEST

I hereby bequeath all blankets, sheets, pillows, pillowcases, and bedding that can be found in my old man's house to the Cattaraugus County Sheriff's office in East Angler on the condition that they be used to give comfort to the prisoners, among whom I counted myself more than once in those dark days. The paper-thin wool blankets that they give out up there aren't fit for anything except scratching the very hide off a man, and those pillows are like limp bags of sand, which doesn't give him a chance to rest or sleep even one minute. I know that I didn't deserve any comfort in those days, and there are those that say that jail is meant to make a man suffer, but given all that I've been through since, I tend to think that at least some of the incarcerated are just good old boys fallen on hard times that don't have the creativity or the spark or the helping hand to make it up out of the hole they've dug themselves. Anyhow, I hope that the donation reaches those that it's meant to and that it gives them the half-step they need to get back on the right track.

As I was telling it, Sheriff Haney showed up less than an hour after Joby discovered me and Danny in the barn. I was still a walking mess, coming back to myself, but uttering incoherencies about how

I was the boy's father and that there wasn't anybody that could take that away. Or so they tell me. Turns out I was wrong anyway. On the basis of your statement the night before, Bill Haney arrested me for assault and endangering a minor and took me on in to the station in East Angler. They took my fingerprints and my picture—which ended up in the papers the next day—threw me into the holding cell with the other drunks and held me through until the following morning when I was arraigned before a judge in Cattaraugus County court.

I saw you scurrying out the front doors of the courthouse, a bandage on your head and holding your belly as if someone had socked you in the gut, averting your eyes and pretending not to hear my pleas, just before they walked me into the courtroom, and I knew that you must have been talking to the prosecutor. I still had no idea of the consequences of what I had done, and I was hopeful that I could plead my way back into your heart and back to the way things were before. And I sat in that courtroom for a good hour until the bailiff called me up and the judge gave the floor to the prosecutor, who might as well have slapped me in the face for what he spoke about what had happened that fateful night.

"Your Honor," he said, "in an intoxicated rage, Mr. Higgins attacked his wife, Sarah Danner Higgins, striking her in the face and fracturing her jaw. Then he proceeded to forcibly kidnap his three-year old son, holding him hostage and forcing him to spend one of the coldest nights of the year on the floor of the Danner family barn, where he contracted extreme frostbite on his extremities, which are still being treated. The doctors are of the opinion that young Danny Higgins will lose at least one toe, as well as part of his earlobe and possibly a part of his nose as a direct result of the actions of Mr. Higgins. Wherefore, the people submit that Mr. Higgins represents a danger to himself and this community. The people ask that he be remanded without the possibility of bail."

I started shouting to the heavens then that that young prosecutor was a goddamned liar, that I hadn't laid a hand on nobody, and that my boy was just fine the previous morning when old Joby had come and taken him up to the farmhouse. The truth is that I hadn't quite worked out what was the grim reality from what I wanted it to be. The judge yelled for order and proclaimed that I was to be held on two-hundred thousand dollars bail and brought down his gavel. And he told me in no uncertain terms that if I were released, I was forbidden from coming within two hundred yards of you or little Danny. With that, the deputies took me away and threw me back in the holding cell, where I continued to scream at the iron bars against the truth that I just couldn't accept, though deep down I knew that eventually I would.

It took a couple of days for the public defender to work out the bail with the bondsman. And it took another two weeks for fat old Horace to get the papers on my old man's house in proper order so that I could put it up as collateral. When it was done, they set me free on the jailhouse steps and gave me back the vomit-stained clothes of more than two weeks prior. I remember standing there, my breath coming out in great billows of condensation and blinking up into the rare appearance of a January sun, and realizing that I didn't have any place to go. I couldn't go to you—you wouldn't have me and rightfully so—and the judge had told me flat out that I'd end up back in jail if I came near you. I couldn't go to Joby and Celia—I had burned all my bridges with your family, Joby had made that clear, and there wasn't any way to build them back. Besides, I didn't have any transportation as Sheriff Haney had impounded my F-100 as evidence and wouldn't let me have it back until I went to trial, if then. I didn't have more than fifty bucks in my pocket and I wasn't at all sure that I wasn't stone cold broke otherwise, what with all the drinking that I'd been doing in those days.

It was about two miles out of town to my old man's house, and although I knew that the same demons and the sorrow were waiting there, I also knew that I'd have to end up there eventually. I turned up the collar on my shirt and started off down the road until one of the boys from the East Angler varsity team recognized me and gave me a lift the rest of the way, though I could tell that he regretted it as soon as my stench hit his nose. He asked a lot of questions about playing in Syracuse and those few games I threw for the Yankees, but he didn't say anything about my having been in jail, though I knew from his gaze that the news had made the rounds. I didn't say much. There wasn't much to say, given all that had happened.

Once I got in the front door of the old house, I realized that there wasn't any heat, and so I set about gathering up anything that was worthless and flammable from the piles of junk that were lying about: papers, clothes, broken furniture, you name it. In my searching, I came on a stash in the corner of the old man's top dresser drawer that he must have hidden for hard times and never got back to before he froze himself to death the previous year. I pulled out the two half-full bottles of Johnny Walker Red and popped one open, just to give it a sniff. Well, it was no Jameson, but beggars can't rightly complain, so I set them both down next to the wood burning stove and started pulling off of one to get a bit of warmth into my bones while I stoked the flames.

I got her built into a good blaze within a few minutes, though it was hard to keep her revved up, what with all the paper and clothes that were burning quick in the belly of that iron monster. But the warmth felt good on my face and, when I got a good set of coals going from the remnants of an old kitchen chair, I closed the damper to keep in the heat and pulled the old man's tattered recliner next to the stove and just sat and drank and watched the sun go down through the weather-stained picture window of the front room. I hadn't slept more than an hour at a time in the jail and the heat of that fire and the whiskey in my belly after so long put me right out. When I woke up three hours later, I was dry and prickly and cold, the fire having long since died down.

I think sometimes that sleep is the cruelest thing that can happen to a man. Not the sleep itself, of course, but the void from which you're forced to return when you awake. It always takes me two seconds after I open my eyes to remember back over the past few days and realize what horror I've committed and how my life has been sent down some dark, new path that I never intended. It was especially bad at that time, waking up in my old man's house, with him dead and gone, and you and Danny somewhere out in the dark, hating me for what I'd done to you both. I piled on top of that hell the fact that my career was over, that I had a bum left arm for the rest of my life, that I had no money nor prospects neither, and that I was hung over to boot. I thought at the time that it was about the lowest that I could get. But I got creative after that and sunk my life even lower still.

Up to that point, there was only one way that I knew—that I'd been taught—to handle life's problems and that was to keep tipping up the bottle until you see the clear bottom or life doesn't hurt you anymore. And so that's what I did. By the time I was half-finished with the second bottle of JW, I was feeling a warmth again, and I had come up with a typically whiskey-soaked plan to turn it all around. I knew that you still loved me—that you still remembered all the good and loving times that are contained in these pages—and

I knew that, if I could just talk to you as we used to talk, I could win you back and we'd stand together to face all that was coming down on us, and we'd make it through somehow.

It was heading on midnight at the time, and the temperature was hovering about zero again outside. I was smart enough to grab an old pair of Carhartt's out of the old man's closet and pull them on before I headed outside. I stuffed whatever loose money and change I could find into the many pockets of that suit, grabbed the quarter-bottle of whiskey that remained to me and headed out the door. It was a long, cold walk back to town and there weren't any cars on the road at that time of night, or at least none that were going to offer a ride to a strange man in Carhartt's carrying a bottle.

It took me almost an hour to reach the Sheriff's station, where I walked around back and found my truck penned up in the little impound lot that Bill Haney kept back there and that wasn't hardly ever used for anything other than overflow parking during the Wild-flower Festival. I slammed back the last of the whiskey and jumped the fence, tearing a hole in the sleeve of the Carhartt's on the barbed wire up top. Once inside, it didn't take me but a minute to feel underneath the wheel well for the spare key that I had hidden in that truck ever since I locked myself out of it three times the previous year, and then I was inside. She turned over nice and smooth and I waited for her to warm up, quietly toeing the accelerator, before I took aim at one of the fence panels ahead of me that was chained together to keep what was inside inside and what was outside out. I put her in gear and gunned the engine and the fence tore away like a sheet of plywood, although it made quite a racket as I drove on through and out into the soft lights of Main Street. I thought for a moment that the noise might have roused Bill Haney from his bed two blocks down, so I sat for a minute and waited to see if the lights in his house would spring to life, but all was silent. A light snow had begun to fall by then, and I set my mind to the task ahead of me. I pulled out onto the street and pointed the nose of the truck toward Collins and you.

I didn't see more than a wandering doe and a handful of cars on my way over the hills from East Angler and there wasn't any indication of a soul stirring that night until I approached the Village Pub, where I knew that young Tommy was still slinging drinks at the bar, the old jukebox was singing away, and the night was young. I was growing dry once again, and I figured I'd need a couple of shots in order to properly pour my heart out to you, so I pulled on up into the parking lot and killed the engine.

The surprise was evident on the faces of the boys shooting pool in the corner when I walked through the door, and I knew that word was out for three counties about what I had done to my wife and child. But I kept it together, nodded at the gawkers that paused in their game and those that interrupted their conversations at the bar, and said a cordial hello all around. Then I set myself atop an open barstool at the far end of the counter, slapped down a twenty, and nodded to young Tommy.

"Mr. Higgins," he said, coming up to me and looking for the bat that I knew he kept taped up there behind the bar, "are you sure you're supposed to be here?"

"Mr. Higgins was my father, Tommy," I said, loud enough for all those who were interested to hear, "and that poor bastard's dead as the winter is long. Besides, there ain't but two years between us, so you've got no cause to be calling me 'mister.' And it's called bail, my friend. I haven't broken out of jail or nothing, so give it a rest and stop looking for that damn bat. It's over in the corner where you left it, you fool. Now give me some of the good stuff."

Tommy looked only partially relieved at what I had to say, and the conversation in the bar never did return to its normal level as long as I was there. The poor kid's hands were shaking as he poured me a tumbler of Jameson, whereupon I slammed it back and nodded to him to fill her up again. He did, and I did, and I gave him the twenty and told him to keep the change, which was about a ten dollar tip for him. Then I motioned him in real close.

"I need you to sell me a bottle, Tommy. Now don't shake your head or nothing, just hear me out. I am one sorry son of a bitch right now, and I need your help. I lost my chance at playing in the bigs again, I near about lost my arm, I've lost my wife and little boy, and it looks like I'm gonna lose my freedom. And that bottle's been my only friend for a number of months now. Now, I ain't a begging man, so either you're going to find it in your heart to take this forty dollars and leave me a bottle out the back door, or you're gonna have to call Sheriff Haney, because I'm going over the top of you to get it. But I hope you'll be a friend and see fit to help a man out of a hole."

And he did, as I knew he would. Young Tommy was a good sort, and I knew that he'd sympathize, even if it were with the devil himself. Anyhow, I slid off the stool and walked slowly outside to pick up the bottle that was dutifully laid at the baseboards of the back door. Thus reloaded, I climbed back in the cab of the truck and headed on toward our home, thinking that with a little courage I could talk you into loving me again. I admit that it was a stupid idea, but I hadn't been in my right mind for quite some time at that point, and I didn't have much to lose.

I wasn't so drunk that I couldn't see that your car wasn't parked in the driveway when I pulled up to the house, and so I left her idling and hopped out to peek through the windows and assure myself that all was dark and quiet. When a light popped on at the house of that old couple the Murray's across the street, I hightailed her out of there, knowing they wouldn't hesitate but a second to call in Sherriff Haney after what I had done, even if it was my own house that I was casing.

There was only one place you might have run to with little Danny, and so I pointed the nose of that truck down the road a piece toward Joby's farm. Sure enough, I saw your car parked up under the eaves of that old barn, almost out of sight for someone that wasn't looking for it. It was getting on three o'clock in the morning now, and I knew that I'd have some explaining to do to Joby and Celia, but I wasn't going to let a little thing like reason dissuade me from my goal. I pushed the bell and watched the lights click on inside one by one as Celia made her way downstairs to the door. She looked through the glass pane to see who might be disturbing their sleep at such an early hour, but when she saw my ugly mug she came full on wide awake. She didn't move to open the door, but talked to me through the glass.

"You shouldn't be here, Lem," she said quietly, and she turned to mouth my name when old Joby ambled up behind her, asking what bastard would ring a man's bell at three o'clock in the goddamn morning.

Joby pushed past her and opened the door and slid out onto the porch, closing the door behind him and telling Celia to head on back to bed.

"She don't want to see you, Lem," he said to me, his breath coming out in big white puffs in the cold night air, "especially not at no three o'clock in the morning. And you know that the judge'll throw your ass right back in jail if he finds out you're here. Why don't you just head on back to your old man's place and give it a few days. Then we'll see what happens …"

I had planned a moving soliloquy in my head on my way over from East Angler, but I didn't expect to have to give it to Joby and it came out all jumbled and slurred and dirty and the only point I could get across to him was that I loved you and Danny both and I wanted to make it up to you.

He knew by the time I stopped that I was dead drunk, and he looked desperately at me for a moment like he was pained to see me falling apart so. And I know now thinking back on that look that Joby was always a true friend to me, though it didn't register in my thick head at that time. But you were his sister too, and like the Godfather says, there ain't no taking sides against family. When he realized that I wasn't going to take no for an answer, he straightened up and stuck his finger in my chest and told me to get on home and sober up before he put a hurting on me that would make me forget about those boys in Iowa. Then he turned back inside, locking the door behind him, and turned off the porch light.

Not to be deterred, I walked around to the front of the house, where I watched old Joby turn off light after light, reversing the order that Celia had turned them on, until finally he flicked off the bedroom light. And I was about to go sleep in the cab of the truck and wait until morning, when I saw the light flick on in the old bedroom that you and I used to share. A shadow passed before the window and I knew that it was you.

"Sarah!" I yelled, quiet at first, but growing to a shout when I didn't see you come on back to the window. "Sarah! Saaaarraaaaah!"

But you didn't come and the light flicked off, and I yelled some more until I heard old Joby's big, booming voice pissed off and coming back down the stairs to the side door.

I knew that I had only a matter of moments before he came out and put a stop to my nonsense, so I started yelling that I was sorry and that I loved you and Danny both. And I kept it up even as Joby stumbled down the porch stairs in only his robe and his shit kickers and headed toward me telling me that he had enough worries on his plate at the moment, what with Cooperative Foods on his ass every minute of every goddamned day, and that he'd be goddamned if some crazy bastard was going to scream up a storm on his front lawn at three o'clock in the morning. And I knew that I'd crossed the line. He came up on me fast, and I pushed him away with both hands, still yelling your name, but then he came back at me and gave me a right cross on the chin. I stumbled forward to grab him and we wrestled on the frozen ground for a bit, old Joby's private parts flapping in the wind. But I was drunk and he was sober and it would have been an even match at best if we were both in our right minds. We came to our feet again, and Joby pushed me back and gave me a good uppercut that picked me right up off the ground and set me on my back where the world spun and finally went black.

When I woke in mid-afternoon the next day, I was back in the county lockup and my head felt as if it had been split by a two-by-four, whether from the whiskey or old Joby's beating I couldn't really tell. When the pain had subsided enough to listen, one of the deputies told me that the judge had revoked my bail that morning and sentenced me to prison while I awaited trial some two months later. On top of it all, the prosecutor was adding charges for breaking into the impound lot and the theft of my own truck. Don't that beat all, that a man can be charged with the theft of his own vehicle? Anyhow, it looked like I was going to be out of commission for a good long while.

And that was the good news—that I was forced to be sober for those two months—and since I didn't have anything to do but think about my actions the whole day through, it gradually came to me what a horse's ass I'd been acting like ever since my old man passed on. Not that I could take any of it back, of course. What I had told young Tommy was right on: I'd lost my old man and any chance I had to make it up with him, I'd lost my career, I'd shattered my arm, I'd lost the only love that I had known in this world and my own son as well, and by that time, I'd lost my liberty. And so it was that at twenty-four years old, I passed the longest, darkest, heaviest, and most despondent eight weeks of my life.

ELEVENTH BEQUEST

I haven't slept in a dog's age, Sarah. I spend morning, noon, and night staring out the window at those clouds that continue to build on the western horizon over Lake Erie, and I know that it's a matter of a short while before they come rolling in. When I can sit up, which isn't often now, I watch the snow coming down in thin frozen flakes that don't come together like the wet stuff but just blow about on the drive beneath without ever settling in any particular place. It seems cold and barren and unforgiving and the days of winter seem to stretch out before us all like one of those long, straight, flat roads that go on for miles and miles through the corn fields of Iowa.

But these days have at least given me the chance to get down the bulk of our story and, for that, I am forever grateful. I've covered just about all that you'll remember, Sarah, and the rest I can guess that you've heard in bits and pieces during these four years that we've spent apart. But I mean to get it all down, even if I have to die with the pen in my hand. When I said so to Celia, she furrowed her brow and gave me a worried look as she tucked the sheets in tighter about me, but I think she understands too that I need to say what I need to say to you before all is said and done. She even told me on the sly that, while she can't tell me where you've gone because of the promises that she made, she'll get every word that I put down on paper into your hands as soon as possible. It was something of a relief to hear, and I thanked both God and Celia for putting my mind at ease.

I have to admit that writing isn't as easy as it was when I started a week ago. It feels like my entire left side is on fire now, and I can't move an inch without making it flare up so that I have to look over and be certain with my eyes that the bed isn't ablaze. And I notice that the use of my right side is going as well. And I think it isn't any wonder that I'm losing control given that my body's swollen up like a watermelon in June. Doc Tyler tells me that it's my body's reaction to the infection, that it's trying to fight, but that it's losing the battle. I give it credit all the same because it's allowed me to get this far in my story to you. And Doc keeps pumping me full of antibiotics, but even he's stopped talking to me about all the research that they're doing on AIDS. It's been more than a year now since the government finally identified the virus and promised that they were on the edge of finding a cure. Whatever comes of it, I'm afraid that it'll be too little too late for little old me.

I had to ask old Joby to double up on the morphine this morning, thinking that it was the only way that I was going to get pen to paper. It took the pain, as it does, but it's taken a few hours for the stupor to wear off, and I don't know how long I have until I can't stand it anymore. All I can do is what I can do, I suppose, and so I continue.

I hereby bequeath any monies that remain in my checking account to Darren Beals, that young public defender that came down from the city to save my ass from six more months in prison. I know that the kid worked near on day and night for a few weeks before the trial and I know that it was his talk with old Joby that ended up getting me out of there after only two months. Not that I didn't deserve more—I'm sure that I did—but if the criterion is whether it was time for me to put my life back in good working order, well then I have to think that they got it just about right. Anyhow, I owe quite a bit more than the few hundred dollars that I might have in the bank to that boy, but I give it to him with the thanks of a humble man, a changed man, a man that owes him something that can't ever truly be paid back.

Now, it seems stupid to say it out loud, but prison isn't all that it's cracked up to be. There were days when I was awaiting trial that I tried to look at it objectively, especially considering that I was likely to be there for some time. It was three square meals a day, I didn't have to work—at least not at anything anyone cared two shits about. I was safe day and night—there aren't any murderous criminals in the Cattaraugus County lockup—and I had all the time in the world to sit and think and write or watch movies or draw or paint or whatever the hell else I wanted to do. But being alone with one's mind over an extended period of time is a matter for European philosophers and Buddhist monks, I think. I was locked in a cell with my sober self, a man I hadn't known for a good two years, and I didn't much like what I found.

I argued with myself—it was inevitable—over whether it was you and my old man who had betrayed me and left me hanging out to dry or whether it was the other way around and I had taken you both down into the depths of the world with me. If I had been able, I'm sure that I would have fought with myself over the accusations that I was making and the conclusions to which I was coming. And the only realization that I ever really came to was that a man makes his own decisions and it doesn't do any good to go about blaming half the world for your misfortunes. And so, starting from that prime reason, I began the long climb back into the world.

I saw Darren every other week or so. It turned out that he had grown up in Almira, just over the southern hills from Collins, though he was practicing in the city where the bigger cases were to be found. He knew of your family, and it seems that his brother might have played football with old Joby once upon a time. Anyhow, he told me that he was trying to get my sentence commuted to time served, but that the prosecutor who had come down from the city was pushing for at least six months' additional time. It appeared that he had political ambitions just like they all do, and he didn't want to appear soft on crime, especially as I had messed with the law by breaking into that lot and taking my truck. I listened to Darren when he told me, but I was dealing with weightier problems right then, what with my nightly battles against myself, and I had the feeling that it might all be coming to some good, and it seemed to me that maybe another six months might just about get me right. But I gave Darren the encouragement that I knew he wanted to hear and told him to keep on plugging away for a commuted sentence and then I went back to considering how I was the lowest scum that ever walked God's green earth and how in the hell I was going to pull myself up by my bootstraps after all that I had lost.

As the trial date approached and it didn't look like a deal was going to be done, I got nervous thinking that I didn't know what I was going to say to you at the courthouse. Well, that's not quite true, I was planning to tell you that I was truly sorry for all that I had done and that I accepted all that was about to befall me. But then it didn't matter, because when I showed up, you and little Danny were nowhere to be found. It wasn't until later that they told me that you had taken him down to Virginia to your cousins' place to leave all that I had done behind you and start again. I should've known that you'd find the right way through my mess for our boy, and I'm damn proud of you for having the strength to stand up and do it. No one would tell me the name of your cousins or the town, nor have they to this day, that's how much love there is about these parts for you and little Danny. And while I wish I could have made this plea in person, I understand why that's not possible after all the pain that I caused, and I respect that all of them in Collins and East Angler too love you as I love you and have only your interests at heart.

Judge Eustace Miller was a wide body, even at sixty, and it seemed like he'd been meant to play offensive line in his younger years. He was cue-ball bald at the top of his head, which was fringed with black hair about the sides in a horseshoe. He had those hanging jowls that you might associate with his kind, and to me he looked just exactly like fat Horace was going to look in another dozen years, and I wondered if it wasn't some sort of prerequisite for the law. He had a booming voice that read out the list of charges that seemed like it was never going to come to an end. But it did. Then he addressed the prosecutor by name and asked if he was ready to begin. The prosecutor stood—he was a tall, rich, politician-looking fellow of about thirty-five, and he pointed to me as he spoke to the twelve members of the jury to his right, and for the first time I noticed that they were all staring directly at me and trying to figure out whether I was the evil scoundrel that they all expected me to be. I didn't know any of them by name, but I recognized some of their faces. The town wasn't that big that they'd be able to get twelve people on the jury that didn't know me at least by sight or reputation.

He delivered his opening statement and it was theatrical in all the right ways. He told the jury that I was the most evil, drunken devil that had ever walked the streets of East Angler, that, while in an inebriated state, I had assaulted my wife and broken her jaw and forced her to leave town, that I had taken my own three-year old son on a drinking binge that ended when we were both discovered at five o'clock in the morning covered in excrement on the floor of old Joby's barn. He said he had doctors that were going to tell them how my drunken negligence had caused my boy to be permanently disfigured. Then he said that, drunk yet again after I'd been set free on bail, I had broken into the impound lot and stolen my truck—which was being held as evidence—using it to go and fight with my brother-in-law, who was housing his sister at the time. He said that he had witnesses for all of this and more, that I hadn't even denied the charges, and had admitted them in most cases. It was an open and shut case, he said, and they should have the members of the jury home before lunch the following day if he did his job right and they did theirs.

Then young Darren got up. He was nervous, and he stumbled a bit, but he cleared his throat, leaned on down into the jury box, and he said,

"Those were some harsh words from Mr. Cantrell, who came all the way down here from the city. And I'm not even gonna tell you that they're untrue, because for the most part they are. But what I am gonna tell you, folks, is that you know this boy. He's one of your own, born and bred here in East Angler. And like a lot of you, he hasn't had it easy. He lost his father only two years ago, a man from whom he was estranged and never got the chance to make things right. And he's lost his arm and his baseball career, partially as a result of his own infirmities—nobody's gonna argue with that—but a double blow to his young life just the same. And now he's lost his wife and son, all through the excess of the bottle, a bottle that he's sworn off now and forevermore. He is, in all honesty and frankness, your very own prodigal son, a boy who had lost his way and now comes back to you for a second chance."

And he continued on to list the weaknesses in the prosecutor's case—that they didn't have any evidence of an intent to harm and that even little Danny had said that he stayed with me of his own free will and a whole load of legal mumbo-jumbo that I didn't understand then and still don't—but I saw the faces of those jury members soften toward me after what he said about the hard times I had been through, and I knew that the prosecutor saw them too, as he sat scowling away at the table and shaking his head slightly with each point young Darren made against him.

When Darren was done, the prosecutor got all formal and stood and cleared his throat.

"May it please the court, Your Honor, the prosecution calls Mr. Joseph Danner to the stand."

Now there was so much going on at the time that I hadn't even seen old Joby sitting not five rows behind me along with the rest of the public and the local press. It was near as much a shock to see him dressed in a shirt and tie as I'm sure it was to see me in chains. But he strode on up to the witness box and the bailiff read out the oath and Joby said he would and he sat down. He was a bit nervous, which I could tell right off because I saw him nibbling at the inside of his cheek like he does when he's out of Copenhagen and can't take the time to run to the store for another tin. He looked down at me and where I thought I'd see hatred, I saw only confusion, and truth be told I didn't know what I was in for, I only knew that he'd tell the truth as he always does.

"Mr. Danner," the prosecutor said to him after the introductories, "will you please tell the members of the jury about the events of December eighteenth last, beginning with the call from your sister?"

And Joby went right into it, just as if he was reading a script, telling them that Sarah had called him screaming that I was drunk and had hit her and there was blood and I had taken little Danny only God knows where. And there wasn't any detail that the prosecutor left unturned or old Joby left unsaid, from the state that he found you in to the calls to the police to the hours of searching through two counties that night and finally to what he found in the barn that next morning. And he finished up with the cold soaking that he gave me in the milk house just before he handed me over to Sheriff Haney.

With every word, I felt myself sinking lower in my seat, withering like a flower in the dog days of August before the gaze of those members of the jury that were constantly looking from old Joby to my face for a reaction to what was being said. He was right, of course, right in every detail, and hearing it spoken so made me think that jail was precisely the place that a monster like me belonged. I even leaned over to say something to young Darren to that effect before he shushed me and continued scribbling notes on his big yellow pad. And when the prosecutor had asked his last question, Darren fairly jumped over the table to get at old Joby.

"Good morning, Mr. Danner," he said, "I have just two questions for you. But I want you to take your time and answer in the most complete manner that you know how. After all, it's a man's liberty that's at stake here. Can you do that?"

Old Joby said that he could.

"Mr. Danner, do you believe that Mr. Higgins loves your sister and their boy?"

Old Joby looked at his shoes for a bit, and for the first time I noticed that they weren't the usual shit kickers that he wore about the farm, but a nice new pair of black Buster Browns, that still had

155

the shine of the store shelf on them. When he looked back at young Darren, everyone in the courtroom could see that his eyes were full of depth and understanding. And so he spoke.

"Well … Lem has been a part of our family for going on five years now, and I don't think there's a day that he was in town in all that time that he didn't spend it among us as a brother and a husband and a father. So I've seen my share of kisses and private moments between them, and I think that Lem here loves his wife and his boy both in every way that he knows how. That don't excuse what he's done, of course, not to Sarah nor to little Danny neither. Whether you pour milk into a broken cup or pour it right up over the rim of a solid one, you still end up with milk all over your floor. And that's what I think about old Lem—he don't know how to reconcile his love with the loss of his father and all of his dreams that were laid low not so very long ago. He did the wrong thing and turned to the drink, and maybe he has his father to thank for that. But it wasn't a lack of love that led him to be sitting here in this courtroom today, that much I can say for certain."

Young Darren was watching the reaction among the jury and nodded slightly in satisfaction, it seemed to me, as he noted the further softening in their eyes at what Joby had said. I saw that the prosecutor was looking over that way too, but his expression was more stern and I knew he didn't like what he was seeing. Darren turned back to old Joby and continued.

"Do you think that he's paid for his sins, Joby?" he says.

"I ain't the one to judge, counselor. I think you'd have to ask that of my sister, Sarah, or little Danny, or of God himself. But I will say that I've seen Lem lose a lot over the past year, maybe more than any man I've known. First there was his old man, then his career in baseball, then there was the arm and all the normal

156

abilities that went along with it, and to that you have to add the estrangement from my sister and his little boy. Truth be told, if you put old Lem away for another six years, I'm not sure that will even make the top five worst things that have happened to him recently. So, has he paid? He's paid with darn near everything he's got. Does that mean he's forgiven? Well, not by me and surely not by Sarah. But do I personally want to see him put away, well … the answer to that question is no. I think he's had just about as much as a man can take in one lifetime. If ever he's gonna pick up the pieces of his life, it'll be now."

There wasn't any mistaking the teary-eyed gazes of almost all those in the jury box then, and I thought I heard the prosecutor swear softly under his breath. He asked for a recess to prepare his next witness and young Darren took off behind him as he stomped out of that courtroom. Judge Miller asked the jury to file out during the recess and they all stepped past me, looking into my eyes for some indication of whether Joby had spoken the truth. I was left alone to ponder old Joby's words that had stung me to the core. It wasn't the thought of going to jail that affected me—old Joby was right that I was basically numb to it at that time—it was the thought that you would never forgive me, Sarah. And all of a sudden my throat clenched and the sobs welled up in me and I doubled over to let it out as silent as I could.

They came back in after five minutes and as soon as the jury was seated, the prosecutor stood to call his next witness. But then he didn't.

"May it please the court, Your Honor, the prosecution has offered to recommend a sentence of time served, with six months suspended sentence, and two years of probation. The defense has accepted."

I looked at young Darren and he gave me a wink and I asked him if that meant that I could go home. He shushed me and told me to listen to the judge, who was about to render the verdict and my sentence. And so he did. Looking down at me from on high, with his hanging jowls flapping with every word that he spoke, with a fire in his eyes, and with spittle flying down from his bench on the tiled floor beneath, Judge Miller told me that the bond between a man and a wife was a sacred one and that the blood tie between a man and his son was the most basic connection in all of nature and humanity. For breaking that bond, I had lost the love of both my wife and my son, which is penalty enough for any man. But I had broken the law as well, and that was his concern. He looked me squarely in the eyes and I hunched up my shoulders, thinking that he was about to unleash the furies on me, but he humphed hard and gave his great head a shake and told the courtroom that he'd accept the prosecutor's recommendation.

"But, Mr. Higgins," he said, shaking a fat finger down at me for emphasis, "if you ever darken my bench again for any reason, I will be sure to give you the maximum penalty allowable under the law."

I nodded my head and thanked him most humbly, calling him "Your Honor" and telling him that he wouldn't never hear from the likes of me again. And I meant it.

And there was the bang of a gavel and it was over just like that. I thanked Darren for all the good work he'd done on my behalf. He explained all about the restrictions of the parole and how I'd have to report to a parole officer, and I shook his hand, and he walked away as proud as ever walked any peacock dressed in a three-piece suit. And after a while, I was left alone on the courthouse steps, still a broken man, but free once again.

And for the first time in over four years, I took a full, sober breath of the clean spring air that comes down off the hills of East Angler in March and squinted up into a cloudless blue sky. I didn't want to waste a moment of my newfound life, and I vowed with the most solemn promise that a man can make to himself to pick up the pieces and fly straight. I knew that you were out of reach to me at the time, and you wouldn't have spoken to me even if it hadn't been so, and that was what I could expect for some time to come, if not forever. But I saw that old Joby still believed in me, and I knew that he was among the first bricks that had to be set in my long road back.

But I didn't go to Joby at first. Instead, I went to my father's grave up on Vermont Hill Road, where I gathered a handful of budding pussy willows from the edge of the cemetery and tied them together with a piece of birch bark and laid them on his grave and spoke to him for the first time in almost five years.

"It's me, old man," I said, staring down at the plain stone set into the ground at my feet. "I guess you probably know about all I've been through lately. Well, I had a good long time to think about all that passed between us, and I want you to know that I forgive you for all that you did and all the you left undone and all that was said and left unsaid and I apologize for my own part in it all, which wasn't so small either."

I paused for a moment and I felt the warmth of the sun on my back and shoulders as it peeked through the clouds above and I heard the rustle of the branches as the wind played over the newly-awakened birch and oak and maple that stood like sentinels over that cemetery day and night, and I saw the tears that came leaking from my eyes splash down onto the marble stone beneath.

"The truth of it is that I didn't know you back then, old man. I didn't know your pain in losing little Colleen and Ma and all of the dreams that you had built around them. I couldn't know it then as I know it now and so I couldn't give you my hand and for that I'm truly sorry..."

I was breathing hard and the words were pouring out of me in great gasps. I wiped the tears away with the back of one hand and settled on down to business.

"But I need to ask your help now, old man. And you know what I'm asking. You abandoned me and them during your life and so I figure it's only fair to ask you to watch over them now that you're good and dead. You bring them back to me if you can, but you watch over them even if you can't and after that I'd say that we're even. How's that sound to you?"

I didn't get an answer, of course. We hadn't said two words to each other in five years and I didn't expect him to turn all chatty on me now. But I felt good for having asked and it seemed as if the world about me felt the better for it too. A warm breeze picked up from down the hill and turned the pussy willows on his grave and I felt a part of the burden lift from my shoulders. I felt his forgiveness within me too, and I knew that I was on the right path. And I have to admit that he's kept his part of the bargain because there you both are safe down in Virginia. And I thank him and God truly for that simple fact.

I returned to his house before dark, where I found the same mess that I had left, plus a kitchen full of critters that had moved in again while I was in prison. Strangest of all, I found a family of raccoons living large in the space underneath the kitchen sink, and I had a hell of a time chasing them out of there and into the open air, them snarling and hissing at me all the way. There wasn't any electricity, so I set about gathering candles. And while the light still held, I opened all the windows and doors and began to give that house a top to bottom spring cleaning like it hadn't had since my mother had passed near on twenty-three years before. I went from room to room, piling trash in the corners and sweeping out all the critter shit and dust and broken glass of that long stretch.

I piled anything that was flammable and non-toxic next to the wood burning stove, knowing that I was in for some cold nights until I could get the electricity turned back on. And I piled up several dozen empty bottles in a box on the front porch, dumping the contents of any that were still half-full right there on the front yard. When I got done I was pretty near certain that there wasn't a drop of alcohol in the entire place. In the late afternoon, I walked the two miles into town to the Red & White to get a smattering of groceries with the little cash the state had given me when I was discharged and some extra candles for the long, dark night ahead. When I got back, I peeled the label from a can of chili, poked a couple of holes in the top, and set it in the fire to cook. After I had fished out every last bean, I washed out that can and mixed in some instant coffee, which I set to heat on the top of the stove. I spent that evening stretched out on my father's mattress, recently beaten clean out in the front yard by my own two hands, and I felt that the place was my own, and I decided right then that I wouldn't sell it, at least not right away.

Old Bill Haney had given me the schedule of the local chapter of Alcoholics Anonymous that met in the basement of St. Mary's on Main Street, so I made the long walk back into town the next morning to sit and listen to others like me that had thrown away the good in their lives on account of the bottle. I was surprised to see a number of familiar faces in there, faces from school and afterwards, and I'd tell you all about them if I could, but I can't, and it isn't my place anyhow. I didn't say much that first meeting and I wouldn't for a couple of weeks yet, but it was a comfort to know that there were others out there battling the same demons, and I kept coming back week after week. I haven't been out there in a good while now on account of the sickness, which I'll get to, but it ain't for lack of want, and there are some of them that'll stop by every now and again to lend me a bit of support.

When I had made it through my first meeting, and I was buoyed by my planned return to a sober and productive life, I made my way over to the sheriff's office, where my truck was waiting for me. Sheriff Haney asked me how it felt to be a free man, and I told him that I was learning to appreciate the little things about life all over again. He looked me in my eyes, nodded his head, wished me well, and handed me the keys to the truck.

"You'll find her out back," he said to me, "but don't go getting into any more trouble, Lem. This town has only so much compassion, and I get the sense that you're right up against the limit."

I thanked him and told him that he didn't have to worry about me none. I had only one goal in life and that was to make amends for all that I had done to you and little Danny, even if that meant that I never saw either of you again. Like a dozen others, he told me that you had headed on down to Virginia to be with your cousins after all that had happened, and that I should just leave you be. I nodded agreement. I knew that you were out of my reach just then, but your brother Joby wasn't. I thanked old Bill again and headed out the door to reclaim my life.

The truck turned right over. I saw that it didn't have but an eighth of a tank of gas, and my means were severely limited at that moment, but it was enough to get me over the hills to the farm, and that was the only destination that I had in mind anyway. I stopped by the Red & White again and spent what little I had on bread and peanut butter and crackers and tuna fish to last me a week. I stopped by the house to grab some old blankets and a pillow out of the closet, and then I was on those familiar roads that wound up and over the hills to Collins.

I didn't feel that I had any right to be on that farm anymore, given all that had happened there and between us. And I knew that there was a good chance that Joby would tell me to get the hell out of there and never come back, a rejection that I just wasn't willing to chance at that moment. And so, I parked across the street from the driveway and turned off the engine and just sat in the cab staring out at the farmhouse and the smoke pouring out of the chimney above and over the muddy fields behind. Devon saw me as soon as I pulled up. He was sixteen then and half a head taller than Joby, who poked his head out of the barn not two minutes later. I waved a tentative hand at him, but he wasn't interested and turned back to the barn, calling Devon on in after him. And it was as I expected, so I sat back and switched on the radio and made myself a peanut butter sandwich to wait out his anger for a chance to apologize.

I slept in the cab that night, covering myself with the blankets as best I could in the chill of the March air. I ran the engine at intervals, just to get myself warmed up and not catch pneumonia while I was doing my penance and waiting out Joby's feelings about me. The next day, I watched him and Devon walk to the barn in the dark of the early morning, lit only by the spotlight over the door to the farmhouse. They must have gone back and forth half a dozen times that day, and each time I saw Devon point to me from the shadow of the barn and old Joby shake his head. I slept in the cab that night too. And the one that followed that. And on the fourth day, I ran out of both food and gas, and I was starting to think that I'd have to give up on the waiting and go begging for one or the other at the door. Just as I was practicing my apologies, I heard a knock on the window and Devon's face was there, the hint of a scraggly mustache about his upper lip. He smiled and motioned to me to roll down the window. He was tall and growing broad about the shoulders and you could tell that he was coming on to being a man.

"Hey Lem," he said, "welcome back."

I said I wasn't at all sure that I was welcome, now that he mentioned it.

"You just keep on, Lem. He loves you like a brother, he does. And sooner or later, he'll let you back in. Just stick it out. In the meantime, he says that I can ask you if you need anything out here."

I told him that I was out of food and gas both, but I needed the food more as I didn't have no plans on going nowhere. He winked at me and ran off to the farmhouse, returning not five minutes later with a picnic basket full of sliced roast beef and bread. And when he told me that Celia had set it aside last night for me, I knew that their hearts were still open to me, if only the tiniest crack.

"You just keep on, Lem," Devon said to me again as he ran back towards the barn. "It won't be long now."

It was Devon that woke me too the next morning, when I found him pouring a three-gallon can of gas into the tank of the truck. When he was done, he hopped into the passenger seat and handed me a plastic bag that had containers of rice and beans and even some oatmeal that was still warm. I thanked him and told him that I was sorry for all that I had put his family through. He still had the resilience of a child then and he told me that he knew it and that he thought I'd be okay so long as I stayed away from the whiskey. And I told him that I would, come what may. Then he asked me to show him some finger holds for his curve and slider and he told me that he was at the top of the rotation for varsity that year. I could see all the dreams of a kid in his big, brown eyes and they took me back years and made me miss you so bad that my guts ached. Finally, Celia came to the door of the farmhouse and called out to him. I stepped out of the cab and stood in the street and waved to her and thanked her for the food and watched her incline her head in response. It wasn't a greeting, but it was an acknowledgement of my being, which is more than I'd gotten from her or Joby in more than a week.

I had to report to my parole officer the next morning, so I made the trip back over the hills to East Angler, where I checked in first on the house to make sure that none of those critters had moved back in. All seemed in order and I drove downtown to see the parole officer in his office that was adjacent to Sheriff Haney's. He was a good old boy and told me that I could call him for support any time of the day or night. I thanked him and took his number and then I rolled right into an AA meeting at St. Mary's right about noon and recharged my determination. And so I wasn't back at my post before the farmhouse until near on two o'clock that afternoon.

Joby's truck wasn't in the driveway when I got back, and I thought that he must have been out at the feed store or maybe checking on the condition of the outer fields, and so I sat back and waited as I had become accustomed to doing over that week. I saw a black car parked down the road a piece in front of the old Hamil place, and I thought maybe they were having a party or it was their little boy's First Communion or they were letting someone hunt pheasant up back behind their house or some such thing, so I didn't pay much attention to it at first. Then, just as I settled back into place and made myself a tuna sandwich out of the supplies that I brought from the Red & White, I saw a shadow skirt around the corner of the farmhouse. It wasn't like Joby or Devon or Celia to be sneaking about their own place, and the fact that there weren't any cars in the drive made me nervous. I saw him come out from behind the house then and stand with a circular red object in his hands, then he stuck it between his knees and scribbled in a little black notebook that he pulled from his jacket pocket.

I was out of the truck now, and the slamming of the door caused him to look back across the road toward me. Then I saw him winding up that tape measure in his hands and he began to walk quickly toward the woods. I yelled to him and this only caused him to pick up the pace until he was fairly running behind the barn and across the fields toward the sugar bush. Well, I had been sober for almost three months at that point, and those extra pounds that I had put on from the drink were just coming off me like the butter that they were, and it didn't take me but three or four minutes of running over those furrows to bring the guy down by his collar. He threw up his hands like he thought I was going to go to beating him right there in the middle of the field.

"Don't," he said to me, "it's just my job. I don't have anything to do with it."

I asked him what in the hell he was talking about, and he blinked up at me through his forearms like he couldn't tell whether or not to trust me quite yet. I asked him again what the hell he was doing there, and he told me plain out that he was surveying. And when I took him in he looked like a surveyor—khaki pants over boots that didn't have a scuff on them, with an orange vest over a white sweatshirt, and round spectacles through which he squinted at me from eyes that were set too close together over a pointy nose and thin lips. He couldn't have been more than five and a half feet standing on his tiptoes.

"Like for the Town of Collins or something?" I asked stupidly.

It sometimes takes me a minute to catch on.

"No," he said looking at me like I was an idiot, and I admit that I deserved it, "it's for Cooperative Foods. They've got me surveying half a dozen farms out here that they're foreclosing on next week. But I ain't got nothing to do with it, I tell you."

He paused and raised his arms again like he expected me to rain blows down on top of him for being a simpering tool of Cooperative Foods. I could tell that he'd been in this situation before and had come out of it with a particular distaste for the scuffle that must have ensued. Then, as we were sitting there in the middle of the north field and I was thinking what in the hell to do with him, I heard the crunch of tires on gravel and turned to see Joby's truck pulling up into the drive. Devon was riding in the passenger seat and I could see the wolf-like silhouette of Woodchuck in between them. Joby saw us right off and cocked his head to one side as he stared at us through the windshield. I pulled the surveyor to his feet and told him to follow me on back to the farmhouse before he lost his way and starved to death in those woods. He looked at me uncertain and I knew he was thinking that he should take his chances in the cold forest, but I repeated the command and he followed along like a wounded dog behind me.

As we got up toward the drive, I saw Joby turn and say something to Devon, who disappeared into the farmhouse behind. It'd been a good bit since I'd had a conversation with Joby, but it didn't seem right to get into all that I had to say, what with this stranger following along behind me and the bomb that he was about to drop on him.

"What say, Joby?" I said as we got within a few paces.

"Hey, Lem," he said in reply and nodded toward the stranger. "Who's that you got there?"

And I told him how I saw this little man sneaking about the house with a tape measure and finally ran him down up in the north field, where he got to shaking like a leaf.

"Mr. Danner, I have nothing to do with this, sir. I'm only doing my job …," he stammered and trailed off as he saw the door open and Devon come on down the stairs with Joby's shotgun in his hands.

"Oh, I know who you are, Mr. Sampson. There ain't an independent farmer within fifty miles of here that don't know who you are by now. And I hear Jack Miller gave you a good beating when he found you slinking about his place last week, ain't that right?"

The little man shuddered at the memory and kept his eyes firmly fixed on the shotgun that was changing hands. Old Joby wasn't angry, at least not that you could tell, and he kept his voice down low and soft and matter of fact, like he was in complete control of himself and the situation. He spat a stream of tobacco juice at the little man's feet.

"Now, I'm not a violent man, Mr. Sampson, and I realize that this is just your job. But I want you to consider that this isn't just my house nor is this farm just my place of work. You come nosing about around here and you might just as well be feeling up my wife or—in your case—making improper advances toward my young son here in the men's lavatory. So, whether it's your job or not doesn't really matter to me one bit."

As he said this last, he shouldered the shotgun and pointed it down the road at the black sedan that sat off to the shoulder near the Hamil place and pulled the trigger. Sampson jumped about a foot in the air and let out a little squeal. The windows of the car shattered with the impact of the birdshot and the air hissed out of the back tire that was closest to us. Old Woodchuck was still in the cab of Joby's truck and he set about barking and growling and pawing at the door to get out and into the fray. Meanwhile, Mr. Sampson covered his face with his hands and sank to his knees, and I believe that he was seriously prepared to meet his Maker right there on old Joby's driveway. But your brother isn't like that, as you well know. He picked the little man up by his elbow and led him out to the end of the property.

"Now you be sure to tell those boys at Cooperative Foods about the reception that you got when I found you out here trespassing over my property. And you let them know straight from my mouth that I won't hesitate to shoot them right in their tiny peckers and miniature ball sacks if I ever catch them out here. And the same goes for you, Mr. Sampson. I'm a merciful man, but my patience has been sorely tried by those boys, and I'm not sure how much longer my sweet nature is going to win out. Now get the hell off my goddamn farm."

When old Joby let go of that man's elbow, it was like a gate had risen out at the horse track and Sampson sprang from that spot and started running at top speed down the road toward the town center. Joby took aim with the shotgun once again, and I thought for a moment that he meant to hit the poor bastard, but when I heard the birdshot rain down on the yellow curve-approaching sign on the other side of the road, I knew that he just meant to goose the man a bit. And it worked too, as Sampson fairly doubled his speed and disappeared into the dip down the road, still running all out.

I half-expected Joby to be smiling when he turned back, but he wasn't, and the full impact of what had transpired hit me then. Joby was about to lose that farm. He looked old to me for the very first time since I had known him—the lines in his face deeper, the bags beneath his eyes darker, and the sorrow in his expression more profound than any I've seen before or since. He looked at me, and I could tell that he had no energy for the emotional exchange that we were due to have, so I cut it short.

"I'll help, Joby. You don't have to pay me or nothing. I owe you more than I can ever repay anyhow. But I'll stay sober and you can put me to do anything you like. I ... I just want to help, that's all."

He looked at me for a moment, then spit a stream of tobacco juice to the side. Then he nodded his head and started on back toward the house. He took Devon by the shoulder and led him up the stairs of the front porch, where he stepped inside. Devon followed along behind, pausing at the threshold of the door just long enough to holler back to me.

"Nice to have you back, Lem."

And they were gone.

TWELFTH BEQUEST

There's really not very much that's left to give away. But old Doc Tyler raised something in a private moment of absolute honesty a few days back. He's always talking about all the research that they're doing over at Mercy and around the world trying to find a cure for AIDS like they said they would over a year ago now, and though I always pictured myself as a beneficiary of that research rather than a contributor, I had to admit that old Doc was only being logical in what he was suggesting. I certainly don't need this inflated bag of pus and infection where I'm going, and if he thinks that it can aid in the effort back here on earth, well then they can have at it. On one condition, I told him. If he can keep me breathing and half-conscious long enough to see this letter through, well then he and his buddies can have this broken body of mine to do all the cutting and poking and prodding that they can stomach, and when they're done they can give the pile of bones and meat that's left over to Joby for a proper burial. We both knew that I wouldn't hold him to it. But still Old Doc nodded and told me that we had a deal and then the darkness of the topic settled down on top of us and I think we both spent that afternoon feeling hollow inside over what was said.

Anyhow, the day after Joby chased little Mr. Sampson down Hampton Holmwood Road and just about made the poor son of a bitch mess his pants, I returned to my father's house to pick up a few changes of clothes and personal items. I didn't even ask to sleep in the farmhouse, knowing full well that I was going to have to go some distance to win back the trust of Joby and Celia before they'd treat me like they used to. And so, I set myself up in that little corner of the milk house that always seemed to have my name on it, the same corner that had seen me curled up and sobbing as Joby washed me down only three months before. It wasn't the most comfortable of accommodations, I realized now that I was sober, but Celia let me up to the house to take a hot shower every couple of days and it felt good to suffer the lingering cold of that March, like I was doing my penance, which I took to mean by extension that there might be a period of forgiveness at some point in the future.

Old Joby talked to me plain and simple that next day and told me that, aside from all the requirements of the State of New York, there were going to be two inviolable rules to my conditional parole in the House of Danner. He gathered up Celia and Devon as witnesses and made me swear them both on the family Bible, the same book that he'd read from when your father passed. First, I swore that I would stay sober, meaning no drink and no drugs unless they were prescribed by Doc Tyler no matter how much my bad arm was hurting or how sick I got sleeping in the cold out in the milk house. And second, and the more difficult of the two, I swore that I wouldn't go snooping around or asking about the whereabouts of you and little Danny.

"If she's ever gonna speak to you again, Lem, and I have my doubts that she will," Joby said, putting emphasis on the last part, "she'll do so in her own good time. She and Danny have got more healing to do than you have a right to understand, and so I want you to leave them alone. You hear me? Good, now swear it."

And I did. I kept the first promise day in and day out from the time that my hand touched that Bible to this very moment, though I admit it's a bit difficult to claim that I'm any sort of drug free when I'm so pumped full of morphine that I could probably stab myself through the arm with this pencil and not feel a thing. And I kept the second promise for as long as I could, which was a good many months, until I felt that I was becoming part of the family again, when I started asking Celia on the sly if she actually thought I had put an end to our marriage or if she saw some way of our coming back together. She didn't ever answer me straight and still hasn't for more than three years now. Her response is always the same.

"All that you can do Lem is continue to fly straight and put your trust in the Lord."

Though they'd taken me back on the farm, Joby and Celia remained distant with me for a good while yet, which is what I expected, but Devon and I picked up right where we had left off. In fact, I'd venture to say that we were better friends after those several months in jail than before. It seemed almost that the kid had grown up in the time that I was gone, and I could see the dreams of an adult deep set behind the flat marble of those eyes that he took straight from Joby. It was a difficult time for him, what with the upheaval that I'd caused and Cooperative Foods sitting like a hungry wolf just outside the chicken coop and ready to break in and tear it all to hell as soon as Joby's back was turned, and I got the feeling that the kid sometimes felt lost between the cracks of all that was going on and was looking to me, of all people, for some guidance.

Devon had just gotten his driver's license, which wasn't as momentous as it might have been for another kid his age, given that he had been driving old Joby's tractors all about the farm and even into town to the feed store since he was about ten years old. But a license meant real freedom and, given the difficulties that were being endured on the farm at that particular point in time, he didn't mean to waste a moment of it.

Over the course of two weeks in early April, he and I fixed up an old Chrysler Newport that he bought off a neighbor for fifty bucks that was just about falling to pieces. He didn't care—to him it was a regular Bentley just off the assembly line in old England—and he gave me a bear hug so tight when that old bucket first turned over that I thought he might crack a rib. And so, with plastic bags over the broken windows and a piece of plywood over the gaping hole in the floor, Devon drove in and out of the farm at least five times a day, running off to see various friends, occasionally getting into trouble, and just looking for some interesting way to spend the energy that's pent up inside any sixteen-year old boy that's looking for some way to define himself.

I remember that there was one day later that April when we were milking the heifers under the harsh fluorescent bulbs of the milking hall while a warm spring dawn crept in through the open windows and Devon told me about a girl named Corinne that he had been seeing from over in Aurora.

"There's just something about her, Lem. She's not the most beautiful girl in the world ... I mean ... that's not to say that she's not beautiful, because she is, but there are others that are better looking. But she's fearless, man, and she gets me. And when I spend time with her I feel like I want to jump around and dance. It's like when we're together, we're both right there and not nowhere else ... not even in our minds ... and it's like that even if we're not doing nothing, just sitting together on her mother's couch or parked outside the movies or just about any damn thing. There's just that something about her and about us together."

When I heard him it was like hearing my own voice piped through a loudspeaker over the intervening five years from the time just after we met, Sarah. The kid wanted to spend every waking moment over at Corinne's mother's house and he had even taken to picking the girl up after school when there wasn't any baseball practice. And the truth hit me like a pair of lightning bolts that fell right out of the sky. First, I could tell by the careful choice of his words and the gleam in his eyes that he was making love to this little girl that couldn't have been more than sixteen. That fact alone explained some of the change that I saw in him, I thought, as he was coming to understand some of the ways of the world. And second, I realized that the little girl that I had pictured in my head couldn't have been much younger than you were when we first came together and took on the life of adults before we were meant to do so and brought about the birth of little Danny. And while Devon had taken on some of the characteristics of an adult, in most ways he too was still just a child making big decisions and not fully understanding the potential consequences of them. And so were we, I thought. So were we.

Well, of course I gave him the best advice that I could and told him to be careful and even talked in general terms about what had happened between the two of us, not wanting to make him cringe by telling him too much about his aunt's love life. And I think he heard me, and he thanked me for the advice, and I started to think that maybe I was cut out for some of the life of a parent after all. Devon was a good kid with a kind heart and, more than Joby even, he remained my friend through the good and the bad times, and I loved him just as if he had been my own little brother. And looking back on it now, I think that there was some base wisdom in his young soul that let him see beyond the mess of knots and trouble that we sometimes created for ourselves, or I created for us both, to focus in on all that was good and solid and right in us.

And where I had failed you and, in many respects, Joby and Celia as well, I tried to stay consistent with Devon at least and show him that I deserved his friendship. I never did tell any of his secrets, and I figured that that's how old Joby would have wanted it as well, as he never could stand a snitch himself. Gradually, I think Devon came on to trust me as a brother too. He brought Corinne around to meet the family not too long after our conversation in the milk house. She was a petite girl, much like you, with small breasts and just the barest hint of a curve to her hips, which confirmed my impression that she was still mostly just a girl. Her hair was brown and she wore it long, and she had bright blue eyes that peered out from a face that was attractive even if the features were set just a pinch too close together. As soon as we were introduced, she jumped up and planted a kiss on my cheek so quick and sweet that I knew the kid was right. The energy about that little girl was infectious.

After he had made the introductions, Devon announced that they were headed down toward Johnson's Falls to see if the water wasn't warm enough to swim, though the last snowfall was only six weeks behind us then. Well, just about the whole room exchanged glances then and each one of them was full of meaning. Corinne looked at Devon and I could see the corners of her mouth turn up for just a split second as they shared what I'm sure was a common picture of the two of them rolling together on the mossy bank of that creek or entwined in the pool beneath the falls if they could stand the cold of that spring water. And Joby looked at Celia as if to communicate to her that their little boy was growing up too fast but that there wasn't a damn thing that he or they could do about it. And I looked at Devon and pinched my eyebrows together to tell him to remember our conversation and be safe in all that I knew that they were doing then and about to do. And Corinne realized that just about everyone in the room knew what they were up to and shifted nervously and looked toward the ground. And though time seemed to stop then and an uncomfortable silence fell over the room, the moment eventually passed, and Corinne looked back up and said how wonderful it was to meet everyone and that she'd stop by to say her goodbyes before she left that evening. And the happiness in their eyes as he walked her out the door made everything about them warmer and brighter, including us.

Though he was focused on Corinne like a laser, Devon's life had grown in other ways as well. All those afternoons that we had spent throwing the ball around behind the barn had apparently done the kid some good as he led the rotation on the Collins varsity squad that spring, though he was only a sophomore. He even asked me to pick him up from practice one Saturday that his car was laid up, and I was happy to do so, as I recognized that Joby and Celia were needing to talk about what was going on at the farm, what with Cooperative Foods ready to take advantage of any momentary weakness. When I pulled up to the ball field in the F-100, they were just finishing up a scrimmage, and I watched Devon throw a couple of respectable curveballs from the mound that left the batter cursing at himself and kicking at the dirt on his way back to the dugout.

I threw the truck in park and walked up to the first-base line, where your cousin Owen was coaching. It was the first time that I had seen him in more than a year, which was before the trouble that I'd created for you all. Back then, back before the trouble, he'd always been glad to see me and jumped at the chance to introduce me around as family. Now he saw me coming and looked at the ground and I could see the wheels turning in his mind as to how he should act with me. I watched one fist clench and unclench and recognized the anger that I'd created in him as well.

"I don't know where she's off to, Lem," he said coldly and without turning around when I got to within a few feet of him.

"I'm not here to ask you about her, Owen. I'm just picking up Devon, that's all," I said to try to calm him some. "But I owe you an apology as well, brother. It ain't no secret that I was messed up and I'm sorry for all the pain that I caused."

"That don't make it right," he said just as I heard the clink of the aluminum bat and saw a double drop into the gap between right and center field. Devon cursed on the mound and Owen turned away to wave the runner on to second. He paused for a moment and then turned toward me again once the runner was safely on the bag.

"Look, Lem, not everyone's very happy about you staying with Joby and Celia after what you done, running Sarah and Danny away. And I count myself among them. Now I hope you stay straight and work out all that you need to work out, but I wish you'd do it somewhere else because this family can't take any more."

I was about to tell him that I understood and didn't blame him and all that I wanted in this world was to make it up to those that I had hurt, including him. But the head coach called an end to the scrimmage and Devon yelled for me as he came off the mound, telling me to hold on and that he wanted to introduce me around to his teammates. Owen shook his head and stood sullenly off to one side as I said hello and they asked me if I had really played in the majors and what I had done to get there. I told them that it was hard work and discipline and the scoff that I heard out of Owen at that moment cut me right to the core. But I couldn't blame him. There never was nor ever will be anyone to blame but myself.

The head coach wandered up to the group that was growing about me and introduced himself as Tom Julian and reminded me that he had played third base for Collins along with Owen way back when, meaning that we had faced each other down a handful of times over the years. He said that I had done a hell of a job teaching Devon to throw the curve and that he was among their best pitchers though he was only a sophomore. Then he surprised me by asking if I wouldn't be interested in helping out with the Collins varsity that spring.

"Owen and I can teach the boys batting and fielding, but there's nothing like a major leaguer to teach the pitchers how to throw. We've got a good shot at the state title this year, Lem, and we sure could use the extra help. What do you say?"

I was about to say that I had a couple of projects of my own and that I was honored but that I really couldn't that season but maybe at some time in the future, when Owen jumped back into the conversation and cut me short.

"Lem's got his own issues to deal with right now, Tom," he said loud over the chorus of voices that had jumped in to agree with their coach's proposition, "and we don't need him bringing them here."

The group went silent and it was impossible for me not to recognize that every one of them knew of my problems with the drink and the embarrassment and the damage that I had done to those that I loved most.

"Er ... thanks, Tom, but not this year," I said. "Owen's right. I have myself to work on right now."

"Well you keep us in mind," Tom said kindly and nodded. "Offer's always open."

I thanked him, but the silence settled back over us and turned awkward. The boys that had been so jubilant only a moment ago spit tobacco into the dirt at their feet and scuffed at it with their cleats. I thanked them all for their kindness, wished them the best of luck in the upcoming playoffs, and asked Devon if he was ready. We walked back to the truck in silence. I wasn't used to feeling like I was under someone's heel, especially not on the baseball field, and it was enough to make me thirst for a drink, though I pushed the thought aside almost as soon as it was formed.

I'm sure that it had nothing to do with your cousin Owen or my realization that I was a pariah in your extended family, but that night I took sick and got laid up in bed for the first time since I had left the hospital in Chicago. Devon found me the next morning shivering away under my blankets in the chill of the milk house and Celia insisted that I be moved up to the farmhouse at least until I was feeling better. And if I remember correctly, that was the very first day since we had moved out more than three years before that I spent laid up here in our old room, though I was nearly delirious with the fever and don't remember much of it at all.

And so it was that April that I first noticed the changes in my health that wouldn't fully materialize for some time yet. That I had caught a cold in mid-April wasn't at all unusual, as you well know. Pretty much half the town of East Angler walks about coughing and sneezing and blowing their nose during the changing of the seasons. What was unusual was that it laid me up for two weeks and caused an infection in my lungs and had me taking the strongest antibiotics that Doc Tyler could prescribe. Old Doc took some blood samples then, but he was looking for common viruses and bacteria and he didn't have them tested for AIDS, which had only been discovered the previous year and was still being called the "gay cancer" and "God's gift to the sinners" and other such things. And while I was certainly a sinner, I wasn't that kind of sinner, and consistent with the arc of my life, it would take something greater and more violent to bring that particular truth to light. Anyhow, even after the fevers subsided, I couldn't seem to shake it entirely, and I went about coughing and wheezing for pretty much the whole of that spring. It wasn't until the long, warm days of summer that my lungs got dried out and I returned to some semblance of normal, but by then everything had changed.

THIRTEENTH BEQUEST

Insofar as a man is able to will away his dog, I hereby bequeath old Woodchuck to my son, Daniel Conor Higgins. I didn't deserve him in the first place, but old Joby said that it was only right that I have him given that I helped discover that hole that Devon pulled him out of. And as I'm pretty much all alone these days, I didn't argue. Old Woodchuck's been a friend to your family, Sarah, for as long as I have, and he's acted with a sight more honor and dignity to boot. It's Woodchuck that lies by night at the foot of my bed and sits up and gently paws at me when I'm lost in either dreams or delirium. And if I don't wake up and give him a pat on the head he goes to barking his head off until old Joby or Celia arrive to put things right. He's a hell of a smart dog, and I know he'll make the best of friends for little Danny, just as he's done for Devon and for me.

Well, old Woodchuck would tell you if he could that I've been dreaming more lately and that my dreams are generally about you. It's almost like there's some parallel us that I can tap into once I put the cares and sorrows of this world aside and slide into soft-feathered existence that lives only in my mind. Or maybe that's just the morphine. A near constant stream of the stuff has me more comfortable now, and I'm sleeping more than twelve hours a day, though I'm trying to keep my senses so that I can finally put it all down here for you and Danny. But when I sleep, I generally dream and the dreams have grown sharp, almost as sharp as real life. And because I dream mostly about you, I look forward to them.

And it may seem silly to write it, but I hope against hope that that's the place I'm headed for once all is said and done. If so, I look forward to spending eternity in your arms and if not, well, I guess I'll never know it. Anyhow, it shouldn't be long now.

After the game last night, I had Joby give me another shot, and I slipped into a kind of half-consciousness until my failing body pulled my mind down with it and it wasn't long before you showed up. You and I were part of the bowling tourney out at the East Angler Lanes, and we were bowling against Owen and Jenny for that stupid championship trophy with the green-painted egg on top that they always kept in a glass case out front. Well, it was the final frame and the game was close and I needed to pick up a split that I had left on my second ball, having driven home a strike on the first. I tiptoed up to the line, brought the ball behind my hip and threw it out with all my might thinking that my only hope was to knock the left-most pin against the back wall and out to take down the right. And just as the ball left my hand, I saw that the pin setter was reading the wrong frame and the pin guard came down and we all sat stock still as the ball just trucked full speed on down that lane and plowed into the guard, sending sparks all over the place. The guard came off its hinges and the collision carried it on through the back of the lane, taking those two pins with it and smoking and smoldering like it had just been beaten to death. And the entire Lanes went quiet. It was quite a sight.

I looked over to Owen, who just shrugged his shoulders, took a pull from his beer, and looked back at Sharon that was staffing the shoe-rental counter out front for some reaction. Then the scoreboard clicked over to the tenth frame and registered the spare and declared us the winners. And we all started laughing until we were rolling around on the hardwood floor and just about pissing ourselves.

When we got back under control, you kissed and hugged me tight and then told me that my thumb was bleeding, and I held it up to the light and saw that the blister that I'd been working up all night had finally come apart and the tender skin beneath was torn. The blood was flowing freely and leaving small red freckles on the linoleum floor, so I grabbed a napkin off the side table and went to wrap it up. But as I grabbed at it, it disappeared, and I was left grabbing at the air over and over, trying to figure out where my stupid thumb had got to. When I woke, I found myself sitting straight up in bed, Woodchuck barking his head off, and me grabbing at a thumb that was no longer there. It hasn't been there for more than three years now. But I still felt the sting of that blister, and even the blood slowly running down the hand that isn't there any more either. I don't mind telling you that I didn't get back to sleep after that.

Anyhow, just after Devon first brought Corinne around to meet the family, the rain came down in sheets for about two weeks straight. The creeks were swollen and running over their banks and into the fields, generally making a royal mess of things. Old Joby was cursing up a storm for having to put off the planting while the soil dried out, and he was worried that we were only going to bring in two crops of hay that season instead of the three that we needed. After the incident with Mr. Sampson, Joby knew to a dead certainty that Cooperative Foods had it out for him and for the farm, and if he didn't bring that mortgage current, they were going to foreclose. Losing two weeks of that season to the rain made him think that it wasn't just the forces of capitalism that were arrayed against him but God and Mother Nature too.

But the price of milk crept back up for a week or so, and Joby was able to sell off one of the old balers that his father had bought way back when. It hadn't been used for more than a decade, but it still worked, and Joby wasn't the only one struggling to bring in a crop in the face of threats from Cooperative Foods, and so he got a good little bit for it and was able to come up with the money for another month on the mortgage and so hold off the wolves. But he was just holding on by the skin of his teeth and it seemed if we didn't catch a break soon, those bastards were going to swoop in and close us down. Although I knew they'd send the sheriff out next time, rightly thinking that old Joby wouldn't hesitate to blow their heads clean off if they came to take his farm away for good.

We all did our best to keep it together that spring, but it was impossible not to feel that knife blade that was being held to our throats, and I fear that we all grew a little twisted in one way or another. As I've mentioned, Devon was restless, as a sixteen-year old boy should be, but more so because he sensed an uncertainty and a desperation in his father's manner. I think it was the first time that he sensed weakness in the man that had always seemed a pillar to him. It happens to the best and the worst of us. Or it may be that Devon finally got over the death of his grandfather and decided that life was too fragile not to live for every moment. Or it may be that he was just so juiced up on life and the love of that little girl Corinne that he was out to suck it all up at once. In any case, his restlessness soon turned to recklessness, and I was a witness to it.

Though he seemed to pull away from Joby and Celia with all the troubles at the farm, Devon and I continued to grow closer together as a result of the time that we spent together milking the heifers each morning and his successes on the baseball field. He'd generally bring me up to date on his victories and other new adventures during the milking hour, before the sun came up and when his father wasn't around to disapprove. And I came to understand through his own telling of his life that he was hell bent on showing those around him that he wasn't scared of anything. He was packing on the muscle in those days, his shoulders and back growing wide from spending long hours with that used set of weights that Joby'd bought him for his birthday two years before. And he was the type of kid that would take any dare just to prove that he wasn't one to be messed with. I learned, for example, that our little game of chicken years before wasn't the only one that he'd played, and over the course of that spring I started to notice new dings and dents in the front and side panels of that old Chrysler that we'd fixed up together.

Whether the stories were embellished or not, I don't rightly know, but he had my mouth hanging open on more than one occasion. There was one bright morning in May that I remember in particular.

"You ever been up to Niagara Falls, Lem," he asked me out of the blue. "I mean the big falls on the Canadian side?"

"Yup," I said, working on the udders of big Sheila, who was developing a bit of an infection and needed extra massaging to get the milk flowing into the pipes.

"I swam it last week," he said with a smile, peering around big Sheila's hind quarters to look me in the eye, and I could tell it was the truth. "About a mile above the falls, I did. None of the other guys would dare to do it. Pussies."

And with that, he moved on down the line, squatting beneath the next heifer and turning up the cups to her udders. The pulsing of the vacuum in the tubery running up to the milk house seemed to keep pace with the beating of my heart. Now, Sarah, you know well that it's no joke to swim the Niagara River in any season, much less in the spring when the water is up and still carries a chill and the current can carry you off and over the falls in a heartbeat. A handful of idiots die every year trying the same stupid stunt, their bodies broken into nothingness on the rocks below as thousands of horrified tourists stand with hands and cameras pointed into the churn and tumble of the water. But I held my tongue, reminding myself that I was his friend and not his father.

"It carried me near a half-mile downstream," he continued yelling to me under the bellies of a half-dozen cows. "I could hear the roar of the Falls and see the mist rising from where I pulled up on shore. It took everything I had, Lem, I kid you not. I almost didn't make it. Corinne had to carry me up the bank to the car."

Now I thought about telling Joby, but again I let it pass. It's hard for me to think on it now, hard to know if I might have said something that would have changed the course of things. Part of me thinks that it was just him. Lord knows that the stories I heard about old Joby down at the Village Pub make me believe that playing the daredevil is just a family trait that runs particularly strong in the Danner men. But part of me thinks that the kid was also reaching out for some attention during a hard time and I might have been there to guide him back. But I didn't and it's too late to change that. It gets me to feeling bad even though I know that I don't carry the blame for what happened next. None of us does.

I know you've heard the story and cried over it along with Celia and Joby, but I'll tell it in brief just the same, given that it explains all that came after. He was a good kid and I miss him. It was a Sunday afternoon in May of that year that he disappeared. He'd been hanging about the farm with Corinne and a group of their friends, both male and female. The boys had begun well enough by stacking up some of that old hay in the top of the barn, making room for the cuttings that would be coming in about six weeks down the road. But they cut out about two o'clock when Corinne and the girls pulled up out front. I last saw them headed off to the north fields and, I assumed, to the creek and the swimming holes beyond.

Old Joby and I were putting the finishing touches on a new hay wagon in the barn some two hours later when those two boys came running in the door so out of breath that we couldn't hardly tell what they were trying to get across.

"Devon—" the tall one said and took a gulp of air—"he ain't come up ..."

Old Joby stood straight up and ran past them to the door of the barn and only stopped when he heard the fat one mutter the word, "beaver." Then he changed direction of a sudden and ran into the house and returned with that old shotgun in his hands, fumbling with the shells that he stuck in the pocket of his jeans.

"Where?" was all he asked at first. But not getting a response, he took the tall one by the shirt collar and screamed into his face, "WHERE, GODDAMIT? SHOW ME NOW!"

Joby dragged the kid over to where the four-wheeler was parked just inside the door. He jumped on with that shotgun in his lap and yelled at the kid to get the hell on behind. They were out the door in ten seconds flat, running that machine full bore over the uneven and muddy ground that was just getting ready to be planted. Me and the fat kid lumbered along behind on foot and found the four-wheeler parked at the northern edge of the field about ten minutes later, the engine still idling.

I knew the way down to the beaver dam by heart and could have found it in the dark of night if need be, so I plunged right on

188

ahead and kept yelling at the fat kid behind me to be sure that he could follow my voice. When I reached the shore of the enormous lake that had been created by the beaver among all that runoff, I could see two heads bobbing up and down out near the dome that had been newly built for the beaver kits that were on their way at the time. One was Joby and he was screaming the boy's name each time he came up for air and was pretty near hysterical. The other was Corinne, who didn't say a word but came up to look hopefully at that bank and gulp some air every minute or so before diving beneath the water again around the other side of the dome from Joby.

The tall kid was standing guard above, that old shotgun in his hands. And the two other girls were cowering against a big old maple off to the side, hugging against each other and letting out sobs every now and again as they looked off toward the water. We heard the slap of a tail near the beaver hut and I watched as the tall boy took a hurried aim with the shotgun and fired off a round into the water beyond. I yelled to him to be goddamned careful what he was shooting at knowing that Joby and Corinne both were down there somewhere in the murky depths.

I still didn't have a picture of what had happened to Devon, and I didn't have time to wait for the fat one to catch up, so I grabbed the shotgun from the tall kid and asked him what the hell was going on. He had caught his breath by then and told me that they had seen beaver kits learning to swim just outside the dome and that had caused him to tell Devon about some kid out in Oak Park that had actually raised a beaver as his pet. And so Devon took it as a dare as was his habit and got it into his head that he was going to steal himself a beaver pup from out of that hut and raise it back up at the farm just like he had done with Woodchuck.

On his dive, the kid told me, Devon had found the underwater entrance to the beaver hut and stuck his head up to take a look around, but it was too dark for him to see clear and he turned back. Then he went back a second time after closing his eyes for a few minutes in order to see better in the dark of the hut. And it was that second intrusion that caused the beaver to swarm. He popped up once yelling that they had hold of his leg and then he was gone under again. To their credit, Corinne and both those boys jumped down into the water to try to save him, but he never came up again and the water was too murky to be able to see anything beneath. Despite the danger and what they had just seen, Corinne continued to dive even when the boys climbed back ashore. They found there wasn't any blood in the water, and they thought that maybe Devon had been dragged back into the hut, where at least he could breathe. And so the two boys set to tearing that hut down branch by branch until they had a good hole worked in it and the female beavers scattered with their pups out into the water below. But there was no sign of Devon. It was then that they had come running back to the farm for help.

I got only part of that story in the moment and the rest of it later. But as soon as I understood the half of it, I gave the kid back the shotgun and jumped in alongside old Joby and Corinne, feeling along with my hands and legs under the water for the body that we knew was down there somewhere but prayed had somehow made an escape of it. Joby stayed nearest the hut and I worked my way out along the dam back towards shore. The fat kid finally came lumbering up to us and I yelled at him to start kicking down the dam to let the water drain. And so he set about it. I was a good fifty yards from the hut and treading water beneath me when my foot hit on something softer than wood, but more solid than the mud of that lake. I took a breath and dove down head first to feel along about five feet beneath the top of the dam with my hands. I heard another shot reverberate through the water and my hands fell on denim.

I swallowed hard, then I took hold with both hands and pulled to no avail. Then I set my feet against the dam and pulled back into the water, but the body didn't budge. He was set into that dam as tight as could be. I came to the surface and yelled to Corinne and Joby that I had found him and couldn't break him loose. Old Joby went into a frantic overhand crawl with Corinne coming along behind him and the tall kid came running over, and in a flash they were all beside me. It took all four of us under the water and pulling for all we were worth to wrench the body free. I think old Joby was so shaken that he was pulling with the strength of five men. When we finally got Devon to the surface, we could see that he had been chewed up pretty badly. His clothes were torn to shreds and there were bite marks on his face and along his arms and legs.

Joby was screaming then, and thumping on the chest of his boy, pushing the water out through his mouth and nose. Corinne slumped next to him, exhausted and praying quietly under her breath. Joby gave him mouth to mouth and CPR while I took the four-wheeler back to the house to call for an ambulance and waited what seemed an eternity for it to arrive. And he was still pushing on that boy's chest when I brought those EMT boys back through the woods near on an hour later, the blood being pushed out the boy's eyes and nose. And he kept muttering to himself, Joby did, driving himself deep into the no-thought of insanity where no mention of the physical world could reach him. It didn't take five minutes for the EMTs to pronounce your nephew dead and cover the body with a blanket while they talked about how best to get him out of the woods.

Joby never really came back from that day, although he goes

through the motions now as much as ever. Somehow he got it into his head that the boys from Cooperative Foods were responsible for the death of his boy—that the stress of almost losing the farm had pushed Devon over the edge and caused him to take the kind of risks that ended in his death. It wasn't so, and we tried to tell him— Celia and me and even Corinne—but he wouldn't be persuaded back then. I'm not sure that he still doesn't blame them for what happened to his boy, even after all this time.

He spent a week in bed, with Celia tending to him every minute of the day and night. I took charge of the farm, making sure that the cows got milked and that the first planting was made just in time to bring forth the three cuttings we'd need to pay the mortgage. It wasn't easy given the waterlogged state of the fields and the fact that I was pretty much on my own. Your brother didn't eat, he didn't sleep, and he only left the house to go to his boy's funeral and see him lowered into the ground next to your father beneath the grand maple. But even at the funeral, he didn't speak to anybody, including Father Murphy, slinking away in the middle of the sermon to sit alone in the cow pasture to the south, the cows circling him like something alien and out of place. He had become a hollow man and he knew that he had better stay hollow or he'd have to face a world of pain in accepting the death of his boy.

Corinne came by a couple of times that first week after the funeral to share in the pain of Devon's loss and see whether there was anything that she could do to help. But, try as we did to hide it, I think she got the sense that her presence was more a reminder of Devon's absence than anything else and she stopped coming soon after. Celia asked me to move up to the house for good the day after the funeral, if only to help her keep an eye on Joby. And so I did.

It was a week to the day after we put Devon in the ground that

I heard the floorboards creak outside our old room in the dead of night. I looked at my watch, and it read three a.m., and I thought maybe it was Celia, that maybe something had happened to Joby and they might need my help, so I jumped up and opened the door, still in my boxer shorts. Old Joby looked back at me from the top of the stairs, fully dressed with a bundle of newspaper under his arm and what looked like a mason jar of liquor in his hand.

"Joby, you okay?" I asked.

"Go back to sleep, Lem. Ain't nothing wrong with me. Just can't sleep is all."

"You sure you don't want to talk or nothing," I pressed. I knew he wasn't quite right in the head yet, and I was worried about what he might be cooking up in the dark of night, especially loaded with some bathtub-produced, low-brow liquor.

"I'm sure. Go on back to sleep. I'll see you for the milking in a couple of hours."

He actually sounded like he had come back to himself a bit. And I'm not one to be giving lectures about the evil of the drink, Lord knows. I thought he might drink himself to sleep at the kitchen table and there ain't no harm in that. So I did what he suggested and lay my head on that pillow again until the alarm woke me two hours later. I threw on a pair of jeans and an old flannel shirt, grabbed a bite of toast and a glass of orange juice out of the fridge, and sat down in front of the door to pull on my boots before I headed out to the barn.

And it was then that I saw it. Through the window of the front door, the sky to the west was all lit up like a red dawn on the ocean or the coming of the northern lights. Now I knew that it was still too early for the sun to be rising, and we sure as hell weren't far enough north to be seeing no northern lights, and as soon as my mind had checked off those unlikely possibilities, it hit on the answer. I was out the door the very next second, the laces of my boots trailing along untied behind me. I sprinted past the milk house door and over the rise in the pasture to look down on the old sugar shanty that was throwing flames fifty feet into the sky. The sound of metal twisting and bricks popping filled the air. Old Joby was sitting as quiet as could be cross-legged atop the rise in the south pasture, the very same spot that he'd run to during the funeral, and he was watching the scene with a smirk over his newly-gaunt features and tossing rocks along into the flames every now and then. He waved me over and patted a spot on the ground next to him.

Now my first thought was to run back to the farmhouse, wake Celia, and call Dean Jacobs down at the volunteer fire department over in East Angler to see if we couldn't save some of the old shanty that had stood for three generations on that very spot. But I looked at the blaze again, and I knew that the hour it would take those boys to get out there would cause them to pull up on a smoldering pile of ashes. Besides, I was more worried about old Joby than anything else, and I wanted to make sure that he got himself back inside the house without running headlong into the flames or setting fire to something else.

"What say, Joby?" I said, walking up to join him on the rise. I saw the mason jar sitting next to him empty and the scent that arose from it let me know that it wasn't any low grade liquor, but kerosene. "I thought you loved that old shack."

"Damn right, I did. Loved it too goddamn much to let those bastards at Cooperative Foods get their hands on it. Hey, Lem, you remember where we stashed those two barrels of kerosene we bought last winter after when the power cut out?"

"Joby," I said softly, "there ain't no fire that's going to bring him back. Even if you torch this whole place and half of Collins besides, he's still going to be gone."

"It ain't got nothing to do with Devon, Lem. This is about war."

And he believed it, and that's how we spent the next two months, Celia and me, working against fate and Cooperative Foods and Joby too to keep that farm running and bring in the pittance that milk was fetching at market. And work as we might, we continued to fall further behind every day. Joby generally kept to his bed during the day, like he didn't feel that he had anything in common with the waking hours anymore. But he came awake every night, sometimes drinking a bit but just as often dead sober, and we'd chase him about his own farm trying to keep him from blowing himself up right alongside the structures and machinery that he seemed hell bent on leaving a pile of ruins.

You'd think that talking to him would have been like talking to someone who'd just plain lost his mind or slurred nonsense the way I used to when I'd reached my drunk limits and beyond, but it wasn't so. The truth is that he made as much plain sense then than in any days before or since.

"They're gonna take it, Lem," he said to me one night after I watched him pull down one corner post of the old barn with the big John Deere. The lumber of that barn had stood in place for more than a hundred years, and I watched it come down like a pile of burnt matchsticks. "They're gonna take it, and I'll be damned if there's gonna be one wall standing or one piece of machinery that can be made to work when they do."

I found him another evening long about midnight stumbling his way through the dark fields toward the old beaver dam calling out for his boy like a pup howling for its mother in the lonely light of the moon. He was covered in dirt and cut up from head to toe from all the tumbles that he'd taken among the seed rows and all that blood and dirt mixed with the tears on his face where he kept wiping away with the back of his hand until he looked like something straight out of a horror show. But the sound of him was worse yet. It just about broke my heart to hear him wail on the way that he did. And it took all of my strength to turn him around and refuse the bottle that he offered me every two steps in spite of his own inviolable rules. I knew that he needed a friend, but I had made you and little Danny a promise, and I'd be damned if I was ever going to break another one of those, whether or not you ever saw fit to forgive me.

Anyhow, neither Celia nor I could find a way to talk him out of his plans for total and utter destruction of the farm. It didn't help any that his predictions came true one after another. Less than two months after we had put Devon in the ground, they were served with a complaint for foreclosure of the property. The process server practically sprinted off the front porch and down the road after handing the envelope to Celia. And looking down, she read that the name on the complaint was Cooperative Foods.

Each new setback seemed only to renew Joby's appetite for structural violence. And so, by the middle of June, the only buildings still standing were the farmhouse and the new barn, and I knew damn well that the only reason they were still around was that old Joby couldn't bring himself to risk the beings that lived inside them. But it was only a matter of time until he hatched a plan to turn the heifers loose and pull that barn down to the ground, and that would be the bitter end of all our struggles.

The morning after the foreclosure papers were served, I left Celia tending to the heifers, and I trekked on into East Angler to talk to fat Horace. I had been to school with his oldest daughter that was quite a looker until she started to put on weight like the old man. Anyhow, Horace told me that we had about four months before the court would grant the foreclosure and we'd be cleared off by Sheriff Haney in preparation for the sale of the farm at auction. We had up until the date of sale to come current on the mortgage and pay the various penalties and court costs. After that, there wasn't anything that we could do but bid against Cooperative Foods and any others at auction.

"Not goddamn likely, Horace," I told him with a note of disgust in my voice. Christ, I thought, for an educated man, he sure was stupid. It was the lack of money that had us in the situation that we were in in the first place. But I held my tongue and thanked him for his time. All in all, it wasn't anything but more shitty news piled on top of all the other problems that we had right then.

When I got back to the farm, old Joby was sleeping, and Celia and I sat at the kitchen table wondering aloud what the hell we'd do with him when they came to run us off the place. He had lost the will to live and, worse, your sweet-natured brother had grown violent with the anger that came of losing his boy and that tale was told nightly in the destruction that he was engaged in about that farm. Celia couldn't handle him herself anymore, and even if she could, they had no place to turn. While it was midsummer then, winter was less than six months away, and it looked as though neither the human nor animal populations of that old place had a roof to shelter under.

And that seems just about the right spot to end this part. I can barely hold the pen in my hand anymore. It seems like I've only got a couple of hours of productive work in me by day—the rest is just pain and the avoidance of pain that makes me stupid. I know that Joby's upping the morphine on me even when I haven't asked him to do it. Anyhow, you tell Danny that I love him and that I always have. It'll be a while before I'm able to write you again, but I'll do it the very moment that I'm able. I love you, Sarah, and I'm sorry about all that's passed between us.

FOURTEENTH BEQUEST

This isn't exactly a bequest in the legal sense, but I feel I need to put it down on paper just the same. I tell you, Sarah, it's an odd circumstance that I find myself in here. It isn't any secret that I'm dying, but I've asked Joby and Celia to keep that quiet until I'm gone. They don't like it, especially Celia, who says you and Danny have a right to know, but so far they've obliged me, and I know that they'll continue to honor my wishes after all that's passed these last few months. There isn't a damn thing any one of us can do about it anyhow, not even those doctors in the city, and the last thing that I want from anyone, including you, is pity. It's enough that I'm wasting away here in the bed that we once shared, that the body that once sustained me and us—the same body that I had pinned a thousand dreams on because I knew that it was solid and could take the weight—that same body is pretty near whittled away to nothing but spots and sickness. It won't be long now.

It's an odd circumstance too that you're going to be in before long—widowed at twenty-five with a seven-year old boy to chase around, and I want to be sure that I leave my feelings clear before I'm gone. Now, you'll probably jump for joy when you hear that I've passed on. Even though you're all the way down there in Virginia, I can feel your hatred towards me for what I did to you and Danny near on four years ago now. I can almost feel it seeping through the phone line when I eavesdrop on Celia who talks so low and soft to you down in the kitchen. What she doesn't know is that the heating duct from that kitchen leads directly up into the bedroom here and, while I can't make out but every third word, I've heard enough to know that you aren't coming back of your own volition any time soon.

You'll probably say good riddance and begin your life anew and never look back to say what might have been. But just in case that isn't what comes to pass—just in case you read these lines and get to feeling bad and maybe come to understand some of all that led to our destruction and can find it in your heart to forgive me—just in case all that happens and you start to feel the loss of all that was, I want you to know that you deserve to be happy. And so does Danny. And that means that you shouldn't sit by like some wallflower at the dance—not that you ever were a wallflower as you're too beautiful and too intelligent to ever simply blend into the background. What I mean to say is that you deserve a husband that will love you and treat you right all the rest of your days. And Danny deserves a father that will love him too and treat him better than I've done and raise him up strong and tall and straight and make him a man. So don't you worry about what we've been through or about any promises that we made to each other along the way—Lord knows that I've broken just about every one that it's possible to break, though I haven't ever touched another woman as long as we've been together, I want to make that clear. But you go on and live the happy life that you were meant to live. And take the High King of Tara along with you for the ride—bring him up in a house of loving discipline—and don't give another thought to what's past.

Joby's been watching that old black and white with me in the evenings. He's a different man today than he was back in the summer of 1982, when he was intent on leaving this farm a pile of smoldering ashes. He'd been on a tear for two months or more, plotting little midnight missions to destroy any useful structure or piece of equipment about so that those bastards from Cooperative Foods would have no choice but to raze the entire thing and start from scratch when they finally came and kicked us off. And, rather than getting cooler with each explosion, the violence seemed to feed old Joby's anger just that much more. So, when Celia finally showed him that foreclosure notice, he lost his shit—pardon my French. Though I'm pretty certain that he'd feared it for years and actually expected it for several months, seeing those words on the page made it all come home to him. He was going to lose this farm that your grandfather's grandfather had pulled up out of the naked earth just after he came home from the Civil War. And the blame was set square enough on old Joby's shoulders that I think he felt the gaze of five generations of Danner men staring down at him from on high—it was a heavy load to carry, as you can imagine.

Well, it all came to a head that July, but I remember it as clear as if it were yesterday. It was warm that afternoon, and there wasn't a cloud in the sky. Old Joby told me later that he had been down to the grand maple to talk with his father and try to figure out some way to just keep on, and his shirt was soaked clean through with sweat and tears. He was drinking that day, and he was quite a sight rambling up to the house and onto the porch, where Celia and I were talking in whispers about the foreclosure notice that we held between us. We looked at each other and then at Joby. He swore a blue streak at us, though most of it was unintelligible, and he told us that even falling down drunk he was still the head of the family, and he'd be damned if anyone was going to keep secrets from him on his own farm. And so, I handed it over.

Joby read it through bleary eyes and sat down hard on the wood of that porch just as if someone had punched him in the gut. He couldn't catch his breath for a good five minutes and Celia set about rubbing his back and telling him that they were still together and that everything was going to be alright. But he knew it wasn't. I saw him choke back the tears that came on him, and he waved Celia off and headed on inside where he grabbed a hat and, he told me later, he headed straight to the Village Pub, where he threw back more whiskey than any man should in a single afternoon or two such neither. Young Tommy finally threw him out sometime that evening, just as the sun was headed down behind the hills over towards East Angler. Somewhere in between shots of the hard stuff, old Joby had decided to finalize the destruction of all that your family had built over a hundred and forty years. It took him almost an hour to get back home, and he was stumbling in and out of the ditch the whole way, or so he told me later on.

The house was quiet when he got back. It was long past milking time, which Celia and I had taken care of every day since Devon had passed and Joby'd lost interest in just about everything save destruction. We'd also managed to put up the first and second cuttings of hay that season too with the help of them Dickerson boys. But at that moment, we were out looking for Joby in all the known corners of Collins and beyond. We figured out later that we might even have passed him in the ditch—he was so out of it and we were in such a state of anxiety that we wouldn't have noticed each other one bit. Joby stumbled through the house alone, shouting our names to be good and sure that there wasn't anyone around. When he was satisfied, he turned on his heel and pushed through the screen door on the porch and out into the heat of the July sun beyond.

Now most of what I'm about to tell came to me later from old Joby himself, but while I was in the middle of it, it all seemed a great confusion. Joby went straight on into the barn, where the big wall-mounted fan was humming away upstairs, where I had left it on to dry out all that wet hay that we had put in just the afternoon before. He walked down the milking floor and opened all the stanchions and led big Sheila out into the fields. The other heifers followed soon after as they always did. We didn't have any chickens or pigs that year—at least not since Devon had left us—so the cows were the only living beings that needed to be turned out. Once he saw the last swish of a tail through the back gate, he closed her up and headed upstairs to the barn.

There was a small can of gas mixed with oil sitting next to the small push mower that we used to cut the grass in the front yard. It wasn't much, but in his inebriated state Joby figured it would be enough to get the job done. He knew that the second cutting of hay would be half dry by then and so it wouldn't need but a bit of a flame to send up the whole shebang. Unsteady as he was, it took him a good few minutes to get up the ladder to the hayloft of that barn, and he was downright shocked to see all the hay that was stood up in it. He told me that he swayed there uncertain for a moment, thinking of all the work we'd done to get it on up there and letting the wind from those oversized blades wash over him and drain some of the crazy that was oozing out of him like sweat. He thought that it was a hell of a shame that me and Celia had put so much effort into that season that he was about to send up in flames, but it didn't deter him for long. He was focused on Cooperative Foods, and he meant to send them a message that they'd hear all the way over in Minneapolis or wherever those fat assholes were sitting down to champagne and caviar after taking away the pride and livelihood of good, hard-working families. Of course, it wasn't any political platform that he was speaking in his head at that moment, but more like the slither of a river of molten lava and whiskey that was spilling out his ears.

It was about then that we came on back to the farm after having looked high and low for Joby through about three counties. Later we figured out that we must have missed him at the Village Pub by no more than an hour. Anyhow, his mind was set on the destruction that he saw clearly in his head and he set about sprinkling that gas mixture on the hay nearest that old fan, which he knew would spread it fast and furious about the loft, giving him only a few moments to scamper down the ladder and out of the barn to safety before the whole works went up. He upended the gas can until there wasn't a drop left inside and he reached to his pocket for that lighter that he was in the habit of carrying around to heat frozen sections of the tubing in the winter. But his hands came up empty except for an old Skoal tin and he set about looking for some other way to light that fire.

Now, Joby told me that even in his inebriated state, he knew that if he left that hayloft in search of a flame, he might never make it back up. It was enormous, the gravity of the thing that he was about to do, and he knew that his nerve was subject to change, especially if me and Celia realized that he was back and running around the barn and we followed him out to have a chat. And so, he set about looking for resources closer to hand, of which there were few. He told me that he thought about striking the pitchfork against the side of the fan to create a spark, but that didn't seem likely. It wasn't flint after all. Then he zeroed in on the cabling running to the bare bulb that dangled from the barn's rafters above his head.

Without taking any time to consider whether it was a smart move or not, old Joby piled up two bales of hay and ripped the cabling from the four-by-eight along which it was stapled. He told me that it came away completely with two or three good tugs, and he felt three things happening all at once. The first was that the light went out all along that string in the hayloft, leaving only a distant glow from the far side of the barn where the lighting was on a separate cable. The second was that the bales beneath him were upset by all the tugging and he was falling toward the floor below. And the third was a loud pop, followed by the shower of blue sparks that he saw and felt come down around him as he was tumbling towards the floor. And then the world went blank on him.

At the same time, Celia and I came to the realization that Joby was back because he had left the front door to the house wide open. At first, we ran through the house calling his name, checking into every room on the chance that he was passed out in some dark corner and wouldn't hear our cries. When we didn't find him at home, I ran outside and headed for the barn, where I stopped dead cold when I saw smoke pouring out of the western wall of that hayloft. But I came on after just a beat, running through the milk house past the empty stanchions and scrambled up the ladder to the floor of the barn above. I headed straight for the second ladder that led to the hayloft, but the smoke was coming out of that hole thick as night and I could see flames licking down the rungs of the ladder from above. I grabbed the extinguisher off the wall and let fly from below, but after half a minute, I could see that I wasn't making even a dent.

"Goddammit, Joby," I was shouting the whole time, with every right in the world to do so, given how foolish he'd been acting lately. "Goddammit, Joby, where the hell are you at?"

Desperate to get up there where the flames were building before the whole barn came crashing down, I climbed the ladder opposite into the overflow space that we sometimes used for extra hay, but mostly just used for storage. I could feel the whoosh of the air over my face as soon as I pushed open that trapdoor, the wind being sucked from that side to the other by the whirring of the fan blades. The fan was nearly as tall as a man and equally as wide, but it was narrow, as old Joby'd bought it special to set flush into the dividing wall of that barn and you could see right through to the other side when the blades were revved up to speed. And it was only when I got right up to the face of that fan and looked through that I saw old Joby lying unconscious on the other side.

Now, from what Joby's told me about his little operation, I figure that the bales nearest the light bulb and cabling must have caught from the sparks that showered down over him as he tumbled ass over teakettle. And by the time I got to him, those flames had grown and were working their way back against the wind and licking at Joby's boots. Though the fan was blowing from the storage room into the hayloft, I could feel the heat coming back through the walls and cooking me right there as if I was a chicken in a pot. On the other side, old Joby was out cold and all of my shouting just washed over him like so much rain water. I was shouting at the top of my lungs and it came through the blades of that fan all broken and flat and mechanical sounding as it always does.

J-j-j-o-o-o-b-b-b-y-y-y-y, y-y-y-o-o-o-u-u-u s-s-s-t-t-t-u-u-u-p-p-p-i-i-i-d-d-d b-b-b-a-a-a-s-s-s-t-t-t-a-a-a-r-r-r-d-d-d.

Not getting any reaction from him, I started running about that storage space like a chicken with its head cut clean off, looking for some way to shut down that fan and get on over to Joby before he was burned alive, which seemed imminent. I could see the fan switch on the wall opposite in the other room and I shouted louder for old Joby, hoping that he might wake and shut her down. But he was dead to the world and all my shouting wasn't going to change that. I grabbed your grandfather's old rocking chair and broke it up and threw one of the legs in among the fan blades, but that big monster just broke it into five pieces and shot it back out at me. And again, I grabbed an old two-by-four from a pile of discarded wood that was lying up in one corner of that space. I jammed it in there good and at first it was kicked back just like the chair, but on the second try, I managed to get it between the blades, where the top blade cut down into the board halfway.

With the fan stopped, the fire receded a bit, though it continued to spread more slowly from bale to bale behind him. I watched the blades grind against that two-by-four for a moment, and I reached on in there with my left hand to grab Joby by the collar and pull him through. Then, just as I had a hold of him, the board starting creaking and whining as that blade cut its way deeper into the wood. With a crack, it came apart, the two halves flying back into the two separate rooms of the barn, and I had just enough warning to pull my arm back through before it would have been cut off. As the blades whirred back up into their cycle, I scanned the room again and again for a bit of steel that wouldn't give way. But I knew that we didn't keep any tools up there and that all that I was likely to find was some old discarded wood. And that's exactly what I found.

Now, old Joby was about coming to at this point, mumbling something that was probably about Cooperative Foods, as usual. I couldn't really hear him through the whirring of the fan blades. But he had sense enough to pull his feet up toward his body and away from the flames that had come back strong and were consuming the entire loft at that point. I was screaming at him from the other side of the fan to hit the wall switch and turn the machine off and crawl on through to my side, but he was in no condition to comply. After a couple of minutes of yelling, I realized that it wasn't any use.

By this time, Celia had followed the sound of my voice and crawled up beside me, wailing away for her husband to wake up. Truth be told, I haven't ever heard a sadder or more desperate cry than hers right that minute, and I don't know why, but I thought of you. Like maybe that was the sound that you were making inside when I broke your heart and our family too. And it was the thought of you and all that I had lost that did it. Suddenly, there wasn't any question in my mind about what I had to do, and there wasn't a second to lose in doing it. I gritted my teeth, took aim, and threw my left arm through the supports and into the whirring blades of that fan. The first pass took half of my hand clean off and I brought it back out spurting blood from every vein and artery. All that I can remember is the pain, but Celia says my scream must've been heard for three counties and it raised the hairs on her neck. But I tried again in spite of the pain—thank God that I did—and the second time I managed to get through the supports and past the blade, which knocked against that titanium rod in my forearm and stopped dead in its tracks.

Now, I was losing blood fast, and the flames were coming on stronger now that the fire had built itself into an inferno. But Celia managed to drag Joby's body through the blades and into the storage room over on our side. Old Joby crawled part of the way, but he passed out again almost as soon as he made it into the storage room. Meanwhile, I was stuck and tug as I might, that arm was locked into that blade. And for a moment, I thought that I was done for—that I would burn to death right there—but I wasn't afraid, Sarah. I knew that I deserved it for all that I'd done, and I swear that I was ready to make my peace with God. But Celia wouldn't have it. She started pulling on me as well, and we could hear the blade scraping against the surface of that titanium rod beneath the skin and muscle as we made a slow progress. She tells me that I was screaming my head off as the flesh was peeled back from my mid-forearm right on down to the wrist. And when that blade got to frail human bone again, well it just chopped my hand clean off. It was a hell of a price to pay, but I was free.

With the flames licking at our backs, Celia ripped her blouse and tied a tourniquet just above my elbow, and the two of us managed to drag Joby to the ladder. Celia went down first, while I lowered his unconscious body down through the hatch with my good arm. I came down after and we dragged old Joby's ass out to the yard through the big doors that opened into the drive, where we all collapsed in a heap. Celia told me later that I looked a bit like Arnold Schwarzenegger in *The Terminator*, with this shiny silver rod coming out of my upper arm. But I was still losing blood, and a lot of it, and it wasn't long before I went into shock. And that's how the EMTs found me, shivering on the ground before the biggest blaze that year for three counties, with half an arm cooking upstairs as the flames ate their way through the barn. They warmed me up as best they could, they hung an intravenous solution, and we headed on toward the clinic in Springer, where they put me on the emergency chopper for Mercy Hospital in the city.

In the hospital, they put me under and gave me two quarts of blood and took my arm from just below the shoulder. The doctors told me later that there wasn't any choice – they couldn't have saved the sorry remains of my arm even if I had demanded it. It wasn't a surprise to me. I guess I knew from the moment I decided to stick my hand into those fan blades that I was going to lose it. But it's a small price to pay for old Joby's life.

Back at the farm, they hung a drip on Joby too, and it wasn't too long before he started coming around. He was right confused for a few minutes, until he remembered his plan to burn down the barn so that Cooperative Foods couldn't get their hands on it. And Celia tells me he looked at the smoldering pile of ruins that was the barn that your great granddaddy had built, and he set to crying right there. And that's how they took him away, crying like a woman over a barn that he had just burned down with his own two hands. It wasn't until later that day that Celia told him how we had just managed to save his life. And he was grateful.

The East Angler volunteer fire department went to work and managed to save both the milking floor and the milk house, though the barn above was a total loss. Joby and Celia came back the next day and, strangely enough, the fire hadn't affected the milking system or the gutters one bit. Joby tells me that they kept a watchful eye on the charred ceiling above, but managed to get the heifers in and out for milking late that morning, their udders filled to bursting with the stuff, which they trailed out behind them all along the field and onto the milking room floor.

Now, it goes unnoticed, but your sister-in-law, Celia, is a right whiz with the accounts of that old farm. And she never missed a payment on the insurance, even with Cooperative Foods breathing down old Joby's neck. But old Joby was surprised enough when Joe Nowecki, the Allstate man, showed up to take a look at the fire, armed with a report filed by the East Angler volunteer fire crew that said that the cause of the fire was an electrical short that no inspection would have turned up no how. Old Joby nodded his head to all the right questions—and while he didn't volunteer any information, he'll tell you that he didn't tell one lie—and the agent saw him for the good old boy that he was, and signed off on that report and cut him a check right there for near on a hundred thousand dollars, with the balance to be settled up later on.

With the insurance money from the fire, your brother should have been able to pay off a good chunk of the past due balance on the mortgage. And at Celia's insistence, he swallowed his pride and went on his knees up to see those old boys at the local office of Cooperative Foods, where he told them that he'd sign the check over right there and asked them for an extension on the balance. But they knew what he'd done, even if they couldn't prove it, and his little farm wasn't anything but an annoyance to them anyhow. And they might have thought that an extension would just give Joby more time to do in what little value was left in that piece of property. Or maybe they were just cold-hearted bastards that couldn't wait to cheat an honest man out of his family's heritage. I tend to think that it was the latter. And so, where he had left with his hat in his hand, but his heart full of hope for a new start on that place after all the bad that we had passed, he returned more defeated than ever.

But that isn't the whole story. It was a full week after the fire, and I was back from the hospital and firmly installed in the very bed from which I write to you today, when I watched old Joe Nowecki pull into that drive for the second time in a week. I figured that he was there to settle up with old Joby, though I knew more or less the value of that old barn, and I thought it was more than likely too little too late. Instead, he came upstairs with Celia and sat down on the edge of my bed.

"What say, Lem? How you holding up?"

I told him that I was getting along just fine, but that I thought it more than likely that my pitching days were over. That got a chuckle out of him and I was proud of myself, for he's known as a serious man all around.

211

He told me how everybody knew that I had dragged Joby out of those flames and that I was a hero for three counties so that I could make a living just doing local appearances for a fee. I laughed a good bit at that and told him he must be set on being my agent. Then he settled down to business. He came with a briefcase, he told me, and in that briefcase he carried a check, and when he handed that check over, he said it was on account of losing my arm in the employ of the farm. I saw Celia peeking over his shoulder at it, trying to get a better look at the number that was imprinted thereon. It seems she'd done such a good job of running that farm that even she had no idea how completely she had insured every moving part of it. I took that check between the fingers of my right hand, which I was still uncomfortable using, and I held it close to my face and read the figure there, which was $75,000.00.

Celia started blubbering about how I could make a new start or send that money down to Virginia to put Danny through college, or buy my own little piece of land down the way, but I waved her off and asked her to go call Joby. When she left, I asked Joe for a pen and went to work on the back of that check and made a notation in the space for the memo as well. When both Joby and Celia come back, I handed it over to him. He read it and looked up to me like he was about to cry. It said, "Pay to the order of Joseph Bartholomew Danner," followed by my signature. On the opposite side I had badly drawn a hand with the middle finger raised and scribbled the words, "Screw Cooperative Foods."

Old Joby said no, and I told him he too could take his no and stick it where the sun don't shine. I told him that I'd pay twice that much just to know that those boys at Cooperative Foods were out of luck in their evil plans and that they wouldn't ever get their hands on this piece of land that they wanted so much that they were salivating over it. Joby smiled and nodded, then started dancing a jig right there on the bedroom floor, and told me that—so long as I was sure about it—then me and him were partners in the farm from that moment on. And he made good on it too. Even before he took that check down to the local office of Cooperative Foods, he signed over full on a third of the outstanding shares in the farm to my name and let me know that he was taking it on to old Horace in town to have it properly registered. I told him that it was too much, and he told me that there'd be neither a Joby Danner nor a Danner Farms if I hadn't been around, so I'd take a third interest whether I wanted it or not. Then he called me his brother, and it was my turn to go to blubbering like a girl.

And so Joby headed out for town and to the local office of Cooperative Foods for the second time that week. He told me later that he thought through all kinds of scenarios about how he would tell them when he got there. He thought about stapling the check to a bag of dog shit or blowing it up to one of those novelty checks that you see on the telethon and calling out the local press to be present when he gave it over. In the end, he waited twenty minutes for the regional vice president to see him—they thought he was there to beg for another extension and they figured he could wait forever—but he handed over the check and gave him a simple, "Now, you can go to hell," and he came on home. I would have given just about anything to see the expression on the man's face.

FIFTEENTH BEQUEST

I hereby bequeath my partnership interest in Danner Family Farms to my son, Daniel Conor Higgins. I want you to hold little Danny's interest in trust, Sarah, until he reaches his twenty-first birthday, and I want you to make all the decisions relating to your family's farm, along with Joby and Celia, of course, up until that day. It might not feel like it after so long, but this is your home and Danny's too, and I won't be around to keep you from it anymore. Once it's done, I think you both have to put the past behind you and look toward the future, for even the land has a memory that only reaches back so far. Lord knows that there are plenty of things that need to be done around here—there are cows to be milked and equipment to be mended and fields to be plowed next spring and Joby's even talked about tapping the sugar bush again and trying to bring out a small batch of syrup. But he and Celia can't do it all themselves. They need help. And more than help, after all that's passed, they need family. So come on home, Sarah, and let the boy work the land as is his right.

I know that it looks downright delusional to Joby and Celia, but I've taken to talking to little Danny when the pain gets too great or I'm in the depths of the morphine and can't rightly tell reality from the fictions that I create in my mind. He's seven years old now, that much I do know, and he should be going out for Little League soon. And in any universe where I hadn't failed him and you so unforgivably, I would be teaching him how to choke up on the bat and keep his eye on the ball, playing catch with him in the backyard and teaching him the rudiments of throwing a curve. Of course, all those things are impossible now and they became so the minute my lips touched the bottle that cold day in December almost four years ago and maybe even earlier. But here and now, when I'm not coughing up a lung or lost in the depths of sleep, which is my only occupation aside from writing in these pages, I've taken to talking the game through with him, and I pretend to myself that I'm teaching him some of all those things that a father is meant to teach a son. And there are certain fleeting, blissful moments when I get lost in the delusion and I close my eyes and try to hold on, but something or other always brings me back to my reality and I get to realize my failure all over again.

But I've got baseball covered, at least. You see, last week I asked Joby to invite your cousin Owen over for a visit as there was a favor that I wanted to put to him. Owen's attitude had softened towards me after he heard about how I saved his cousin and helped bring the farm back from the brink of foreclosure and, in any case, we were friends once upon a time, and I knew he wouldn't refuse a dying man his last wish. And so he and Jenny came over for dinner on Tuesday and they came up the stairs to see me just as another overcast day was fading into the blackness of night just a little sooner than the day before.

Now, the decayed state of my body doesn't get much of a reaction anymore from Joby or Celia or Doc Tyler and so it's only the people that haven't seen me in a while that give me some sense of how truly horrific I now look compared with what I was when I was playing ball and even afterwards when I was putting on the weight of the drink. Though they both tried to hide it, their eyes went big as saucers when they saw the sickly state of my body, which is thin as a scarecrow now, with odd bulges where my lymph nodes are swollen to the size of baseballs. And the sores and lesions just about cover my body like giant freckles at this point so that I look like the hide of a cheetah, where the skin hangs tight about every angled bone. I look like death, is what I'm saying, and I could see the disbelief in their eyes as soon as they walked in the door.

Jenny was sweet and held it in as she leaned down to kiss my cheek and held my hand and asked how I was doing. I told her honestly that I'd seen better days, but that it was nice to see her again after all the time that had passed. She forced a smile and told me that she felt the same and missed our days all together, but pretty soon she looked desperately at Celia, who understood at once and jumped up to ask Jenny to help out in preparing the venison steaks that they'd pulled out of the freezer to thaw earlier that day. I've never seen such relief as when Jenny said her goodbyes and hurried on out the door and down the stairs. And I thought I heard a gasp and a sob between her footfalls and the creaking of the stairs. I don't blame her one bit. I frighten myself sometimes.

And Jenny wasn't the only one. Even Owen had trouble looking me in the face, and he kept tripping over his words and telling me how sorry he was that I was laid up. To make matters worse, I launched into a dry coughing fit with every movement from the bed and every attempt to speak and I couldn't seem to get out the first word, much less put the question to him that I was meaning to ask.

"So, Lem, when does Doc think you'll be back on your feet?" he asked me after another fit that had me on my back and gasping for air as if I was breathing through a straw.

He looked doubtfully at Joby, who sat impassively at the foot of the bed, and I realized that Owen didn't have any idea what was wrong with me or how short my time actually was. It's true that I had asked Doc and Joby and Celia to keep the fact of my disease quiet, knowing what sort of reaction a case of terminal AIDS would have in a town as small as Collins, but I didn't expect that they would keep it from family. I should have known that Joby's word is his bond and that he wouldn't tell you or the Pope himself if I hadn't given him permission to do so.

In answer to Owen's question, I just shook my head and he understood enough to not go on asking silly questions. Instead, he prattled on about the World Series and the Royals' comeback and what a phenom that Bret Saberhagen was, when I finally put my hand on his arm to slow him down. What would have held my attention for weeks on end in years past didn't mean a thing to me now. I had other, more mortal concerns on my mind, and so I pulled him in close and took a long, even breathe and asked him what I wanted to ask him.

"I don't have the right to ask favors of you, Owen ... I know that ... but I'm going to do it anyway. If Sarah and Danny come back after I'm gone, I want you to teach the boy baseball. You ... nobody else ... you. Will you do it?"

"Of course, Lem," he said, nodding his head. "Of course, I will. But it can't be—"

He stopped in mid-sentence and went quiet as he came to the full realization of the significance of my question. I bowed my head and closed my eyes for a second to give him my thanks. Knowing that I was past the point of exhaustion, old Joby told him that they'd better be getting downstairs before the girls over-seasoned the venison. Owen was still awkward, but he said a quick goodbye and told me not to worry, that I could count on him to keep his promise, and it made me feel lighter right away. And as they walked out the door and down the stairs, I realized that my only remaining task was to finish what I had begun putting down on paper here. And it was a good thing too, because I was damned tired.

We're almost to the end, Sarah, and there's really only the story of my untimely demise that remains to be told. It came most unexpectedly just when it looked like everything had finally turned around for the farm and for me. We received the note on the property about three weeks after Joby's last meeting with Cooperative Foods and, as dark as were the days leading up to his breakdown, those that followed our paying off that mortgage were lighter than any that we had spent since my very first days on the farm when I was falling head over heels in love with you. There was a tremendous amount of work to be done in getting the last of the hay in and preparing the farm for the coming winter and everyone was anxious to get at it. I was laid up in bed for the first while, of course, and I had lost my left arm, but I was also still blissfully ignorant of the virus that was coursing through my veins, and I still had thoughts of a distant, prosperous future where I was able to make it up to all those that I had hurt and lead the straight-laced small town life that was left to me. After all, I was a partner in Danner Family Farms, and I didn't mean to squander the second chance that God had seen fit to give me.

It was then that I started asking Celia about you, thinking that my actions might have earned me some credit with her that I could cash in for information and the chance to make it right with you. But she didn't ever budge, as I've mentioned, and I've never known people to keep a secret better and closer to their hearts than she and Joby have kept yours.

Anyhow, once the tension with Cooperative Foods had been defused, Joby came fully back to himself and took charge of the farm just as he had before he spent those months trying to burn it all down. He and the Dickerson boys put up a temporary shelter for the equipment and that third cutting of hay that they brought in while I was still laid up. Celia took charge of the milking both morning and night, which isn't an easy chore for one person. In truth, I can't tell how they got it all done, what with caring for me night and day as well, but they seemed to have a renewed energy about them in spite of all that had happened. They even starting flirting with each other and scurrying away for the occasional midday interlude. Now, I don't mean to suggest that they forgot about Devon and all that had happened, as they both made daily trips up to the grand maple to visit with him and they shed a river of tears together, especially during that first year of his absence. But when they weren't remembering their lost boy or putting things to right about the farm, they ran around like a couple of kids in high school—like we did not so many years ago—and they talked openly about the possibility of having another child. Knowing Devon as I did, he would have wanted his parents to be happy and not to go about half-dead as a result of anything that he had done or left undone.

The summer passed quickly on into fall, and it was a picture-perfect day in early September when the leaves had mostly turned to red and gold and the air was dry and there was just the barest hint of a cold front on the wind coming down from Canada that Doc Tyler pulled his big old Cadillac into the gravel drive of the farm for the first time in months. Joby and I were in the driveway tinkering with that old conveyor belt that was nearly as old as I was and prone to crapping out at least twice a season when we most needed it to get the hay bales into the furthest recesses of the barn. Truth be told, I wasn't much use without my left arm, and I mostly just sat on the ground handing tools to Joby as he went to work on her. Celia was out there too, hanging sheets on the clothesline just to the right of the front door of the farmhouse and I could see her throwing mischievous glances at her husband every minute or two through the sheets that were gently waving in the wind. But we all stopped when Doc Tyler pulled up and threw her in park off to the side of the drive where the old barn used to sit.

I'd been seeing him in town every two weeks as part of my rehabilitation and all seemed to be going well, though I had developed another lingering head cold that I couldn't seem to shake no matter how much rest I got. He had prescribed the usual medications and then antibiotics when I started coughing, and he had even taken a few blood samples to have analyzed in the city to be sure that the cold wasn't the result of some latent complication related to the amputation of my arm. But he had told me just the week before that all those tests had come back negative and that it was his opinion that I was just more susceptible to colds now that my body had been weakened by the trauma of the summer and that's just the way that it would be for a while. I didn't have any reason to disagree with him, and I thought surely that it was just a matter of time and rest until I was fully back on my feet and able to contribute more about the farm.

"Afternoon, folks," he said holding up one hand in greeting, while in his other he carried the black bag that seemed another part of him. "Can I impose on you to invite me inside so that Lem and I can chat for a few minutes?"

Celia took Doc by the arm to lead him up to the house and Joby told me to go on ahead while he washed the grease and grime from his hands in the milk house. By the time I walked into the kitchen, Doc Tyler was already seated at the table with a steaming cup of coffee in his hands and chatting away with Celia about the need to change out the tires on his car in favor of the studded snow tires that would get him through the winter. I took off my boots and took a seat at the kitchen table, where Celia handed me a cup of coffee as well. When there was a break in the conversation, Doc smiled at me in that sympathetic way that he has with his patients, and I knew right away that the news that he brought wasn't good.

"Celia, I'm very sorry to be so rude, but would you excuse Lem and I for just a few minutes? There's something that I need to go over with him in private."

"Of course, Charles," Celia said with a look of concern. "You boys just holler if you need anything."

She looked questioningly at me as she walked toward the stairs. I shook my head and raised my eyebrows to let her know that I had no idea what to expect, though inside my guts had begun to tighten with the expectation of bad news. The truth was that, even with all that I had lost, life had been too easy through the end of that summer and into the fall given all the turmoil that had preceded it, and I felt like there was an anvil ready to fall on top of me every time I walked out of the door. It turns out I was right, though I wouldn't know for another minute or two exactly how heavy that anvil was.

"Lem, I don't know how to tell you this," Doc said, turning that sympathetic smile on me again, "so I'm just going to come right out and say it, okay?"

I nodded, anxious about what was to come and the patter of Celia's steps up the stairs seemed to match the beating of my heart.

"I saw an article in a medical journal last week about contamination in the nation's blood supply. Maybe you've seen news of the government's efforts to develop a test to screen for blood contaminated with AIDS?"

I shook my head and furrowed my brow and wondered just where in the hell this conversation was going.

"Well, it doesn't matter. There was one line of the article that mentioned that infections by transfusion had largely occurred in urban areas, like Los Angeles, New York ... and Chicago."

He paused to see whether I was following him, and I was, but it still took me a while to catch all the way up with his meaning. You see, the amputation of my arm at Mercy Hospital in the city was fresh in my mind, and I thought that what he was giving me was good news in that Buffalo wasn't on the short list of cities where transfusions had led to infection. And so, I was nodding along with him, not really understanding what he meant to tell me. I had almost forgotten Davenport, where they had patched me up after that last bar brawl. The doctor there had told me that I'd lost more than a liter of blood on the barroom floor, and that they'd had to send to Chicago for bags of O-negative to infuse me with. My heart sank into my feet as I finally realized what Doc was driving at.

"But I was fine after I came back, Doc," I said. "For God's sake, that was more than four years ago now."

"I understand your confusion, son," Doc said kindly, "but that's the way the virus works. It can sit dormant for years until it develops into AIDS and the symptoms begin to show themselves."

"But how can you be sure? You said yourself that it could just be that the trauma made me more susceptible to colds for a while. Didn't you say that?"

My voice was rising as the realization was sinking deeper and deeper into my conscious mind and I fought harder and harder against it. I wasn't thinking clearly, and if I had been, I would have realized that this was a just penalty for all the pain that I had caused or at least that there was a sense of justice in it. But, after all that had happened, I was clinging to life once again and, as I said, I had big plans for how I was going to continue to turn it all around and bring us back together as a family. The thought that those plans were never going to come to fruition was simply more than I could process at the time. And so I continued to try to argue my way out of it.

"I did, son. And I wanted to be sure before I came out here. I wouldn't give this news to you if I weren't one hundred percent certain. I called the hospital in Chicago, where they told me they had diagnosed cases of HIV contamination by transfusion in Chicago from around the same time period. Then, just to be absolutely certain, I sent some of your blood to Mercy to be analyzed. Two separate samples. Both came back positive. I'm sorry, son."

I bowed my head and covered my eyes with my good hand in disbelief. I felt Doc's hand on my shoulder at the same time as I heard Joby come in through the back door on the other side of the kitchen. He paused, grunting as he untied his boots and then came on stomping as he does through the foyer and toward the kitchen where we sat. He paused when he saw me bent over in shock and Doc's hand on my shoulder.

"Can you give us just a minute, Joby?" Doc asked him kindly.

"Uh … sure, Charlie," he said looking at me with concern. "Um … I'll be upstairs if you need me for anything."

Well, we sat in that kitchen alone for a good half hour, with Doc giving me all the details. He told me that my immune system was weakened as a result of the infection, but that he hadn't seen the symptoms of full-blown AIDS as of yet and that I could spend years that way, leading a normal life, if I was willing to take some precautions and go on to Mercy for treatment on a regular basis. And he spoke about the research that was being done all over the world and the fact that finding a cure for AIDS was at the top of everyone's list and that eventually someone would find the answer and it might come any day and that was another reason to keep myself as healthy as possible. To all this, I nodded and tried to raise my own spirits, but I was still in absolute shock.

Eventually, he asked if he could bring Joby and Celia down and tell them so that they would know what to look for and how to care for me. It was vitally important, old Doc said, that they not handle my blood or treat me without wearing gloves. And I agreed that they had a need to know, though I asked him to keep the fact of my disease from anyone else and he said that of course he would and that was part of his job.

Joby and Celia were just as shocked by the news as I was, and they both sat silent for several minutes before they realized that I was still in the room and started talking both at once about how I had years remaining to me and that a cure was surely in the offing. I nodded. They listened attentively to Doc as he explained how careful they had to be in not coming into contact with my blood, but that otherwise they could treat me just like they had in years past. And Joby tried to lighten the mood by asking whether that meant that he'd never get the chance to lay me out again like he did the night I came screaming for you. They all chuckled nervously at that. And I wanted to laugh along with them, but I couldn't find the strength and the mood in the room fell lower still. But at least I was talking again by the time Doc Tyler left later that afternoon, and I thanked him and promised him that I'd make contact with the specialist that he recommended at Mercy the very next day to get a jump on my treatment.

I won't go into all the trips that I made into the city, sometimes with Celia or Joby and sometimes alone, but over the course of three years, the number ran into the hundreds. From the first, I asked Joby and Celia not to tell anyone, including you, about what had happened. And though they disagreed with keeping it from you and little Danny, they honored my wishes for privacy just as they've honored yours all these years. We limped along on the treatments that I was given and the promise of a cure for two years or more with only minor overnight stays in the hospital when I had infections that my body couldn't seem to fight off on its own. Then, just over a year ago, I noticed the first lesion on my face. I didn't have to consult Doc Tyler or my doctors at Mercy to know that was a sign that the virus had become AIDS, and I watched helplessly as I started dropping weight and my body disappeared before my eyes.

My stays in the hospital became longer and more frequent until there were months where I spent more time there than here. And always there was the promise of a cure. But I always came back to this room, which they kept for me, and to the care of Joby and Celia, who in addition to all the other pains that I'd caused them over the years, were saddled with taking care of a dying man. It was about three months ago that the doctors at Mercy let me know that I had entered the terminal phase and that, short of a miracle, there was nothing that they could do but try to prolong my life and keep me comfortable. They recommended that I stay in the hospital full time through the end, but I talked it over with Joby and Celia and they understood that I didn't want to spend my dying days in a sterile hospital room, with sadness and death all around me. And while the doctors disagreed, they admitted that it was my decision and they let me go.

Well, that's about it. I figure I've got one entry left in me. My all-out, no-holds-barred, give-it-all-I've-got apology for what I did to you and little Danny more than four years ago now. You can see by these pages that I've spent most of the time from then until now trying to make up for it in one way or another. I've grown to love Joby and Celia like my own brother and sister, but make no mistake, I've done it for you. And if being here on the farm is as close as I can get to you, then so be it. I swear that I'm going to spend the rest of my short life planning and scheming ways to make up to you what I did and bring you back to my side, though I'm afraid that the hour-glass will run out on me before I can do so. In any case, rest assured that the farm is here for you and Danny when you need it. Joby says he'll keep it safe for you.

CONCLUSION

The snow has been coming down for nearly two days now. The clouds hang great-bellied and heavy, so low to the fields that a man feels he has to duck his head when headed out the door. It's the start of that long, cold winter that I told Joby was coming along early this year. And I can see in my mind's eye the spray off the great grey white-caps of Lake Erie being scooped into the sky by the air currents swooping down over the plains from Canada. The spray becomes a mist and tumbles up into the clouds, where it becomes lost in the towering wall of grey and seeks out particles of dust to cling to for the long trip back to earth. It's a journey that each droplet, each molecule, has made time and again as it cycles through this world, gaining and losing itself, but nothing ever diminished, until it is newborn but retains the memory of its former state. The droplets grow cold and solid and heavy and begin to angle down, back through the soft opaque space about until the world opens before them, the air grows lighter, and they tumble down to land briefly upon my windowsill, where they sit still for a moment as if to let me regard them, and their white perfection reminds me of you, Sarah.

I feel that I too have grown cold and solid and heavy, that I am tumbling back toward some world that the core of me remembers, even if the rest is almost new born. And I know that those newborn parts of me have spent too much time on what might have been. What might have been is gone as the perfect snowflake that melts on the warming windowpane is gone, its remains sliding slowly down the glass to be re-frozen with its brothers and sisters in a mass of ice at the bottom. It's gone as the leaves of autumn are gone, taking with them the best part of themselves and leaving only a soggy, broken reminder for us to find at the end of the cold season. What might have been is gone, and I am left with *what is*, broken and sickly, barely breathing and flanked by the long bony arms of the reaper that leans poised to take unto himself the soggy detritus that is left behind.

The infection sits deep within my bones now, my breath comes only by force of will, and it is surely just a matter of days. Old Doc Tyler told Celia that there isn't much for them to do but wait patiently and make me comfortable. Old Joby's giving me enough morphine to kill a horse, and Doc told him that he can give me a triple dose and let me go when the time is right. But I told him that I got a bit of the poet-sinner in me still, and I want to get it out before I say goodbye.

I see now that I held on too tight to what I thought was real, Sarah. To my old man, to my dreams of being a ball player, to you and to Danny. And in holding on so tight, I lost you, one and all. And maybe that's my nature, and maybe there's not a damn thing that I could have done about it, but I'm not at all sure about that. It seems to me that I made my choices, and I sit in the harvest of them. There isn't anyone to blame about these parts but me.

It sure seems funny that those things that I didn't value as highly as I should have seem to have fallen in my lap. I've got no right to claim a friend like old Joby, especially considering what I did to his only baby sister. And I almost lost him too. There were long spells out on that road, just sitting in the cab of the truck and watching him watching me from the dim light that shown through his bedroom window, that I thought he never would let me back onto the farm. I felt like a man that has slid down the rungs of a ladder and has a hold of the very last by one bloody hand as he dangles over the precipice of eternity. And I didn't know whether the rung would hold my weight nor whether I'd be able to swing my other arm to and haul myself up out of the abyss. The truth is that I still don't know and never will, because suddenly there was a hand that came from out of the darkness and hauled me up by my shirt front and that was Devon. I sure hope that I've paid back some little bit of the debt that I owe him and Joby, though I'll never be able to pay it back entirely, especially now.

And to have a part of this farm that has become my home over the last five years seems to me just about the strangest thing of all. I don't deserve it either. I was just glad to be about here when Joby lost his senses and tried to burn it to the ground, and I'm glad to have something meaningful to my name to pass on even if I don't precisely call it mine in my own heart. That the insurance was able to pull old Joby from the greedy claws of them bastards at Cooperative Foods surely isn't any of my doing—that was all Celia, who always has run the finances of this farm like a Swiss watch. Even lying here in our old bedroom, watching the snow that continues to fall outside, I feel like I'm on stage and playing that part of some fool that's only halfway there and just can't seem to get his act together.

I don't deserve any of it. And so I feel almost as if the part of me that's leaving now isn't real at all, but is some collage of incidents and catastrophes that have happened since that day that my old man came at me and broke my heart. I think that might have been the very last day that I was me—the me that I've been trying to get back to for all these years. Sometimes I thought I could pitch my way back, sometimes I thought I could love my way back, and Lord knows that sometimes I thought I could drink my way back. But there isn't any going back, and that's just the way it is. And it's just me that sits here, alone and broken, writing out my sorrows because I know that I threw away the only chance that a man has a right to ask and that my life is ebbing away from me through this sickly body that used to carry my dreams.

I've got sorrow. And regret. And I've got them in spades. But I've got no anger left in me, Sarah. I don't believe that I'll be me in any understandable way on the other side, and I don't believe that the universe will take retribution on me nor my old man neither for what we've done wrong. My only hope is that at the end of it all that there'll be an understanding—the sharp point that I achieve sometimes when I'm lying flat in the bed and staring at the ceiling and thinking about how it all could have gone so wrong. And I come full circle in my mind to knowing that it's the pain that I caused that makes me love you and Danny deeper still, and it's the pain that my own old man caused me that makes me think back to those times that we'd sit on the banks of the beaver dam and just be silent together. And for a split second, Sarah, I swear that I feel it in my heart that it's all one, that one begets the other and that nothing exists without its opposite. I hope ... I hope ... I hope that that's the answer, not because I want to put my own mind at ease, but because then I'll know that even if you continue to hate me with every fiber of your being—and you've got the right—that at the end there'll be a forgiveness.

I am one sorry son of a bitch, Sarah. And if it makes you feel better, I know that the very last thought to go through my morphine-soaked mind will be the love that I won and lost in you. But I hope it isn't the sorry that makes the difference. I hope that in the end there's a forgiveness, because one day when we were both as innocent as the two children in love that we surely were, on that day you loved me. And that's forever.

Well that's all that I've got to say. If you can find it in your heart, I sure would like to be buried up near the sugar bush. But whatever you decide, I love you and Danny both.

Joby, I'm ready …

Signed,
/s/ Lemuel R. Higgins

Witnessed by
/s/ Charles Tyler
/s/ Horace Wiggins

EPILOGUE

Now, I told my sister, Sarah, that I didn't think I had no business messing with Lem's words here. I ain't got but a bit part in it, I told her, and it was written direct to her, not to little old me. If I'm the constant in these pages, it's because Lem passed his time here and I'm married to this land just like my old man was before me and his old man was before him, God rest their tired souls. And anyhow I ain't at all certain that Lem'd want these lines that are full of his blood and pus and tears sent out into the big, wide world for every Tom, Dick, and Harry to judge him and go on about what he done right and what he done wrong over all those years that are past. But she wore me down is the truth of it. She kept at me until I agreed to put down a few words and put a sort of period on that story that Lem began over two years ago now. And if it ain't what Lem would have wanted, well I figure I still owe him a jab or two given all the pain that he caused this family. I think he'd agree with that, and I hope somewhere he's chuckling to himself and nodding his head with me as I write these lines.

I gave him the morphine like he asked and more of it with every passing day. Hell, his body was so wracked with pain and infection right there at the end, his breath rattling out of his throat like exhaust through the butterfly valve on an old diesel engine, that I knew it was a mercy that I was doing and I didn't hesitate. I gave him a triple dose when he asked for it and he passed on long about the end of October, just as the cold was settling in at the start of what was a long, difficult, and dark winter for all of us. Truth is we'd been giving him too much for weeks, and old Doc Tyler said he must have the tolerance of a work horse for hanging on like he did. I'd seen him back in his drinking days put back a liter of Jameson before lunch and still manage to seed corn in rows as straight as a preacher, so I didn't have no doubt that Doc spoke the truth.

When old Lem finally let go, I was out at the barn—or what used to be the barn—making sure that the tarpaulins that me and them Dickerson boys had put up were going to withstand the heavy snowfall that I knew was just around the corner. Celia held his hand as he gave that final breath and left his distended body behind. Then she came outside to give me the news and we set about making the arrangements.

It took some convincing, but Sarah came on back from Virginia with little Danny that was about four and a half years old at the time. She didn't want to at first, and I was of a mind to let her alone because the truth is that I never did think that we had a voice in the relations between them. But Celia don't see things that way. She just about tore that phone from my ear and headed on into Lem's bedroom, where she picked up Lem's journal from the nightstand and went to reading it out loud right then and there. I could hear her voice breaking at parts and she told me later that they both had a good cry over all the dark things that had passed and the forgiveness that would never come. Celia tells me now that she could feel that Sarah was holding something back then, like there was a piece of the puzzle between them that hadn't quite fallen into place. Anyhow, it took some convincing, but Sarah agreed to pack up the car, pull Danny from his pre-school, and start on up to the farm that very afternoon. I say there ain't nothing like a death to bring closure to a troubled relationship is what I say.

Once they arrived, we had a tussle about where the service was to be held and where the body was to be buried. It seemed for a while like Sarah didn't believe that old Lem was changed at the end nor dead neither and that he might hop up out of his casket and come at her like he'd done that night that tore their young family apart. But Celia talked her down as they sat by the fire and let her know that we loved her and our care was for the living and we'd handle it any way that she wanted done. Now it didn't change her outlook right away, and she was adamant that we wouldn't show the body in our home, no matter how much me and Celia considered him family. But after a couple of days and a long talk with Danny that she didn't never explain to us, she said it was okay with her that we drop the body in the earth up at the sugar bush next to Devon and the old man just like old Lem had asked of us.

But she had her own condition to state as well, and it wasn't until that very moment that the pieces of that puzzle fell into place and the full force of all that had passed between them came home to me and Celia both. Turns out that Sarah was two months pregnant long about the time that Lem decided to clean out his old man's place, take that bender, and lose his damn mind. The way she told it, Sarah had tried to tell him more than once, but his constant drinking and their fighting precluded just about any chance of a real discourse between them in those dark days. She was confused, as she put it, and not at all sure that she should be bringing another soul into the family given that they were dead broke and Lem wasn't half the man that he used to be when they married.

Well, she didn't lose it immediately, but a little baby girl came out stillborn only a couple of weeks after Lem busted up her jaw and dragged little Danny into the cold winter night. They were in Virginia when it happened and the way Sarah tells it those doctors in Richmond that treated her couldn't say with any degree of certainty whether it was Lem that caused it or just a natural loss, but she held him responsible in her heart in any case. After Sarah got over the shock and the heartbreak of it, which just about tore the soul from her body, she didn't want to talk about it with no one, not me nor Celia neither, and certainly not with Lem. She pushed it all away and focused her remaining energies on little Danny to the exclusion of all else.

Even four years later, she wasn't all back to herself, though she could manage to talk about all that had passed almost without shedding a tear. If there was one good thing that came of Lem's passing, I say, it's that it allowed my sister's soul to heal enough to put her back on her feet and start walking straight again. And, having finally heard Lem's apology in her heart, she was willing to have him buried here on the condition that we'd have a private service for little Colleen, for so she'd named her. There wasn't one of us that could say a word against that, so it was done, but never explained to anyone outside the family until now, which is just as Sarah wanted it.

We held the service at Lem's old man's house, which Celia spent two days cleaning in preparation for the viewing. Now, you'd think that after all that had happened it would have been a quiet affair, but East Angler doesn't get many names in the papers or on television and the folks about these parts always did like to see a local boy make good almost as much as they liked to see him fall. Well, even though it was a Tuesday and as cold as a witch's tit in January, more than two thousand people filed through that house to say goodbye to the only kid that had ever made it to the majors, including all the names that appear in these pages. The line coming out from the door stretched down along Main Street, and every one of them stood patiently in their winter coats and Carhartt's and caps and gloves. Old Sheriff Bill Haney shook my hand like he always does, then he give me a big bear hug and went to blubbering on my shoulder, telling me about how it near broke his heart to see that boy go to jail and that he still wakes up nights thinking that he hears old Lem rattling the chains to the impound lot trying to get at his truck. It was quite an event, I tell you, and I think it softened Sarah just a little bit more to see the wonder on her boy's face at all the friends and admirers of his old man that came on through that place to pay their respects.

Well, I wasn't short on help to dig the grave as everybody and their brother offered to lend a hand. In the end, it was me and young Tommy and Bill Haney that used the Bobcat to put a hole in the earth next to my old man and my son, Devon. I took solace in the fact that Devon loved old Lem like his own brother, and I knew he'd be right glad to have him lie next door beneath the boughs of the sugar bush. And so it was. Father Murphy said his piece about troubled souls and dust returning to dust and I stepped up to say a good word or two. I looked out over the masses that had gathered and told them that Lem always did like to perform in front of a crowd. And Sarah dropped in the first handful of soil and Danny the second, and we came on back after the ceremony to backfill the hole and level her out and place the gravestone that set in the ground just like the other two. And that was that. Except it wasn't.

We tried our best to settle on back into the life of the farm. Lord knows we had a pile of work to do that winter and spring to bring her on back from the precipice and set her on course once again. But there wasn't any getting over the fact that we had all been changed, and putting old Lem in the ground apparently wasn't enough closure for us to move on. We wandered the days lost like some zombies from one of them old movies, not really paying much attention to anything but just going through the motions until our minds could process all that had happened and come out to an awareness of the present again. The weather didn't help much neither. It was right cold that winter and it kept us inside for days on end as the snow came down and piled up against the house and on top of the tarpaulins that was only barely holding together under the strain. Little Danny and I'd go out every couple of days with a ladder and poke at the fabric ceiling with a two-by-four nailed crosswise to another just to try to push some of that snow off and lessen the weight. But the gray and the fog was a constant and it seemed like we were all wandering about in a dream. And I don't think we awoke none of us until the sun peeked out again in late February and we enjoyed two or three days of the spring thaw when the water flows and the birds sing and the buds come on out and you know for sure that the world ain't dead but has only been slumbering the winter away.

Well, just that little spark seemed to light a fire under us all and the clouds seemed to lift and we moved with purpose again. And one day not long after, Sarah come to me and told me that she wanted to help me put the farm back together and make something good out of what Lem had left behind. Her idea was to sell Lem's old man's house that was just sitting there vacant and attracting critters again like it had when the old man had passed and to use the money to rebuild the sugar shanty, but to do it big and right, with state of the art equipment and a set of rooms above that her writer friends could stay in when they wanted to get away from their cities or their jobs and just come on back to nature and good, clean hard work.

237

Now, I'm a liberal man, especially for the sort of folk that lives in these parts, but I didn't want no gaggle of ex-hippies running about the farm and smoking dope and making a mess of things just when I was trying to put it all back together. And I told her so. But when Sarah gets an idea in her head, there ain't no shaking it loose. And she wore me down and promised me that it wouldn't be no trouble at all and that everybody that come would have chores to do and it would be a boon to the farm and another source of income and on and on she went. But she really got me when she told me that some writer friend of hers from out in California was writing a book about Cooperative Foods and the way they was "buying up the American landscape and the disappearance of the American farmer" and all the things that were close to my heart. Well, I couldn't pass up the opportunity to stick it to them bastards one more time and I know that old Lem would have approved. And so it was.

It took Sarah three months to sell the old Higgins place, but she ended up getting a small premium on it from some baseball lover over in Canada that couldn't believe his luck to have stumbled on the home of a former major leaguer. And that and the checks from her book that was rolling in bigger and bigger every day give her enough to do just what she set out to do. It didn't take her but six months to get it up, and now from the window at the top of the eaves of the farmhouse as you look out over the fields to the east you can see the second and third stories of the new shanty. And with a spyglass you can generally see one or two heads looking out those upper windows right back at you, sitting there at their desks and waiting for inspiration to strike.

And even I have to admit that they've been a help in more than one way. They pay a pretty penny to come here away from the city where they can clear their minds and get back to first principles.

And it's part of the deal that they'll spend half of each day helping on the farm. Now, I doubt that I'd have the patience to deal with them for even an hour, and I ain't never tried, but Celia don't think nothing of putting two or three of them at a time on cleaning out the stalls or gathering sap from the sugar bush or minding the boiler or even stacking hay in the summer months. It's a bit more difficult to find easy tasks for them in winter, but they can still help out milking the heifers or building hay wagons or plowing the drive. Anyhow, it's enough that we didn't have to hire out help this season past and I don't see any need for the immediate future. And with the money that's rolling in, I'm not eyeing the price of milk morning, noon, and night like I was, and if it keeps up I think there'll be a right little business for Danny to take over once I get tired of running the farm and spend my days down at the Village Pub drinking old Lem's remaining chits.

And that writer from California was true to his word and put out that book about Cooperative Foods and even thanked me and Sarah in the credits. It caused a bit of a stir and I hear that they're even holding Congressional hearings into the business practices of those bastards as a result. I hope they all go to jail, but I ain't holding my breath. I ain't never been naïve about the world nor politics neither, and I don't aim to start now. They'll probably donate a pile of money to the right campaign and by the time the next big news story rolls around, it'll be all but forgotten. But I think they'll leave me alone now that they know that I'll bloody their noses some more if they go sticking them in here again. And that's worth something.

Beyond the writers' colony, as Sarah likes to call her little vacation business, she's been busy with her writing. Soon after Lem passed on, she put out a set of short stories that were snapped up by all them that read the book about her troubles with old Lem. And then I think the guilt came upon her, knowing as she did that she owed a large part of her success to her failed marriage, but likewise knowing that she wasn't giving old Lem a fair shake out in the big, wide world, given all he had done to try to put things right. And so, one day about a year after he passed, she convinced her agent and publisher both to print the words that are laid down in these pages, old Lem's Last Will and Testament. And she asked me to write a piece to wrap it up.

Now, as I said, I was against the idea right off. It's one thing to apologize to those that you love and leave behind a record of your life for your one and only son, I told her, but it's another to throw those words out there for the whole of the world to judge, especially given that the whole of the world didn't have a positive notion of Lem at that time. But it ain't no surprise that she don't listen to no one but herself.

"Joseph," she says to me all high and mighty-like as she does when she talks about books, "there is nothing so beautiful in all of literature as a man at confession who is making an earnest attempt at amends."

And, despite my own personal feelings, I figured that old Lem would have done just about anything to have Sarah call him beautiful again, so I guess it's alright.

It's been two full years now since old Lem passed on, and ain't a day that goes by that I don't make my way up to the gravestones that sit beneath the old sugar bush to pay my respects to my father, my boy, and old Lem—all the men that have been most precious to me and all of them dead. Sometimes I take little Danny with me and tell him stories about his old man and how once upon a time he played with the best of the best. And we keep the gravestones free of the mud and the leaves and the snow that want to pile up there season after season. It ain't always easy.

Just last week we had near on two feet of snow that fell straight down wet and heavy from off old Lake Erie that don't look as though it's going to freeze this year. I cleaned it off the stones like usual, leaving three nice holes at the edge of the forest. When Danny and I made it up again yesterday just after the morning milking, the sun was making a rare appearance through the dark clouds of winter and the topmost layer of snow had frozen solid so that even my fat ass didn't fall through to the ground. The wind was blowing down at us from the sugar bush, though it wasn't howling anymore as it had been the previous night. And we were just about silent making our way, both lost in contemplation, and we were only ten feet from the gravestones when I saw them and put a hand on little Danny's shoulder to make him stop. And he turned to me and I held a finger to my lips and pointed out toward the holes that I had dug atop those gravestones the previous week.

He lifted his little blue eyes, them same eyes that stared at me out of Lem's head during the years of our trouble, and they grew wide with surprise. For there, lying silent in the holes that I'd dug, out of the wind and insulated from the bitter cold that was whipping about, lay three white-tailed deer—a buck with the broadest twelve-point rack that I ever did see, a little doe, and a yearling—all curled up on themselves and sleeping atop the gravestones in the warming sun of that glorious morning. And there we sat silently reveling in our fortune and admiring God's beautiful creations for full on five minutes, little Danny quiet the whole time, his eyes glued to the scene like he wanted to take in every second, until the buck scented us at last and raised his head and jumped out of the hole and stood up to his full height and snorted to wake the doe and the yearling from their slumber. They didn't bolt right away, but stood their ground, regarding us as we were regarding them, the three holes of the dead lying in the space between us.

Well, finally, that buck dropped his head and pawed at the ground and trotted off into the trees, the doe and yearling following along close behind, their three white tails bobbing along through the branches until they disappeared. And little Danny turned to me with his eyebrows raised and his little mouth puckered up to let out a well-formed "Whoa!" and then he laughed and run up to the grave of his father as if to tell him all that had just passed. And I stood there thinking that I'd better run the fence line and put up a salt lick and buy some more of them No Trespassing signs from the feed store if we were going to ever hope to have that experience again.

Now I don't know if that buck and doe were the same two that Lem seen from his bedroom window over two years ago, but I like to think so. And anyhow, I know old Lem would be tickled pink that his boy got to have that experience and was so affected by it as a young boy should be. And in the quiet of the dark hours of the night, I like to think that Lem is out there calling that buck back to him, telling him that it's safe, that he can bring his young family, and hoping that together they can show the beauty of this world to little Danny, the High King of Tara, even if Lem can't be here to do it in person. I know it ain't rational, but the older I get the more I realize that there ain't much about this world that is. Lord knows that in life we kept kicking old Lem off the farm and he kept right on coming back like he belonged here and there wasn't nothing we could do about it. I like to think that by now he's made it his home and he's set himself the task of watching over his boy from the heights of the sugar bush. And in the wee hours of the night, I promise to do what I can to see that the boy grows strong and straight. And if I'm on the edge of sleep, in that no time between awake and the dreaming where most anything is possible, I feel my friend's hand on my shoulder and I turn to see him give me a nod of thanks.

And then he's gone.

P atrick O'Connor was born and raised in farming country south of Buffalo, New York, where he played sports and worked variously as horse trainer, farmhand, park ranger, waiter, septic tank cleaner, and social worker. In 1993, he worked as a congressional aide in the Washington, DC offices of New York Senator Daniel Patrick Moynihan. After studying English Literature at the University of Richmond, he spent a season hiking the Appalachian Trail before pursuing a degree in law. Then, while studying at Georgetown University Law Center, he joined a fact-finding expedition to Guatemala, where he spent several years climbing volcanoes with his dog and working on indigenous rights and environmental issues. He is currently a partner in the Miami law firm, Harper Meyer Perez Hagen O'Connor Albert & Dribin LLP, where he practices international law and, among other projects, works to procure the return of stolen Maya artifacts to Guatemala. *The Last Will and Testament of Lemuel Higgins* is his first novel.

Made in the USA
Charleston, SC
05 December 2011